TRAVELLERS
IN AN
ANTIQUE LAND

David Creed

TRAVELLERS
IN AN
ANTIQUE LAND

Secker & Warburg
London

First published in England 1982 by
Martin Secker & Warburg Limited
54 Poland Street, London W1V 3DF

Copyright © David Creed 1982

British Library Cataloguing in Publication Data

Creed, David
   Travellers in an antique land.
   I. Title
   823'.914[F]   PR6053.R/

ISBN 0-436-11413-5

Photoset in Great Britain by
Rowland Phototypesetting Limited, Bury St Edmunds, Suffolk
and printed by St Edmundsbury Press
Bury St Edmunds, Suffolk

For Himself, with Love

CONTENTS

Beware of bloodshed. Trust not in that, for blood never sleeps.

Salah-ed-Din

The hand which you are unable to bite, kiss, and pray that it may be broken.

Lebanese Proverb

May God guard the vineyard from its watchman.

Lebanese Proverb

THE BEGINNING

NIGHT. THE city of Beirut, beautiful under a skin of moonlight. A city spreading outwards from its crescent harbour, imposing hotels and apartment blocks rearing up tall and
pale and the lit roads reaching into the surrounding hills.

But look beneath the skin: no ships tied up in the harbour,
they are anchored well off-shore, out of artillery and rocket
range; no lights in most of the hotels, only dark emptiness and
the death-smell of the fires that gutted them in '76; a twenty-
storey apartment block concrete-grey against the night sky,
unfinished, "snipers' tower" people call it because up on the
fifteenth floor – where the windows are brilliant with the glare of
pressure lamps – heavily armed men of one of the Groups,
trigger-happy, search the night for targets; and the roads are
already quiet even now, at eight o'clock on this July evening,
because as soon as darkness comes the people are afraid of their
own city.

He drove the black Mercedes fast and expertly; and the lights
fell away behind and below as the car left the city and climbed
the steep, tight-curving highway into the mountains.

Two men, their jungle-green Syrian Army uniforms showing
NCO's rank. In the half-light within the car the driver's face,
dark-skinned, is young, hawk-nosed and arrogant; his hands,
hard and sure, dominate the wheel. Beside him the older man
sits relaxed, looking straight ahead, broad shoulders pushed
back into the seat, arms folded across his chest; the peak of his
forage cap, pulled down low on his forehead, shadowing the
upper half of his face, leaves revealed a square jaw and a long
mouth surely not made for smiling. He is the leader.

But it is always the younger man people watch (especially
when he speaks quietly). Which he does now, his native Arabic
throaty and quick.

1

"The photographs. She's a beautiful woman." A faint smile thinned his full-lipped mouth.

The other merely shrugged; and turned to stare out of the side window.

"Bhamdoun," he said, gazing down over the sheer drop close on his left to the town two hundred feet below, its lights pooled on a shelf of the mountainside above the valley, whose narrow darkness ran back the way they had come, to open out eventually to Beirut and the sea. "There's a road-block two kilometres on. This time, don't flash the lights or use the horn."

An instant sullenness thickened the driver's face: at the last military checkpoint, on the outskirts of the city, he had secured swift passage by doing both and by leaning out of the window and speaking peremptorily to the men with guns, and had enjoyed that; but now he answered lightly enough.

"We are simply returning to base," he said, meaning to mock but not daring to make it obvious. "– for the record, that is."

The older man did not look at him: he did not need to, reading it all in the tone of the voice.

"Do the *seen* things by the book," he said quietly, "and no one will look beyond them." Privately, he considered the young man beside him unsuitable for the Service; but he had learnt very early in life not to question the decisions of his superiors – and those lessons *not* from the book, those lessons injected straight into the blood, the nerves and the emotions, so that there was never any possibility of them being forgotten.

Twenty minutes later they drove through Saoufar, mountain air coming cool through the car windows, plane trees in full leaf, their straight trunks catching the sliding moonlight; and the big hotel lying back from the road seen ghostly-pale and most elegantly proportioned – then its rather Victorian spell broken by the Russian-made tanks and big guns parked in its spacious grounds, by the massively sand-bagged guard posts flanking the smashed gateway and the shell-pitted façade black-dark to the glorious sweep of mountain country across the valley.

The Mercedes ate up the kilometres of the night, over the mountains, down to Shtura and the Beka'a, and the two men had little to say to each other. They were together only in the plan and its action; and every detail of that was known to each of them, had been shared in discussion. As they travelled through the night the young man let his mind create and "feel" the

2

action, and the excitement of it lived hot in his brain and body; but the older man thought of what lay behind and beyond the plan as well as what lay inside it, and that chilled his heart. He thought of the three men who had conceived the plan; and despaired of ever having the courage to go against them. Much too late, now . . .

The bars of Shtura were still open but the town's streets were empty. He took the Mercedes through them without even changing gear.

And drove on, vineyards on each side of the road, darkly green under the moon and the grapes hanging small and green and hard.

Just before they reached Zahlé the older man said, "Next on the left. You'd better change down."

And they turned off the highway on to a narrower road, unmetalled. Drove more slowly then, bedrock jutting up in places where the summer dust had already blown away. Vineyards still; and groves of fruit trees, cherries and apricots: the land running down gently now to the Beka'a Valley, the Garden of Lebanon (and the route many conquerors have taken since the Phoenicians made rich the ports of their Mediterranean seaboard).

Two villages they passed through, shuttered to the night; and before the third saw its name-board planted to the right of the road: AL-AIN, the flowing Arabic script white against black.

"Drive on through. Stop about half a kilometre beyond."

Houses, two or three small-fronted shops, a café-bar but no lights visible; and then to their right the land running flat away into moonlight, to their left the hills rising sudden, rocky and close.

When he pulled the car on to the verge and switched off the engine they could hear a dog barking, back in one of the farms scattered around the village.

"I didn't see the marker." The young one moved his shoulders, passed his hands over his mouth and chin.

"Says something for your driving," the other commented dryly. "I noted it. Not far back, two-three hundred metres . . . You clear about the way we go out? Afterwards?"

He nodded. "Clear." And grinned, gesturing at the road ahead. "This takes us back to the main road again. Then just keep on going and we can't miss Baalbek." He paused, then

3

added, needling the other, "Go straight on to Syria, if you like."

Both men got out then. The older one opened the rear door, rummaged under a blanket tossed as if casually on the back seat and pulled out the two guns, laid them in their holsters on the roof of the car – Skodai 9 mm, each with silencer attached – and then reaching in again he brought out a bottle of whisky, which he stood carefully beside the guns.

Joining him, the younger man took up the bottle in his hands, turning it to get the moonlight on the label.

"Glenlivet," he read out, and grinned. "For *sergeants*?"

The other took the bottle from him, ripped off the foil and unscrewed the cap.

"It's mostly smuggled anyway – this is the same price as lesser brands." And, tilting the bottle to his mouth, took two or three mouthfuls, savouring each.

"No wonder you Syrians aren't in any hurry to leave Lebanon," the young man said.

The older man lowered the bottle and stood holding it in his hands, looking down at it; there were many things to say but he was not going to say any of them to this kid because it had always proved a waste of time to say such things to people who did not even start with the desire to understand.

"This is a very beautiful country," he said briefly. Looked up then, held out the bottle. "Come on, have some. Then it's time to start."

The young man took the bottle and surveyed it with an expression of distaste.

"Contrary to Islamic law," he said.

The older man turned away impatiently.

"Mm, agreed," he said, and taking one of the guns in its holster buckled its belt round his waist. "Drink, man. If you're going to play the part, get the details right."

The young one drank, as of course he had always intended to do: three large mouthfuls quickly swallowed.

"And – later?" he queried (needling still as he reached for his weapon). "How far do I 'go for real', then? By what you've just said, I should go *all the way* . . . That'll be just fine!" He finished buckling on his gun and straightened, staring into the eye of the moon. "'All the way'," he said again, softly and with relish. "With *both* of them . . . Yes, I'd like that." Laid bare by

4

the moonlight, his face looked much older than his twenty years.

The Syrian took the bottle from him.

"We do what we came to do, nothing more," he said patiently. "Remember that." And turned to put the whisky back in the car.

"But if he will not – *co-operate*?" The young man's voice twisted the last word to give it a secret and vicious meaning.

The sharp click of the carefully closed door loud in the empty silence; and then the older man stood looking into the young and handsome face. And did not like what he saw.

"The *co-operation* is not of vital importance, you know that," he said, holding the dark, hot eyes; and the steel naked in his voice. "We do exactly what we came to do. Nothing else."

They walked back the way they had come, close together but the older man slightly in the lead. Under the moon the road ran pale and clear before them; on their left the land reached wide and flat, heavily cultivated; and to their right sparsely wooded hills rose in steep curves, lost themselves in shadow against the sky. It was very still.

"There's the signpost." The older man pointed ahead. Under the moon, the leaning sign at the side of the road – AL-AIN – the heavy darkness of trees behind it reaching up across the face of the hills. "The turning's just beyond."

They came to the signpost – and a ruin, set back from the roadside. Thick walls of ancient stone dreaming away the night and only grass within; but outside the west-facing wall a small grove of cherry trees flourished, sheltered from the snow-winds, which in winter blow off the heights of Mount Lebanon.

And as they took the right turn the cherry trees went with them but then gave way to a grove of pines. The two men walked along the narrow track with the moon shining in their faces but the thick-growing trees like a dark wall to either side. The moonlight looks in the faces of the men and rides the tops of the trees like a surfer rides the tall green water; but the world under the trees is very dark.

Soon they came to a big wrought-iron gate breaking the wall of trees; and opened it and walked up the curving drive. As they rounded a bend, they saw the house, lights on downstairs, and at once their manner of walking changed; they began to talk together loudly, chuckling.

5

Approached the house. Two men, friends, surely: a little drunk, one with his hand on the shoulder of the other. Laughing.

"Tagarid." Hisham Kurban spoke his wife's name with love as he leaned over her on the bed, outlining the curve of her cheek with his forefinger and then his hand sliding down to caress her throat and shoulder: the lust gone out of it now. "Tagarid: the only word left that can never be defined although it is understood in some deep part of me."

She laughed softly, moving sideways as he slid down to lie beside her then cushioned her head into the hollow of his shoulder.

"Lovely nonsense you talk; I could listen to it for ever," she said dreamily; and then added with sudden intensity, huskily, "You define 'Tagarid' every time we make love. Know that. Know that, beloved . . ." Then from the self behind her closed eyes, up out of the searching, giving love of their bodies the words swirled unthought, running on the ebb tide of the physical joy: "*I would die for you,*" she said.

And felt him move suddenly beside her, felt his hand clench brutally in her hair; and opening her eyes saw his face above hers, angry, appalled.

"That's a stupid thing to say," he breathed tightly, staring down into her eyes.

"So – I meant it." She gave him the words slowly, tense to his gaze. "I meant – that if ever there was dying or living to be done for we two, and the gift of it were in my hand, I would take the dying to myself and give you life."

The anger went out of his face leaving it quiet.

"Lovely nonsense you talk," he said after a moment, mocking gently. And kissed her and then lay back beside her, their bodies touching all the way from shoulder to foot.

I feel as if he is inside my head in the same way as he was inside my body, part of me, she thought; and lay breathing softly, touching him.

After a while he stretched, grinned at her.

"Coffee? What d'you think?"

"Mm. Gorgeous. I'll make it." And swung her legs over the side of the bed.

When she came out of the bathroom he was still lying

6

stretched out on the bed, his head pillowed on his arms. He had switched off the lights and opened the double french doors leading out on to the balcony and the room was full of moonlight; he watched her as she walked across the room and stood silhouetted against the moonlight, looking out over the balcony to the world beyond. Under the moon, she saw the villa surrounded by a thick belt of trees, beyond them in the distance the grey thread of the main Shtura-Baalbek highway, the wide sweep of the flatlands pinpricked by the occasional lights of cars or villages; and to her right, very close, the looming hillsides.

"I can see the ruined tower," she said, leaning back against the door-post, her long dark hair gleaming in the moonlight, her brocade housecoat darkly red and its embroidered golden dragons breathing smoke and brilliant fire. "The moonlight catches the paleness of the stone . . . Let's excavate there one day, I'd like to do that."

Watching her, he smiled.

"Dreams of Roman swords and Assyrian jewellery, of the coins of Iskander –"

"– and the sandals of the Legions beating the paths of victory and defeat from Beirutus to Aleppo to Antioch and back again."

As she spoke, she heard a car approaching along the road which ran past the property, the engine-noise loudening quickly across the quiet of the night and then the lights seen intermittently, caught, lost, caught again amongst the trees; and watched it pass along the road, go on in to the night.

She laughed.

"No legions now. Our twentieth-century traveller journeys to Baalbek to trade in stolen cars or hashish." And as she turned back into the room, thought she heard the car stop farther on down the road. "I'll get the coffee," she said to him, the car already gone from her mind. "Don't move."

She did not hear them come up the curving drive towards the villa; only, as she entered the long, softly lit sitting-room before going upstairs again, carrying the coffee tray in her hands, heard the bell ring. And set the tray down on a low table of pale onyx, wondering who it could be. As she straightened it rang again and she heard a low laugh outside the front door, a man's laugh, and at once she felt her own happiness leap in answer to it; we are here at the village, Hisham and I, in the place where he has been known and loved since the day he was born, so go and

7

see who it is. This is Hisham's place and I am Hisham's wife: there are only friends here.

And moving quickly, lightly, she went to open the door.

"Don't answer it!" – Hisham, urgently, low and hard as he came out from the bedroom, on to the landing above.

But the door was already open. And one of the two men outside had already moved forwards into the doorway so that there was no possibility of shutting the door against them now. For her, for a second, time fractured: against a background of total emptiness she saw his face close to her own, a dark face and terrible to her, eyes narrowed and staring straight into hers with what she knew instantly was male threat. And then – as suddenly – the fracture snapped back into place and time was whole again.

"Peace be on your house," the man said (and she saw with surprise that he was very young). He stood staring at her while the second and older man moved past him into the house to stand beside her and speak also the words of polite greeting.

She smelt the whisky on their breath; and their creased uniforms were Syrian. But their faces smiled now: and the inane grins of the slightly drunk disarmed her. She returned their greeting quietly as Hisham came down the stairs and forward to stand behind her.

"We need water for the car," the older man said to him. "We are returning from a short leave in Beirut and we took the hills too fast." His speech was slurred, but as he spoke his eyes flicked briefly round the room and they were clear and – purposeful?

"That I can give you easily," Hisham said shortly. "Come out to the garage with me, there's a can and a tap there."

But the younger man reached sideways and pushed the door to: the click of its closing a small sound but seeming to her to suggest – an end? Or perhaps (and she felt a thinness sudden in her blood) a *beginning*?

"The coffee smells good," the younger man said. The grin was still on his mouth but his eyes were entirely unsmiling, staring at Hisham, and his right hand close to the holster of his gun relaxed but suggestive. Then he turned to Tagarid, the grin still loosening his mouth. "Perhaps Madame would be kind enough to offer two travellers the hospitality of the house?" he said.

8

"But of course," she responded automatically; and moved away from the door. The two uniformed men followed her into the amber-shaded light of the centre of the room, their booted feet quiet across the rich, dark-red brilliance of the old and beautiful carpet from Mashed. Then suddenly and as if out of nowhere the thought came in her mind that there was a gun in the drawer of the table in the kitchen. *Hisham*, she thought: Hisham put that thought in my head. She glanced at her husband: he was still standing by the front door but his eyes were boring into hers, tense, full of his will; and she knew she was right about the gun.

"We need two more cups," she said carefully, looking up at the older man (she was already afraid of looking at the younger one), "I'll – get them from the kitchen."

But behind her, the young one laughed.

"I'll come with you," he said, moving to look into her face. "I'll come and *help* you." The mockery was plain in his voice; but there was no mockery in his eyes: they met hers with arrogance, and then slowly and lustfully travelled down over her mouth, her body.

"There's no need, thank you," she said desperately. But as she went into the kitchen he followed her. She went straight towards the table but, of course, he sensed her purpose and was there before she could open the drawer. He caught her against him and his hands moved roughly over her body, over her breasts to her groin, squeezing and probing until the breath hissed through her teeth.

At which he laughed and released her, stepping back a little, grinning.

"The cups," he said. "We'll have some coffee – first."

Returning to the living-room, she poured out coffee for them, her hands shaking, and sat down in the armchair by the onyx table. The room pleasant about them, a room reflecting a lot of living, made beautiful with the things discovered, enjoyed and valued during the living of life. The younger man gulped down his coffee at once then prowled the room restlessly, inspecting pictures, picking up ornaments and examining them closely before setting them down again. Hisham and the older man were sitting in chairs opposite one another, as they had been when she came back from the kitchen. She had been aware at once, then, that *some*thing had passed between those two, but

9

she could make no guess as to what it had been; only, Hisham was changed. He seems to have withdrawn totally into himself, she thought, and yet *there is no peace in him*. This discovery set fear running strongly in her; because Hisham had always seemed to her a man of an inner strength not to be defeated, not ever to be defeated and therefore lose his peace. She searched his face, to send her love into him; but he would not meet her eyes.

"What's this made of?" the younger man asked the room at large.

Hisham put down his cup and looked round: a pink-lustred bowl was being held up for his inspection.

"Rose quartz," he answered, turning back and looking down at the floor.

"Valuable?"

"Yes . . . Take it if you wish."

The young man laughed and set it down again.

"Later," he said. And came and stood behind the chair Tagarid was sitting in. His hand slipped under the forward fall of her dark hair, then gripped and pulled so that her head was tilted back; he looked down into her face and then his hand moved over her neck, stroking.

She saw Hisham's eyes come up then; and made to rise. But the hand on her neck stilled, tightened, pressing her down; and the other hand came round her from behind and slid in under the golden-dragoned brocade, reaching for her breast –

Hisham moved convulsively but the older man's gun was out and he eased himself, taut and grimacing, back into the chair.

"Let us get what we came for, do what we came to do, and go." The big man's voice measured, angry and hard; and his gun steady on Hisham.

"There's other things to do first." The younger man's eyes taunted Hisham.

"You think you have time! Search for the papers while I keep this one in his place. We'll finish it then."

But the young man's lust had him by the guts now.

"I won't be long. Keep the gun on him and if he moves, kill him." He jerked Tagarid to her feet and thrust his face close to hers. She saw the lust which she was ready for, but the hatred honed it to a crueller edge. "Won't be the first time for you tonight, will it?" he jeered. And caught the brocade housecoat in his two hands and ripped it apart.

10

Her hands, taloned, went for his eyes, but then beyond him she saw Hisham surge to his feet, she heard his voice "Tagarid! I always –" and then she saw the young man's fist swinging for her face, but it was too late to avoid and . . . her self, her world exploded into pain. Shortlived. In falling, the back of her head struck the wooden arm of a chair and she blacked out.

. . . Into darkness came the knowledge that light exists and that therefore somewhere light indeed existed; into the silence came a small, soft sound that repeated itself rhythmically and repeated itself rhythmically until: "*I* am making that sound. I am alive and I am breathing it."

She opened her eyes: a glow of pleasant light and whiteness above; and blocked in against the lower edge of seeing, hard shapes coloured and unfinished . . . ? There must be a wholeness somewhere; it is necessary to move the head and the eyes in order to discover it.

Turning her head, rediscovered pain. But held onto the light with her will, reaching into it for the shapes she knew must be there, the shapes of reality. Saw colours making patterns and the patterns known, then identified: it was the Mashed carpet and she was lying on it and – ripped brocade and her body naked; blood on both. From her face, her body. Memories stormed in and almost hurled her back into the dark but she fought against them, reaching for and finding then grimly holding on to the one word: *Hisham*?

Holding onto that as the dying to life. But forcing the other memories out and away, heard again the silence, it crowded her close, beating its black wings to shut out the light because there was no sound and silence lives only on death.

Hisham? My love my love? Where are you?

Slowly she pushed herself up, grimacing with pain; and saw him at once. His body across the room from her, lying on the floor close to the front door.

Crawled across to him not noticing that as she neared him she crawled through his blood. He was dead. Already the grey cold in his face. And most gently and carefully she straightened his body so that he lay on his back (as he often lay after they made love, watching her as she dressed or brushed her hair, and the love still flowing between them).

They had shot him twice, but most of the blood had come

11

from his face, for they had beaten him about the head most savagely; and when she had made his body a decency she crouched down beside him on the floor and took his broken head onto her lap. He had been a very handsome man. Now there was nothing left.

"Hisham," she whispered. "Hisham." Her eyes were fey; and she whispered to the dead face of her lover. Husband and lover.

. . . The sun rose and shone into the room through the door that still stood open to the kitchen. The rectangle of sunlight moved slowly across the floor to the place where Tagarid and Hisham lay. When a corner of this golden brilliance slid across her eyes, Tagarid got up and pulled the tattered golden dragons of brocade about her; and walked out of the house and along the sunlit road to the house of her nearest neighbour.

1

"HOW'S THE new PA shaping?" Mustafa Bashir's English, like his clothes, impeccable as always, and he eyed his Assistant Director benignly.

But said Assistant Director, whose name was Matthew Curran, was aware of the iron which lay close under the velvet (as always); knew also that his new PA had been given the post by Bashir personally.

"I'm very pleased," he said at once (which was, in fact, the truth; there was no need to be diplomatically evasive about this one). "Her work's excellent. She's fast and accurate, and of course her languages are extremely useful."

"Glad to hear it." Bashir got up from his white leather executive's chair and padded across pale luxurious carpeting to the window: the Airline Offices were on the ninth floor of a skyscraper block in West Beirut and the view was superb. Clasping his hands behind his back, he gazed out at the spread of the city reaching down to its half-moon harbour. It was mid-August, and a humid heat-haze smudged the mountains of the Lebanon Range that filled the eastern skyline, behind the Christian Sector of the city, mountains still green after the long and unusually wet winter but the green a little tired now, soon to fade altogether and die leaving those slopes yellow-brown arid under the burning high-summer sun.

"Does she seem – do you get the impression she cares for the job?" he asked after a pause. Then, as no immediate answer came (Matt Curran, behind him, wondering how precisely to answer the question, or if indeed his answer mattered at all, the question merely reflecting routine interest in efficient personnel?), he said slowly, "I want to know, Matt. I gave her the job, you may remember. In fact, though, I hardly knew her."

After a moment Curran said quietly, "I think you almost asked, just then, if she is *happy*; and the answer to that is, in my opinion, no. She is extremely withdrawn." He paused, because he was not sure he had chosen the right word; but then moved away from the woman's strangeness, saying more easily, "As to the job, I certainly get the impression that she finds it interesting . . . Why did you choose her, sir? If I may ask."

"Her husband died. About six weeks ago. He was a friend of mine. A very close friend." Abruptly, he turned to face Curran (who saw his face sombre, brooding). "'Died'" – he repeated his own word with bitter violence – "a euphemism in fact. We Lebanese use too many of them nowadays, we refer to our Civil War as merely 'the events' – eighteen months and forty thousand dead and we say 'the events'! We call our forty-odd heavily armed militias merely 'Groups' –" He broke off, consciously re-forming his controls; and then went on, less violently now but the bitterness still there, thinning his voice. "Hisham Kurban didn't just *die*, he was killed," he said. "A doctor; a man of no political affiliations so far as is known, no political importance, simply a good doctor and a good man: and he was beaten up and then shot to death."

Curran was full of questions, but Bashir spoke again and suddenly: "She was there, his wife. They raped her, probably before his eyes; when she came round, she found him already dead." And he stared at Curran as if surely Curran, like himself, would have to reject it because it was impossible to accept.

"'They'?" Curran queried.

The two men waited silent, tense, eyes and thoughts locked; they had never been as close as this before.

And the question perhaps too probing; in this city, at this time, to answer it too dangerous. Mustafa Bashir's eyes slid away from the Englishman's.

"The men who killed him were wearing Syrian Army uniforms," he said; and then, turning away, went over to the bar-cupboard built into the wall and opened its polished wooden doors, stood surveying the array of bottles. "The Syrians promised a full investigation; but it's highly unlikely that such an investigation, if they mount it, will come up with a Syrian soldier as the murderer. *They* are the Arab Peace-Keeping Force; and *they* are responsible to no one but themselves, ultimately." He turned to Curran, smiling affably: the

14

face of business was alive and well again. "Help her as much as you can, won't you, Matt . . . What are you drinking?"

Curran refused the drink; and watched Bashir pour himself whisky. Fifty-two, Bashir, but he kept himself fit playing squash three times a week and the greying of the hair at his temples merely emphasized the authority in his strong, Semitic features.

"Hisham Kurban." Curran tried the name; and then sought for the man (while aware that he was searching for him in order to be able, perhaps, to find a way to the woman who had attracted him strongly from the first moment he had set eyes on her). "Was he Muslim, then?" For he knew she was Christian.

Bashir nodded, drank whisky and then went and sat down again behind his desk. After a moment he continued speaking, slowly, thoughtfully.

"He was a fine man; a fine man and an excellent doctor," he said. "Came of an old-established and respected Muslim family, big land-owners up Zahlé way. Very autocratic, his parents are, holding to the traditional ways of Islam, the total authority of the father . . . He wanted Hisham to stay on the estates – he was the only child, you see, although his father took a second wife – but Hisham refused, he left home and did what he was surely born to do, doctoring." (He is remembering them, Curran thought as he watched the brooding eyes and listened, is remembering the father and the son blood-tied together yet striving against each other.) "It can't have been easy. 'We cut each other to the bone sometimes,' I remember Hisham saying once . . ."

"What was his speciality?"

"Neurology. He studied in Edinburgh and the States, then came back to Lebanon about '72, '73 perhaps, and joined a multi-disciplinary clinic in Beirut . . . He will be very greatly missed."

"When did he marry?"

"A bit over two years ago. The family gave him a villa up beyond Zahlé, then, a place just outside one of their villages. He rented a small flat in Beirut, but he and his wife would go to the Beka'a when he had his free days. Perhaps if he hadn't married . . ." He let his voice trail off into silence. Then shrugged, finished his whisky and set down the empty glass. "No good thinking like that, is it? Pointless." Angry at himself, Bashir.

15

"She's very beautiful," Curran put in quickly; it was unlike his boss to indulge in the "if" philosophy and he wanted to help him out of it.

Bashir looked up quickly, inquisitively; and what he saw in Curran's face tallied with what he had heard in Curran's voice. "Beautiful? Not that, to me. Too strong a face, for a woman, for my liking. But very attractive. Unusual." And after a moment he added, "But I should watch your step there, my friend. If I may presume to give you advice. Go very carefully indeed. She's not, I think, an easy woman to get close to, not any more, anyway; and the Lebanon is certainly not at the present time an easy country for a foreigner to work in."

Tagarid Salamé Kurban placed the ten photocopies on the Assistant Director's desk and stood back.

"There was a call from Mr Massoud's office while you were with Mr Bashir," she said, facing him across the big glass-topped desk, her voice quiet and colourless, her English – like her French – near-perfect. "He asked that you ring him back. Would you like me to place the call now?"

"Any idea what it's about?" Simply to keep her there: he knew what Massoud wanted to discuss.

She was tall and slender and dressed entirely in black, no relieving touch of colour anywhere – except in her face, for her eyes were deeply and startlingly blue in the dead pale face.

"The new freight tariffs, I expect," she answered at once. Stopped speaking then, stood waiting. (And he knew she was aware of what he was doing.)

"Surely," he said; and gave her instructions about that and other routine matters. As he was speaking he went on studying her face: framed in the short-cut, straight black hair, the forehead broad, brows dark wings above the intense blue of the eyes, it narrowed sharply to a pointed chin. She wore no make-up; and in the week she had worked for him he had never known her smile – her mouth, yes, the polite movement of the lips as occasion demanded, but the blue eyes always unchanging, untouched by the world about her, as if she herself were shut away and her dwelling-place surely a desolation of cold. Up to this day he had thought her bitter, ungiving by nature, the cold in her an old wound, an old tragedy with its cutting-edge turned outward against the world; but now that he knew the

16

reason for the cold being there, and how recently her wound had been inflicted, a desire had come in him to get behind it and find, perhaps rescue – something of her *self*.

So that when he had finished the instructions he said quietly, "I'd like it very much if you'd permit me to take you out to dinner one evening."

For a moment she stared at him in silence; and then the rose-pale lips of her long mouth smiled their polite and narrow smile.

"Why not?" she said quietly. Quickly made an effort then (as if she's remembered that after all I *am* her boss, he thought wryly), adding, "Thank you, it would be a pleasure," and agreed that they might go out together in two days' time.

Back in the pleasant modern office she shared with the Accounts clerk, Tagarid Kurban put her notepad down on her desk and went over to the window and stood looking out: this room was at the back of the twelve-storey office-block and below her the streets of the city climbed up and back towards the mountains, the yellow-stone buildings of Beirut University College seen not far distant, surrounded by gardens and trees, the greenness pleasing to the eye. She did not look to the South: the bombed and rocket-blasted desolation around Shiya there, shattered and gutted districts whose ghosts no one dare yet defy, to re-build and re-inhabit. Directly below her ran Hamra, the city's big shopping street and erstwhile tourist paradise; the shops down there still enticing with imported goods brought in legally or illegally, but only the rich can pay such prices (and these days the rich get richer and the poor get poorer and only fools and a few honest men pay their taxes) . . . Turning away, she went and sat down at her desk, was opening a file when Siham spoke from across the room, in the Arabic she preferred to use although her English was excellent.

"I start my leave tomorrow," she said. A young girl, just nineteen, dark and impulsive, still occasionally surprised by the unlooked-for complexities of life. "I've made out the work-schedules for the girls in the typing-pool, as you asked me to. They'll be able to deal with all my work, it's only for a week and they've done it before."

"Are you going back to your village?" Tagarid asked – a politeness merely, she had no real interest.

Surprisingly, Siham's face clouded.

17

"Yes, yes, I'm going home," she answered uncertainly; and then made a swift change of subject, saying with a sort of forced eagerness, "Was your area hit by the power-failure last night, Mrs Kurban?"

Tagarid shook her head.

"No. I didn't even know there'd been one."

"Lucky you. Our electricity went off just after seven, didn't come on again until half-past eleven! So Dina and I lit candles in the kitchen and tried out a new recipe of my aunt's, very complicated and time-consuming."

She was so young and very pretty, Tagarid thought, a truly sweet girl: and realizing she wanted to talk Tagarid rested her elbows on her desk, put her smile on her lips.

"What did you make? And how did it turn out?" she asked. And then while the girl gave an enthusiastic blow-by-blow account of the making of Helwhaat El Jibni with Ushta, watched her dark-skinned and vivid face and thought about her. Siham was a Druze, she knew; her family lived in a small village high up in the mountains of the Shouf; she had two sisters and one brother, all older than herself, but Siham was the only one who had left the village to come and work in the city; and in Beirut she lived with a spinster aunt, and as a young girl her life was tightly circumscribed . . .

"Sounds good," Tagarid remarked as the girl finished speaking; and wanting to show more friendliness than she had offered hitherto – Siham's youth and zest for life suddenly reaching into her and creating a small warmth within her – added carefully (because somehow she must begin to be able to speak about such things again without falling apart emotionally): "You will obviously make some young man a wonderful wife – beautiful, and a good cook as well!"

But the result of this was not what she had expected: Siham's face suddenly went dull; then she hunched her shoulders and looked down at her desk, began moving papers about on it, distractedly.

Alarmed by what she had apparently caused, wishing now to be free of it, the momentary desire to move closer to another person entirely gone, regretted even, Tagarid said stiffly, "I'm sorry. That was rude of me, perhaps." And she half-turned away, reaching for her phone.

But before she could pick it up the words came urgent across

18

the room to her, "No Mrs Kurban, please don't apologize. It's *my* fault, it's just that . . . Can I tell you something? I've no one to talk to at home and I *must* talk to someone about it, I *must!*"

The girl's face suddenly so nakedly miserable. I must try to remember that I do not have the monopoly of personal despair, Tagarid thought; and said, encouragingly if still coldly, "If you want to tell me something, Siham, then do."

"Yes – You see, I've got a, well – I've got a boyfriend. But I dare not tell my aunt or my family. You know I live with my aunt, and she's terribly strict, well I suppose she has to be because it must be difficult for her, I realize that, the responsibility of me when I'm not her child." The words pouring out, the girl near to tears and her face flushed. "But I met this boy in the library, oh nearly two months ago, in the British Council Library, I used to go there with Dina. And now we meet at Dina's house and sometimes we all go to the cinema together, but I *dare* not tell my aunt . . ." Her voice trailed away into silence.

"But what's wrong about all that? You and he can get married, can't you – if that's what you want?"

"He's, he's a *Christian*." Her voice haunting the word with hopelessness.

"But Siham! Surely that's not an insurmountable barrier, not nowadays? There are lots of mixed marriages." In her concern for the girl she said the words quite easily and only afterwards thought of herself and Hisham. Which, when she recalled it later, surprised her.

"You forget: I'm Druze. For us, *never*." The last word a violence; but then the vehemence died away out of her face and body. "They will never let me marry 'outside'," she said dully, her voice bitter with the known and accepted finality of it. "*Never.*"

"But – surely, in the end, they can't stop you? It might even mean breaking with your family for a while, but they surely can't actually *prevent* you from marrying him?"

"Yes, they can." Her eyes wide, fixed, staring into Tagarid's.

"I can't – well, how?"

But the Druze girl shuddered.

"They can," she said softly. Then jerked her eyes away from Tagarid's, looked down at her desk. "They can," she repeated, whispering the words. And then picked up a sheaf of papers and began leafing through them, finally selecting one and winding it into her typewriter. All the time her hands busy.

She is afraid, Tagarid thought: she is mentally and physically afraid!

"Better do some work, I suppose," Siham said after a moment, carefully matter-of-fact. "Thanks for listening to my problems, Mrs Kurban . . . I do over-dramatize sometimes, I know that. I expect it will all work out eventually."

But Tagarid knew she did not really believe that.

Finishing work as usual at two o'clock, Tagarid walked home. Her apartment was in an eight-storey block on Jeanne D'Arc Street, no more than five minutes' walk from the SaxAir offices on Hamra. That day, however, she took a longer way round so that she could buy fruit and vegetables at the street-market she preferred: tall and slender, her severely cut black linen dress emphasizing the svelte grace of her body, the pale dramatic beauty of her face, she was a woman to lure the eyes and many heads turned to watch her after she had passed by. She walked quickly and her black hair moved silkily, no rest in it and none in her blue eyes, either.

The afternoon sunshine lay hot and heavy on the streets and the smell of dirt, of rotting staleness, of neglect was everywhere: the refuse dumped daily at street corners may or may not be collected (it depends on how much the nearer residents will pay), the rats are fat and numerous these days, and streets and pavements remain unwashed until the rain comes and then the rubbish races downhill with the water and finally clogs the gutters and drains and floats on miniature Sargasso seas . . . But the rain will not come for months yet. The rubbish stays where it is and disintegrates slowly and revoltingly under a crawling mass of flies . . .

The stalls of the street-market were heaped with delicious produce fresh in that morning from the countryside: peaches, plums, apricots, still some strawberries on sale and some of the first figs of the year; big bunches of parsley for "tabouli", spinach and purslane, and as young Mahmoud selected a lettuce for her his hands brushed against piled bunches of mint and its aroma burst forth, sudden and refreshing . . .

New bread from the baker's, but from there she had to walk

in the roadway for a bit because the whole of the next corner had been taken over as a command-post by the CMP – a "Group" whose beliefs and motivation were incomprehensible to her, but Nasserite, vaguely – which had marked out its domain with a barricade of petrol drums and iron piping: heavily and ostentatiously armed, the khaki-uniformed militiamen always patrol the first-floor balcony of their guardhouse there, and man the sand-bagged machine-guns commanding all approach roads. That day, in the open space below the balcony, three or four militiamen were grouped round a young man sprawled in a battered armchair, his bandaged foot resting on a bench in front of him, and a teenage youth, fifteen, sixteen years old, in shirt and jeans, stood proudly behind him, clasping a Kalashnikov to his chest . . .

More armed men about than usual. And on the white-washed walls of the command-post four big posters, deep-bordered with red and black, presenting the faces of four men. She remembered, then: four members of the CMP had been re-ported killed a few days earlier, fighting somebody's battles up in the hills behind Tripoli, and this afternoon they would be given their martyrs' funerals. As she went on her way the posters of the four "martyrs" blazed from walls and windows all along the street: three men with young and ardent faces, but the face of the fourth older, thin-featured and hard, the eyes stating a total commitment – to what?

She passed the gutted frontage of a shop fought through five years earlier during the Civil War, its battered sign still announced (in three languages) "High Class Menswear" although it hung at a crazy angle; passed a once-a-garden beside a once-beautiful house, its trees despoiled now for firewood and the rubble of fallen masonry scattered over rubbish-littered weed-infested earth, the spacious balustraded balconies fes-tooned with the washing of squatter families. As she turned into Jeanne D'Arc Street, she noticed a man busy at work among the shambles of the small jeweller's shop which had been broken into and looted one night a week before, and remembered that the departing robbers had left a time-bomb behind them for good measure, she had heard the blast of its detonation crack the night apart. She had learnt from her concierge what had happened but had not asked the reasons behind the destruction of the little jeweller and his business: the people of Beirut do not

21

ask such questions now, they simply give thanks that whatever has happened has happened to someone else . . .

Letting herself into her flat, she crossed the living-room and went straight into the kitchen. Fatmeh, her maid, was there. As always, the tea-tray stood ready on the breakfast-table and Fatmeh, having lit the gas under the kettle on hearing the key turn in the front door, stood staring at it waiting for the water to boil: a thin girl of eighteen dressed in black skirt and blouse, a black-and-grey headscarf totally concealing her hair. She greeted her employer without looking round, then was silent.

Tagarid checked in the fridge for drinking water and meat, then told her maid what needed to be bought the next day.

"Na'am," Fatmeh said. "Na'am." Nothing more: she was a girl possessed by silence; and hers was plainly a silence that had nothing to do with peace or happiness. Tagarid had immediately recognized that cold and brooding withdrawal: like her own fierce need for aloneness, it surely had its source in some happening in life that had cut through most of the roots of being and left the self without life and warmth, clenched tightly into bitterness and the shielding of its own hurt. But the recognition had brought in her no desire to know what it was that had broken the flow of Fatmeh's life, or to make even the smallest gesture of offered kindness to the girl. She had employed her simply because a woman she knew, who worked for the "Back-up" organization, had given her the girl's name as a dependable and honest worker in desperate need of a job.

Going back into the living-room, Tagarid stood for a moment by the window. Her flat faced a different way from the managerial suite of the SaxAir offices but the view was almost equally breathtaking: this time out over the harbour and the sea to the mountains beyond Jounieh, to the coastline reaching northwards; Byblos up there, lost in the haze, then Tripoli. She looked out of her windows often, the big windows of living-room and bedroom: and mostly she looked not towards Byblos – "the oldest city in the world" – or to the northern slopes of Mount Lebanon, but to the north-*east*, because over the mountains in that direction was the village called Al-Ain, beyond Zahlé, where she had lived with Hisham, once upon a time had lived . . .

Hearing Fatmeh come in behind her she turned away from the window and sat down on the pale-green upholstered sofa.

22

The girl placed the tray on a low oval-topped table beside her, and stood back.

"Is there more that I must do?" she asked, the Arabic slow and colourless in her low voice; and she standing with her hands clasped loosely in front of her, looking down at the carpet on the floor by the table, a carpet from Kerman, small, made from silk, old and very beautiful.

Tagarid followed her eyes and felt the anger rise in herself: she had brought that carpet here from the villa at Al-Ain, it had been one of Hisham's presents to her and that anyone else should even look at it was suddenly intolerable.

"Nothing," she answered sharply; and gestured dismissal.

Immediately, the girl left the room, pulling the door to carefully and quietly behind her.

Leaving Tagarid alone. She reached down and smoothed her hand over the carpet, remembering Hisham alive . . . Suddenly shuddered and closed her eyes: had remembered Hisham dead. Sitting back, biting her lips, her whole body clenched in agony, she fought her memories to a standstill.

Emptiness, then. I feel empty in mind in body and in soul whatever that is, she thought. And as usual poured into that emptiness the hatred that had awoken in her since the night Hisham had been killed, rearing up out of despair, seeking furiously for an outlet, any outlet, but finding none. Caged, undirected violence raged in her blood; memories seeking their own death but not knowing how to make it. So she lived through that evening once again: beginning as always with the lovemaking of Hisham and herself; ending as always with Hisham beaten, shot dead, and the horror of it reaching from his battered and bloody face into her hands, his head in her lap and her fingers quiet over his skin . . . And morning sunlight moving across the room.

Standing up, she moved close to the window. Beirut harbour, the mountains beyond, beautiful in the soft light of late afternoon. She seeing none of it. She lifted her right hand and stared at it, the palm open and the spread fingers: the hand that had touched Hisham's face. But Hisham is dead, Hisham is buried. They gave him a martyr's funeral. Up at Al-Ain the people had spoken loud his praises, fired off their guns for him, and the streamers garlanded the village streets with red and white and green and black.

And I? I, Tagarid, his wife, and lover? What can I give him? The question a perpetual torment but no answer had ever yet presented itself.

He is dead, she thought once more; and what can you give the dead? The people of Al-Ain remember him but there will never be any new memories of him made now, and the old ones, like ghosts, will grow dim; the guns they fired for him – well, even the echoes of the guns are silence now; the garlands are faded from the summer sun and already many are broken and trail in the dust of the village streets.

What can you give the dead?

Staring out at the spread city, she saw none of it. The whole of her being was turned inwards, its strength directed into striving to release the answer to that question because surely every question must have an answer.

What can you give the dead? She raised her clenched hands, her face was twisted with the intensity of the desire in her mind – and then suddenly her hands dropped to her sides, her head lifted and her face was gone quiet, open, a softness there, a dreaming.

What can you give the dead?

Death. You can give them a death.

Question and answer. She was amazed at how long it had taken her to formulate the answer to her question. It seemed so obvious, now. Obvious, simple. She perceived beauty in its simplicity, in its directness; and her thought moved forwards swiftly along the paths that seemed made for it.

I will give him a death.

– Whose?

Why, a Syrian death of course. A Syrian soldier, who else?

– It will take a long time.

There's the whole of my lifetime for the doing of it.

– You may be caught.

That does not seem important. Life now is an emptiness, at the centre of me there seems to be nothing – does it matter, to lose that? To give him the death: *that* is important.

. . . Her focus of vision changed and now she saw the city, its harbour and the Lebanon Range rising beyond; the sea was darkly blue with the coming of evening, buildings gleamed sungold pale and mist smoothed the shapes of the mountains. She looked away to the north-east, Al-Ain over there within the shadowed valleys. And she became aware of a new ease in herself, a buoyance come with the realization that there was, after all, something still to be worked for, to be lived for and achieved.

That night she began to dream the patterns of revenge.

2

"ONLY IF we go in my car and to the place I choose," Tagarid had said, smiling, when – a fortnight later – he asked her to drive with him out into the mountains for a Sunday to be enjoyed in cool, clean air. "You bring lunch, fine, but it must be my car, my place."

And it was a lovely place. Not dramatically beautiful; just the sweeps of mountain and valley, some rugged, some gentle, all clear-lined under sunlight wherever you looked; and the cool and the quiet a beneficence after the bustle and heat and filth of the city, after the tension of life lived amidst a divided people.

"It's not that we actually *do* have car-bombs and rockets and shoot-outs every day, well not where I live," she said now, "it's simply that we know we *may* have any – or all – of them at any moment of every day, and every night. So the tension builds up in you."

They had spread their picnic lunch in the deep shade of a tall and splendid tree heavy with dark green leaves, a giant in this place of mostly scrub vegetation. The remains of their picnic lay haphazard on the cloth she had spread upon the big woven-rush mat they were sitting on: cold chicken, sliced ham, kibbé, a bowl of tabouli, salad, cakes and biscuits. They had drunk white wine, a bottle of Ksara; and now held mugs of black coffee in their hands.

Matt Curran looked around him: behind, the hot dry land sloped gently upward to the unmade road – her white Renault 5 parked at the side of it – and then beyond it rose suddenly steep to a long ridge, grey rock up there, stark against the sky. To each side stretched reaches of rolling hills and valleys, wilderness and cultivation, and about a kilometre back along the road was a village they had passed through; in front of him the gentle slope continued on downwards and then he could see the line of its termination and knew it dropped fast and precipitously to a river a hundred metres below. Lying propped on one elbow, he looked out over the huge spread of the Beka'a to the mountains of Syria the other side.

"That village we passed through," he said after a time. "Is it *your* village?" And wondered if she would push it – and him – away, the quick yes or no and then on to a different subject.

"No." She put down her coffee and clasped her hands on her knees: the movements fluid and economical, and her black overblouse and trousers moulding her slenderness clearly against the hot dry browns and yellows of the high-summer land; and after a moment she went on, slowly. "No, Al-Ain is about ten kilometres on from here . . . But most of the land around these parts belongs to an aunt of Hisham's. I know this place."

Feeling her re-living other times, another man, he knew she was using him. But he was already quietly in love with her; and believed that if only he could get her to talk freely she might perhaps break the tight band of cold that locked her into the past, shut her away from him. He hoped she might come out to him then, gradually.

"Yours is a superb country," he said. "Will you show me some more of it?"

She was silent for a while. Matthew Curran, she thought: somewhere in his early forties, she supposed, this tall fair-haired Englishman; narrow-faced, brown eyes direct and warm but with a sudden probing edge to them sometimes; a certain hardness emanated from him – something in the way he moved – and yet he was a man with whom she felt always at ease. She wondered why he had come to her country: very few foreigners did, any more, if they could possibly avoid it. It was not as though SaxAir needed his presence, either, for all their British connections. Perhaps it was this slight air of mystery about him which intrigued her, led her to accept his invitations from time to time. Already she had twice had dinner with him, gone swimming with him at Summerland, had drinks with him round at his flat. After all, she told herself, one had to fill in the time somehow, there had to be some padding round the hard core of life that was simply planning, thinking, waiting – for an opportunity to occur – and that time might as well be passed

27

pleasantly enough. She had never been one who enjoyed the company of other women.

"If you like," she said, finally answering his question, her mind made up. Looked round at him then, blue eyes brilliant in her pale face. Then, "But I will never take you as far as Al-Ain."

"What makes you think I should want to go?" he countered in sudden anger.

"You think you would find out more about me, there."

"And, would I?"

"Perhaps."

"And perhaps you would find out more about yourself, discover –"

"I know what you are going to say," she interrupted. "You are going to tell me that I should try to look forward, not back. That there is a great deal of life yet to be lived. That it is life that is important, not death." Her face was hard, totally against him. "I understand all that. But whatever is going to be done has got to come *from inside me.*" She tapped herself on the chest. "I shall find my own way out." She looked away from him then – away across the huge valley. And after a moment her voice came level and cool. "You see, they will never actually punish anyone for the murder of Hisham."

"'They'? The Syrians?"

"Yes."

"But this is Lebanon. And he was Lebanese. Surely, for the crime of *murder* –"

"Don't be so damned naïve!" she snapped. "You surely know that if they so choose, they *are* the law in this country."

He frowned, got up and went across to her, sat down beside and slightly in front of her. Suddenly, it seemed to him, she wanted to talk, and all at once there surged up in him a feeling of gladness that it was to him she was at last consenting to open her mind.

"I realize that, but it's still pretty hard to accept," he said, looking into her face and swiftly away again. "Surely, though, they must take *some* sort of action?"

"At first," she said, "because of the anger in the village, they promised a full investigation, the certain detection and punishment of the guilty men. And it is true they have paraded the machinery of justice, conducted interrogations, brought me photographs to identify." A quick laugh came out of her, a bitter and angry sound, a sudden denial of such outward show. "But we know that they will never actually *execute* anyone for the murder," she said, and it was a blunt statement of fact. "Even if we could force their hands – by publicity, or by using our friends in high places – to make an arrest, set up a trial, and finally condemn someone to death, even if we got that far such a punishment would never be carried out." (He looked briefly into her face again, saw it expressionless and knew she had gone through all this many times before, the words coming out now without having to be thought newly, they had been with her for a long time.) "The whole affair would merely be transferred to Syria, and the guilty would very soon go free . . . But it will never get that far. They will play it slowly and more slowly until even in the village men no longer care *enough*."

" 'Enough'?"

She looked at him then, blue eyes brilliant and impersonal.

"Enough to threaten counter-violence, to threaten blood," she said. "That is the only way now, in the Lebanon, to get what you want: the threat of violence, made in the sure knowledge among both givers and receivers that the threat will *certainly* be carried out if nothing is done . . . Bargains made with lives and deaths. Deaths, mostly."

She was still looking at him but he knew she was not seeing him. Then remembered suddenly that he had seen the same expression – a cold, self-absorbed concentration, remote but wholly purposeful – on her face once before. It had been that morning as they were driving up into the mountains, they had been waiting in line, moving forwards by fits and starts towards a road-block manned by the Syrian Army: young men those had been, smart and fit-looking, strong country bodies and faces vivid with health: and all the time she was inching the Renault towards them her whole self had been tense, her eyes, every fibre of her being engrossed in her awareness of the Syrian soldiers, and on her face this same cruel and concentrated remoteness as if the spirit of her were not in the same world as her body . . . He looked away and eased himself down to half-lie on the ground beside her. He had just realized that here was something vitally important and perhaps terrible (for her) and that at this moment he could either go on with her and become involved, or withdraw and keep his own freedom intact.

29

"Is it true the men were drunk?" he asked after a moment; going on because as soon as he had recognized that the choice was there he knew himself committed to her.

At the question her head jerked away from him.

"What makes you ask that?" she said sharply, looking out over the valley. "Why do you ask that?"

"I don't know . . . I must have heard it from someone, the doubt."

"You can't have. *I've* always said they were both drunk and – well, there's no one else to say." She grimaced. "Except *them*, of course."

"But – do you mean you *do* have doubts?" he asked tautly. "About them being drunk?"

She nodded, looked at him then, a quick turn of the head. (And he felt that, at that moment, she was really seeing *him*, the person Matt Curran, a man to talk with about herself.)

"Yes . . . Not to begin with, though. At first, straight after, I mean, I didn't think about, any of that. No . . ." Her voice trailed away into silence (and he saw her eyes change, going away from him). She turned to look across the valley again, her hair falling forward partly hiding her face; and only then went on, out of her re-gathered remoteness. "One day, I don't know exactly when, I was thinking about it, living it all over again, and I remembered . . . I remembered the younger man." A small shudder shook her; then she lifted her chin and the black hair swung away from her face. "He *smelt* of whisky, his breath smelt of whisky," she said carefully. "When I opened the door to them, when they spoke and the way they – held themselves: I immediately *assumed* they were drunk, not very, just a bit, surely like any enlisted men returning to base after a day out in town. But later" – her voice beginning to jerk now, but held low and tight – "later, the young one, his eyes, his eyes did not look drunk at all. Later, when he was, close . . . His breath, yes, there was whisky on his breath, but his eyes –" She broke off and there was a small silence. Then: "Now, I'm not so sure they were in fact drunk," she said.

"Have you reported this to anyone else?"

"No. There wouldn't be any point. It would make no difference, now . . . They would almost certainly say I had made it up after the event in an attempt to make a straightfor-ward 'rape-and-murder' case look like – something else."

30

"You mean, to bring politics into it? To give it political significance?"

She nodded.

"And when I think about that, you see, I know that really I must be wrong. Because Hisham would commit himself to no political party, no political attitude *whatsoever*." Her voice strong again, sure. "He was a neurosurgeon, and entirely complete in his dedication to his work. He despised the politics of Lebanon, the Lebanon of now. Like robber barons, our political leaders, he said, continually warring against one another for nothing but personal power, with no thought at all for the long-term welfare of their people . . . They ought to be bigger than that," she finished softly. Then, after a moment, she made a gesture embracing the surrounding countryside. "It is like this over at Al-Ain," she said. "There, they gave him a martyr's funeral, *the people*, that is right and proper. Guns firing and speeches and banners across the streets. But when I was up there last week many had blown down in the wind and the colours had all faded . . . They require revenge, the people of the land, the family. It is their right. But *they* do not know how to set about it."

The emphasis was so slight that he hardly noticed it (though later, he was to remember). He lit two cigarettes, gave her one.

"The family, do you see much of them now?" he asked carefully, recalling what Mustafa Bashir had told him, the autocratic father –

Tagarid's sharp thin laughter cut his thought off dead.

"'Much'?" She jeered at the word. "I see *nothing* of them and I don't suppose I ever will, not any more. Though my father-in-law has conveyed to me that I am welcome to live in his house for the rest of my life if I wish to – as a good Muslim it is his duty to offer me that, therefore he has done it. My God! What a life that would be! Total dependence – on a man who actually loathes me."

"Loathes you?" The repetition jerked out of him by the fierce intensity of her last words. "Why should he loathe you?"

She drew savagely at her cigarette and stared out across the valley.

"Three months after Hisham and I were married, his father

31

summoned him into his presence and demanded to know why I was not yet pregnant." Soft and clear she began, soft and clear she continued (and Curran knew himself entirely forgotten). "And Hisham told him then that we had decided to have three or four years for ourselves first, not to have children till after that. He wouldn't accept it – though finally he had to, of course . . . But he has always believed that it came from me, that it was I who influenced Hisham to the decision – also, that even if it had been Hisham's idea it was 'my duty as a woman' to persuade him otherwise . . . I've only seen Hisham's father once since the murder. 'If you had lived the woman's part in the proper manner,' he said to me then, 'I would have had a son of his now.'" She laughed her small hard laugh again. "And that's true: *he* would have had a son of his," she said bitterly. "Now, he never will . . . Oh yes, he hates me in a very special way."

"Tagarid, is –?" But he broke off, his eyes catching movement on the road above them, a man walking along the road, towards them. "Someone's coming," he said.

The man left the road and came down towards them across the dry, hard ground: a tall big-shouldered countryman in faded overalls, who walked with an easy stride, sure of himself, sure of the land beneath his feet. And when he stood beside them Matt Curran saw the square and strong-featured face weathered by wind and sun, and watched him with interest: a man, surely, of character and some influence.

"Sabah il kheer," he greeted them; and Curran got to his feet and put out his hand, meeting the grey eyes so surprisingly pale in that Arab face, returning the greeting in Arabic.

The man shook his hand but then immediately his eyes went down to Tagarid.

"Ahlan wa sahlan, Madame," he said to her.

She smiled at him and they spoke together briefly. Curran heard his own name spoken, noted the ease between them. And then suddenly the man turned and left them, striding back the way he had come.

"That's Ibrahim, Ibrahim Selim," Tagarid said. "He manages the land here for Hisham's aunt . . . Hisham spent a lot of time up here when he was a boy, and Ibrahim knew him well. Loved him, I think. And he loves me because I am Hisham's wife." She used the word "loves" without embarrassment, indeed almost with pride.

"He's from Al-Ain?"

She nodded.

"He'll be back in a few minutes. He's just gone to get some fruit for us, to welcome us. He was working over there" – she pointed to her right – "on the slopes overlooking the river."

Ibrahim Selim soon returned, carrying a wickerwork basket piled high with fruit, and an enamel jug of water. Tagarid accepted these and invited him to join them.

They sat talking together, drinking coffee and eating the figs and grapes that Ibrahim had brought, grapes big and seedless, very round, pale green blushed with red.

"I have never tasted grapes as good as these," Curran said after a time, with genuine admiration. And Tagarid explained that they were called Tufa'e – "appled" grapes – and were very seldom to be found in the shops of the city. The three of them talked with a sort of reserved friendliness, Tagarid translating occasionally so that the partial language barrier between Ibrahim Selim and himself did not matter too much.

But something between them mattered. Curran knew that almost immediately: the grey eyes of the countryman cool, keeping him at a distance and – *appraising* him, yes, that surely was the word; Curran felt he was being studied, closely. And that the real talk was waiting for Tagarid and Ibrahim Selim to be alone. So after a little while he got to his feet, saying he felt like going for a walk.

"Up there," Ibrahim Selim said, pointing to the hill behind them. "Up there where you can see the grey rock, the other side of that, there's a spring, an artesian spring. It's good up there. Rough going, though, if you're not used to it." And he smiled, a small mockery.

They watched him in silence as he climbed to the road and then began to work his way up the rough stony mountainside: and perceived the tall foreigner, as though in confirmation of opinions already formed, both agile and sure-footed.

"He knows how to walk in the hills," Ibrahim Selim admitted, and nodded to himself; then turned his back and sat gazing out over the valley, waiting for her.

"Thank you for coming," she began; and asked briefly after his wife and family, dark-haired and fresh-complexioned Sawsan and the two sons, both strongly built and fair like their father, eyes Crusader-grey.

33

"Madame, why did you ask me to meet you here?" he asked her then.

The directness in him is as un-Arab as his eyes, she thought; and said, "I need your help."

"It is yours," he answered at once, "you know this . . . Now, even more than before."

"Do not promise so fast!" she said quickly. Then gave a low laugh, to lessen the suggestion of rebuke. Went on: "I know that – because of Hisham – you will always be my friend, will always wish to help me; but it is wiser to hear what is requested before promising anything. Especially these days."

"Unless what you ask of me is impossible, literally impossible, I shall do it, Madame; or, make it possible to be done." He turned his head then, and stared at her; but said no more.

She kept her eyes on the valley (knowing that in him there was love for her, a strange kind of love that existed in a part of him that he shared with no one; and knew it was that love she hoped to use).

"This time I need more than a friend, 'Brahim," she said. "I need an *ally*. If you do what I ask, you will – to a certain extent – *commit* yourself to something that I know is against your principles, against your whole way of life."

"Ask it, Madame."

She heard the grimness in his voice; and remembered he was a hard man and – now, with Hisham dead – a lonely one. Turning to him, she met his eyes: blue to grey; and felt the yearning in him.

"I want a gun," she said to him softly. "A silenced gun. I want a gun with which to kill a man."

"Who?"

Her lips lengthened in a tight and narrow smile and her eyes held his.

"A Syrian soldier."

"Why?" He knew why; but knew also – and immediately – that if he refused her he would almost certainly lose something of her.

"Because no one else will."

"But – there are many soldiers?"

"Any Syrian soldier will do. A death for a death. That's simple justice, isn't it? Countryman's justice; and Hisham was in his heart a countryman . . ." She reached out her hand and

34

laid it persuasively over his where it rested on his knee, and her voice came bitter and full of hatred. "We have had no justice for his death, and we never shall have. Somewhere, the men who murdered him live – free. Two drunken soldiers, 'Brahim, and now they are living out their mean useless lives while Hisham is – dead. Two Syrians, gutter-rats from the slums of es Shams. Two animals coming in out of the night, into a man's house with guns in their hands, looking for loot, looking for God knows what; and then – *murdering*. For what? For what? For, *nothing*. There is no meaning to it. Only, Hisham dead . . . And somewhere, two Syrian soldiers who murdered him. Out of our reach." Her hand left his, went to her own face and she smoothed it across her forehead, fingertips lingering over her eyes. (And Ibrahim watching her.) "It is not right that *no one* should be punished. That Hisham should die with nothing to complete his going: that *cannot* be left – unfinished – as if it were of no importance." She turned away from him then. "Also," she said, looking out over the valley, "because I need to do it. For him. *I* need to do it."

Silence brooded within the shade under the big tree. (And from the grey rocks high above, Matt Curran saw the tree with its shade pooled around it as a small darkness on the sun-bright, burnt-brown slopes of the land; but he could distinguish no people down there.)

"No, Madame." The refusal quiet but firm and she knew at once that it would be useless to talk further about it. "I will not give you a gun."

After a moment she said, "You are – a man of peace. There is no reason why you should involve yourself." It mocked him. She had not wanted to mock but out of the pain and frustrated fury in her came a compulsion to hurt him, and the words were said. She felt him recoil from her, but his voice as he continued was almost expressionless.

"But I will help you –"

"There's nothing else I want." Hating; she hating everything, hating even Ibrahim Selim (for being alive when Hisham was dead).

"Madame, please – a little patience. I do not think the same way as you do, you know that. Our country is now so deep in revenge-killings that there seems no way that peace will ever find its way into our lives, our hearts . . . But you have the right

35

to your own decisions and actions, as I have the right to mine. It is not for me to judge you . . . So I will help you get what you want."

Without looking at him she put out her hand again and placed it over his; and said nothing. They were silent for a minute; and although she knew she was going to get from him what she wanted she felt herself lessened by the manner of the getting, as if something of value were gone from her relationship with this self-contained countryman who had a kind of strength that she could never have.

"In Beirut such things are not difficult to arrange," Ibrahim Selim went on quietly. "I know a man who will supply you with a silenced gun. It can be done quite easily."

When they drove down from the mountains it was late afternoon: as they neared the city the soldiers at the checkpoints were aggressive, ordering many cars off the road to be searched, then searching them with deliberate slowness. They were pulled off themselves once, and got into line behind an almost-new white Mercedes sports car whose driver – a young Arab in elegant pale tropical suiting, handsome and bored – strolled back towards them and propped himself against the Renault, on Curran's side, and leaned down to speak to him.

"Which road did you come in on?" he asked, his slightly accented English revealing a French education.

"Damascus-Syria. We only joined it at Shtura, though. Is there trouble?"

The other nodded.

"Near Anjar, on the Damascus road," he said. Continued in a voice of studied nonchalance; but the dark eyes wary and restless in the smooth well-cared-for face delicately scented with Guerlain aftershave. "Someone drove through a road-block without stopping so they opened fire – with a 20 mm cannon." He waited for the question; it was not asked but the answer was churning about inside his own head so he said it aloud hoping that if he spoke it, it might leave him in peace. "The driver and two women with him were blown to pieces."

Curran had no words. But beside him Tagarid moved, leaning across him to ask: "Who was manning the road-block?"

The Arab's eyes met hers.

"Syrian Army," he answered. "Soldiers of the Arab Peace-

Keeping Force. Keeping the peace in the Lebanon. Preventing the Lebanese from killing other Lebanese, so the Government tells us." It was quietly spoken; but the nonchalance was gone from him, and between him and Tagarid, for a second, passed a current of understanding. Then he straightened. "Nice talking to you," he said to Curran. "They can't be much longer with that Volvo in front of me. Vaya con Dios."

When the soldiers came to the Renault they asked merely for identification papers, car-ownership documents, all of which they examined carefully; waved them on, then.

As they entered Raouché, the streets were a surging mass of Sunday shoppers. Open-fronted shacks lined the roadway, crowded close to each other with their backs to the heavily polluted sea, offering for sale merchandise of every possible description; displayed goods festooned every makeshift wall and overflowed out onto the sidewalks, and the crowds were in holiday mood, dressed in their best, children everywhere and the air thick with heat and dust and noise.

"It's mostly Palestinians here, someone told me?" Curran asked.

She nodded. "This used to be one of the most select promenades in Beirut . . . Then the Palestinians came; and were offered the hospitality of our peaceful land. They took that first; and then they took the land." Her voice was neutral, and he was going to go on with it but she shook her head. "Leave it be," she said, low and hard. "There are too many questions and by now everyone has a different answer. And as the answers multiply, the fragmentation of Lebanon increases . . ."

"You'll come in and have a drink, won't you?" he asked as they drove on, along the Corniche, past the British and American Embassies.

"It's only just six . . . You come to me, my flat has a superb view and I'll serve you yerba maté the Druze way."

She let them into her flat, led him into the living-room and then left him while she went to tidy her hair and wash her hands.

Crossing to the window, he stood there entranced, gazing at the city spread out before him down there, working out the layout of known roads and landmarks . . . Heard the door open behind him and turned smiling – to be confronted by a young girl, thin and dark, wearing a dowdy black skirt and blouse, and her hair scraped back and hidden under a plain grey scarf. Obviously she had not expected to find him there; and standing gripping the handle of the kitchen door she stared at him unspeaking, brown eyes blank and uncomprehending, but totally incurious.

As if I do not exist for her, he thought, as if in her world I do not exist. And so: "Misa-el-Kheer," he greeted her (to prove he existed?).

But – without answering she turned and went out, closing the door behind her.

He stared at the closed door. And it seemed to him that she had left a coldness in the room; he sensed it and moved his shoulders as if to shrug it away. But even after he had turned back to the sea and the mountains, the shadow of it remained in the room, the memory of it in his blood and in his mind.

"A girl came in while I was waiting," he said to Tagarid when she returned, taking from her the tray she was carrying and setting it down on the low table by the window. "Young and dark-skinned, very quiet. Your maid?"

"Yes. Fatmeh." She had changed into black silk trousers gathered in at the ankles, and a high-necked grey silk over-blouse; her short black hair shone newly brushed but she wore no make-up, her face as he had always and only seen it: pale and still, frozen into its possessive and unrelenting grief.

"She seemed – a strange girl?"

Tagarid glanced at him in a kind of surprise (and he wondered if there were any other living person of whom she was truly aware, or if since the death of her husband her world had so narrowed that now it contained only herself and the man-remembered).

"Strange? Fatmeh?" She sat down on the sofa, looking down at the tray; and her hands delicately touching the tea-things there, small movements that appeared to him to be totally unnecessary. "I've never really thought about it." (Not saying "about *her*", he noticed: "about *it*", as if the circumstances surrounding the person were the real importance, not the person herself.) "She's very quiet, yes. She came to me on a personal recommendation, I've never asked her about herself." (And still the maid Fatmeh not truly real to her, Curran thought, she did not even ask me what I meant by the word "strange".)

38

He sat down in a chair opposite this woman he already desired, was (perhaps) already in love with. Why, he wondered – it was surely nearly a hopeless cause. He knew it would take a long time to get close to her either mentally or physically: time he didn't have – No, not necessarily a long *time*, time was not the essence of the thing, it was that he had somehow to *break into* her consciousness, get her actually to see him. Looking at her now, he was aware that he was prepared to work very hard at that.

"Will you pour me some tea, then?" he said quietly, smiling at her. He gestured to the array of strange utensils on her tray. "And while you're doing that explain to me *what* you're doing, if you please."

So she spooned green yerba maté from a small cut-glass jar into the two silver handleless cups, gourd-shaped, narrow-mouthed at the top so that your tea will remain comfortingly hot while you talk, for the drinking of tea is an integral part of the social life of the Druze hill villages. She filled the cups with hot water from the small kettle on its heated stand, and then handed him one of them, together with his "kara", the six-inch hollow "spoon" through whose almond-shaped bowl, perforated with tiny holes, he would drink – the "kara" also made of silver, and at the top of its handle, just below the flattened mouthpiece, he saw two coloured stones set into the silver, each spoon with different colours so that when the company is great all may set down their cups freely yet each will know his own again.

But here in this flat eight storeys above the divided city, they were two. And very separate. He, knowing the separateness and beginning to scheme against it. She, not even aware of it because to her, since the murder of her husband, isolation from her fellow-men had been the natural state of living, sought after and, once secured, well-guarded (because within it she was never alone).

They talked about the country they had just spent the day in, she told him about the crops and the life of the people of the villages, she told him a little about fifty-year-old Ibrahim Selim and his young wife from Baalbek, his first wife put away childless and this Sawsan the mother of his sons.

But at last, he said it. With the talk she seemed to have softened a little, he thought; and if she turned away from it, well, he could easily withdraw. Carefully; to try again later.

39

"And – you, Tagarid?" he asked. "You tell me all sorts of things about your country and its people. But not a single thing about yourself."

She looked away from him then; and said after a moment, neutrally: "Hisham is dead. You know that. So you know the most important thing there is to know about me."

Later, he was to wonder if perhaps she had tried to open a way for him, at that point, into what was beginning to take shape in her. But if so, he did not perceive it at the time, he thought she was simply warning him not to attempt to come too close to the grief in which she existed and had her being. So he said gently, "Not that, girl. I meant, tell me about you, who you really are. The 'you' before you were married." And realized suddenly that he had always avoided using her husband's name to her; that even when he was thinking about her husband he never actually *named* him. "About where you were born, your family . . . Things like that."

She sat without speaking for a minute and then got up and stood looking out of the window. Her hand moved up to her hair, she brushed her fingertips along the edge of the inward-curving bell of dark silkiness. Then into the lengthening silence and still with her back to him, she said, "My hair was long. I cut it off, the day *after*. In the morning, early in the morning." And she stood with the silence gathering round her. Then: "My sister cut hers off when she went to college," she said slowly. "Not for any reason. Just because all her friends had short hair . . . I haven't seen Sana'a for more than a year now . . . At my wedding –"

"Is she like you?" he asked quickly, to stop her going back to the very thing he was trying to lead her away from.

She turned and looked at him, a small smile gentling her mouth.

"You don't have to try so hard, Matt," she said, returning to sit down on the sofa, leaning back into the green cushions and curling her legs up underneath her. "I will tell you about me."

"Not unless you want to," he said. "I'm not just being inquisitive. Believe that –"

"I *know* it." (He felt the word, only slightly stressed, as an acceptance of the possibility of his nearness to her. Relaxing, he leaned back in his chair also; and waited for her.) "I don't come from Beirut," she went on after a pause. "I was born in the

40

South, in Tyre. That's where I grew up. My father was a pharmacist, he had two shops, one in Tyre and one in Sidon . . . My mother was from Zahlé, in the Beka'a; her family had – still have – property in the town and when we were kids we used to visit them, it was very beautiful, cherry orchards and the mountains close behind . . . I came to Beirut in 1973 to study at AUB, a four-year course, Business Administration." She made a face, and a gesture with her hands to show her small world comprehensively destroyed. "In '75, the civil war. Both my father's shops were bombed out, looted . . . He was shot down in the street and died in hospital, in Saida . . .

"So we moved up to Beirut because – well, there was no life left for us in the South, only dying and death." Her voice flat and calm, her face half-hidden from him as she folded her hands in her lap and looked down at them, hair sliding forward, shadowing her eyes. "There was no money so I left university and took a job."

"You said 'we'. Who else is there in the family?"

" 'Is' " – she repeated the word as if it were a cruelty, and then went on quietly, her voice preserving a careful peace. "There *is* my sister Sana'a, who cut her hair short to go to college. Sana'a is in Tripoli now, we have a relative who manages a hotel there and Sana'a helps her, just the two of them and a cook. No tourists in Tripoli any more, but it is good to stay open if you possibly can.

"But if we say 'was' – ah, that is different. There *was* my mother, there *was* my brother."

He closed his eyes, appalled.

"Don't talk about it if you'd rather not. I'm so sorry –"

"Don't be," she interrupted. Looked up at him, her eyes hard and bright. "Life isn't all beautiful but you might as well stare it in the face . . . We moved up to Beirut, as I said; four of us after my father was killed: my mother, my brother, my sister and I. Beirut '75: my brother was eighteen and he went out one day, one afternoon, to buy food. He did not return. Three days later my mother was contacted by the police and the hospital: we have this body, they said, the ID bracelet gives a name that is also yours, and your address; the young man was found in the street bleeding to death from gunshot wounds – if he belongs to you would you kindly collect the body. We never knew what had happened, or why . . . After that my mother went back to

41

the family home in Zahlé. She died there not long after – gave up bothering to live, I think." Her eyes were still hard and bright but she reached out her hand and touched his briefly where it was clenched on the arm of his chair. "Don't dream of being sorry about me," she said again. "I'm in no way sorry for myself. Only sorry that so many people I loved are dead . . . And Beirut is full of faces that have stories like mine behind them. Or worse. Much worse."

As he walked home later that evening the faces of the people of the city possessed a new reality for him. Now I am beginning to *live* in Beirut, he thought. I have ceased at last to be a visitor.

High above the harbour, Tagarid Kurban sat by her window recalling the instructions Ibrahim Selim had given her for the establishing of contacts that would quite soon put into her hands a silenced gun. Now, *I* am beginning, she thought exultantly; and whispered aloud the name of the man with whom it would begin: "Khaled."

In the kitchen of the flat, Fatmeh Mohammad Hamad was preparing Mihshi Warra Enib: a quiet dark girl, carefully wrapping spiced rice in vine leaves, as in the past she had done many times in her own home under the watchful and critical eyes of her adored mother. Now also, dead.

3

THE NEXT morning, looking out of the window of her flat, Tagarid checked her watch by the clock high up on the tower of the American University: 6.45, and the early morning sunlight shining full on the clock-tower, flaring the bougainvillea flowers below it to brilliant purple where they lay massed along the university's yellow-stone enclosing walls. As she turned back into the room, Fatmeh came in from the kitchen carrying a tiny cup of coffee, Turkish, and the delicious aroma of cardomum came with her. Carefully – without word of greeting – the girl leaned across the dining-table to set it down and

– the blast of an explosion close by, a crashing blow of sound pounding through the framework of the building.

– Tagarid's body jerked and she ducked away from the window.

– Fatmeh screamed once, dropped the coffee cup and ran and hid her face against the door.

Silence. Tagarid straightened up and glanced quickly out of the window, but the explosion had come from behind the building and she saw only other faces at windows, stranger-faces peering out, caught up in the violence clawing at them out of the morning sunlight. Looking round she noticed the spilt coffee spreading across the table, dripping slowly down on to the pale carpeting; and Fatmeh huddled with her face pressed against the door, whimpering.

"Get a cloth," she said harshly, and walked across to the table, stood the cup upright in its saucer again.

Fatmeh remained exactly where she was, only raised her arms above and around her head, seeming to draw herself into herself yet further as if seeking vainly to make herself invisible; and her whimpering remained a monotony on the air, a mindless, directionless terror.

But Tagarid saw the girl's continuing fear as merely feeble stupidity. The immediate shock, and stab of fright – until you knew yourself whole and untouched – yes, everyone felt that when a bomb went off close by, in Beirut. But the people of the city had been living with that kind of thing for more than five years now; and if the bomb – or rocket, or whatever – did not kill or maim *you*, and if there was no immediate call for assistance – which you might or might not answer – you simply got on with living your own life. That was the only way to keep comparatively sane in this world gone mad.

"Fatmeh, *please* – go and get a cloth!" she said again. "The danger's over and the stain's getting into the carpet."

The whimpering went on, fretting the silence; and Fatmeh entirely unmoving.

Then, almost, Tagarid went to the girl, to hold and comfort her. She stood in loneliness herself and for a moment perceived a lonely and terrified girl. But suddenly out of the silence the memories grabbed her

– the aroma of coffee on the air another time another place

– blood – coffee – *Hisham dead.*

Her body shook with anguish. And when the spasm was over and she became aware of the girl Fatmeh again, she hated her because she was alive and Hisham was dead. Walked past her without look or touch and found a cloth in the cleaning cupboard, also a can of carpet shampoo, and returning to the living-room wiped the coffee stains from the table and from the carpet, working with deliberate total concentration in order to block off all other thoughts.

When she had finished she took the cleaning materials out into the kitchen. Fatmeh was there now, sitting on a wooden chair at the breakfast table, staring into space. Freshly brewed coffee simmered on the gas-stove.

"I'll take my coffee now," Tagarid said quietly, and went back into the sitting-room again.

In the kitchen, Fatmeh's head moved. For a long minute she stared at the door through which Tagarid had left the room; and a burning hatred gathered in her dark eyes, gradually increasing in intensity as if the hatred were being channelled from all parts of her being to meet in her eyes and become a living entity, growing.

★

44

In high summer the morning freshness is soon gone: it was only 7.30 as Tagarid walked along Hamra on her way to the SaxAir offices, but it was already oppressively hot, the humidity a lassitude insinuating itself into the corners of the mind. Immaculate in black silk shirt-waister and high-heeled sandals, she moved with her own sharply defined grace and an air of personal remoteness.

On Hamra most of the shops are functioning now, four years after the ending of actual and overt civil war, though there are some whose heavy steel shutters, installed in '75 against looters, have never been raised since then. The worn and broken pavements have not been repaired and are dangerous with sudden treacheries but she comes this way every day and – that day, it was different. Ahead, the wide thoroughfare was blocked by a mass of people, a turbulence of men and women milling around, questioning, answering, exclaiming – moving off and standing by – and the noise of their turmoil was unmistakably fuelled by two things: fear, and the raw excitement engendered by destructive violence that has left you yourself unharmed. She worked her way through the crowd, keeping to the left-hand side of the street as she approached the two fire engines and an ambulance blocking the middle of the road, picking her way over broken glass, and looking up to her right saw the ripped-open blackened windows of a line of offices three storeys above, torn curtains flapping and a thin stream of smoke, the hoses and ladders leading up to it and firemen glimpsed working inside.

"Who got done this time?"

"Iraqi Airlines –"

"'They' should keep to the rules, not do it when ordinary people are on their way to work –"

"– many casualties, so they say – two fatal. Many taken to hospital, flying glass mostly, just passers-by –"

"'They' must have been clever, to get it in past the guards –"

Always "they" when you are out in the open; to name names, in Lebanon in the eighties, you need a wall of friends around you and a lot of guns at your back . . .

At her own office-block the security men, in civilian clothes but overtly armed with machine-pistols, nodded to her and let her pass. They should have stopped me, she thought; they know my face but I'm carrying a holdall – not big, but big *enough* – they should have stopped me and checked what was in it. And as she went up in the lift she wondered if at Iraqi Airlines some employee – clerk, PA or cleaner, known and trusted (or perhaps not even that, but the guards bored, lazy or bought) had simply walked in to work with his/her bag and then walked out again without it . . . How easy it is, she thought, how very very easy when you don't care *who* you kill. *That* is the secret of success: that it is not important (within limits) *who*: only, that you do it.

It was a busy morning at the office. At a quarter to nine, when she was called for by Matt Curran, she merely noted the fact that Siham had not yet arrived and hoped briefly that the girl wasn't ill, had succeeded in getting back safely from her visit home; then Curran took her directly into the Director's sanctum to sit in on a fairly high-level conference. Which was interrupted just after ten: the sirens sounded, the street noises – in any case muted this high up, and all windows tight-closed to maintain the cool of air-conditioning – suddenly fainter still as drivers down in the street drew in to the side of the road; and the six people at the conference got to their feet and moved to the windows and looked out (it is always advisable to know just what is happening, if that is possible).

At first there was apparently nothing to see; only, in all the windows opposite, on the flat roofs of lower buildings, other faces looking out, heads turning, eyes questing, and in the street far below the traffic at a standstill. They opened the windows wide, and heard the quiet now punctuated by the blaring horns of other drivers who, caught in the jam, wanted to get on their way. Then, saw the street-faces turning skywards, the faces at the windows opposite getting the message and suddenly everyone gazing up, arms upraised, fingers pointing.

Dog-fight up there in the blue. Planes high up in the far and brilliant skies. White vapour-trails patterning the sky, patterns delineating the savage dance of the fighter-planes in their swooping curves of flight, new images being created as the old ones drifted away and vanished so that all is flowing but incoherent . . . Above the hush of the watching city the snarl and whine of the aero-engines runs brutal (and the car horns suddenly silent).

From the Port area, ack-ack guns begin to bark defiance, but the white puffs of their bursting shells are so far below the

46

committed planes that they seem idiotic (which they are), nothing to do with that drama of death and combat being acted out in the high blue above.

You have sometimes to remind yourself that they are killing each other up there, Tagarid thought. Each highly trained pilot, each highly complex machine a terrible weapon in his country's hands seeking the destruction of its chosen enemy . . . It is all incomprehensible and dreadfully beautiful.

"Whose planes?" Matthew Curran questioned her, without looking round.

"Syrian, Israeli, I suppose," she said huskily. "They both fly regular patrols over Beirut. One of them got the timing wrong today." Shading her eyes against the brilliant sunlight, she added, "Or got it right, who knows. Maybe, one of them came looking for a fight."

Suddenly, one white trail up there – ends: the end seen final against azure blue. And half a minute later – as people hold their breath – a thick, deep thud is heard, far off in the hills but enormously heavy, a great hammer-blow, and its tremor shudders through the ground to rise up into the fabric of the buildings, rattle the windows and strike deep into the hearts of the onlookers. Who know only too well what it means – the shattered metal the searing flame, and the blinding impact reverberating through air and earth to tell them.

"Christ." A statement, not an exclamation. And Matt Curran turned away from the window, stared with disbelief at the calm elegance surrounding him. For a moment he struggled in limbo, unable to make a bridge across the fearful gap between the two realities; then, with an effort of will, he forced his mind to take cognisance of the room about him. Everyone had left the windows, which were being closed now; the men-of-business were all moving back towards the big oval table in the centre of the room, yet for the time being no man spoke to anyone else, each was enmeshed within his own separateness, his eyes avoiding those of his fellow-men while he rediscovered his own world. Through the shuffling quiet the air-conditioning hummed away quietly to itself.

"Whose was it, I wonder?" Someone eventually floated the remark across the silence.

Someone else said, "Syrian. I hope."

As the words were spoken, Curran looked at his PA. And saw

47

her face lift, the blue eyes quickly taking in the man who had spoken them then as swiftly she looked away, in his direction, but he knew she was not really seing him, the sapphire eyes brilliant but, quite blank: herself shut away behind them but something burning in her so fiercely that the blankness was flamed with the potency of it. Indefinable – but obsessive. Gone then; and her eyes slid away and she turned towards her chair, which was positioned slightly behind his own at the table, her hands already moving possessively among her papers . . . *What* had he seen then, he wondered. His mind produced the word "ferocity" in answer and he considered it briefly and then pushed it away as being way-out nonsense. Was pulled back into the business world almost immediately as the Chairman rapped the table, calling the conference into being once more. But his memory held onto the incident, would not let him forget or dismiss it. An unease about her had been born in him. Unease *for* her . . .

The meeting finished at 11.30, and as Tagarid returned to her own office the phone was ringing. Tossing down her notes, still standing, she answered it, identifying herself by way of greeting.

"Who is that? Who is that?" A woman's voice coming over the line, high-pitched and strained.

"Mr Curran's PA. Tagarid Kurban."

There was no response so, thinking that perhaps the caller had the wrong number altogether, she said, "This is the SaxAir office. Who would you like to speak to, please?"

"I don't know, there was this number in her book so –"

"Madame," Tagarid interrupted, "do you want SaxAir or do you have the wrong number?"

"Forgive me, Madame." A short silence. Then, the woman's voice quiet now, obviously carefully controlled: "My name is Ibtisam Rawdah. My sister –"

"Oh, you're Siham's sister!" Tagarid glanced across the room and confirmed that the other desk was exactly as it had been when she had left for the conference earlier that morning. "I work in the same office as Siham but I've been out until just now. I didn't realize she hadn't come in today. I do hope she isn't ill?"

"Ill?" The word repeated sharply, as if it were a strange concept that Siham might be ill; and then repeated again, eagerly this time. "Ill? Yes, yes, of course she is ill, the doctor says she must stay in bed –"

"Will she be in tomorrow?"

"In? What do you mean, 'in'?" The voice rising again, running wild.

"Will she be able to come to work, do you think – tomorrow?"

Silence. Then: "No." Very quiet, the one word. Again, "No" – and then the receiver put down.

Tagarid hung up and stood staring at the phone, baffled and more than a little disturbed. Baffled because the woman – Ibtisam Rawdah – had in fact told her nothing, and her voice had been – surely? – very close to hysteria; disturbed because she had gained a strong impression that Siham was by no means simply and ordinarily "ill". There were car-bombs every day in this city, kidnappings, shoot-outs, everyone was always at risk, one way or the other; also, worse, the girl lived over in the Christian sector very close to the Green Line, and the snipers were often in position above the crossings, ruthless, unpredictable and deadly.

If she does not ring in tomorrow I'll find out her number and ring her, Tagarid decided; but, for the time being, it might be better to leave things as they are. After a few moments she settled down again to her own work.

She met him for the first time that night: "Khaled", the man whose name Ibrahim Selim had given her. Had phoned him the day after she and Matt Curran had been into the mountains together, and a meeting had immediately been arranged: ten o'clock at night, at a café-bar called La Paloma, down a side-street off Verdun. She had been a little surprised at both the time and the place – it was late for a woman to be out walking the streets alone (but he quick to stipulate "alone"), and the café was deep in a hard-core Party area – but she had agreed immediately.

And now as she walked in that direction – a tall, slight figure keeping to the dark side of the empty streets, long-sleeved black shirt worn outside black jeans, her holdall in her hand – she wondered what he would be like, this Khaled. But only briefly, soon dismissing him with a mental shrug. So many "Khaleds". He will give (or sell) me a gun, she thought, her head lifting and

49

the resolve, bitter and hard, twisting her mouth. That is his only importance to me: *he will give me a gun.*

But it was not like that at all.

La Paloma was set well back from the road, with a red-and-white tiled courtyard in front of it. Where this met the pavement, a line of steel posts cemented into concrete at one-metre intervals denied access to vehicles. And as she turned in off the street and began to walk towards the yellowly lit restaurant she noted the four spotlights (dark now) mounted above the entrance; noted also that the courtyard was flanked by the blind side-walls of two six-storey apartment blocks, not even bathroom windows overlooking it; finally noted the three khaki-uniformed militiamen grouped to the side of the restaurant doorway, two standing, the third seated, an automatic weapon across his knees.

The militiamen watched her approach. When she was a few metres from the doorway the man in the chair moved and, although he did not get up or openly threaten with his weapon, she knew it was a challenge.

"Khaled." She gave only the name, as instructed. And the guard's hand moved in a small gesture: go in.

She came to a halt just within the doorway, expecting someone to come forward and meet her. A long room, fairly well-lit down the central aisle and a bar right across the far end, bottles glittering under concealed lighting and a big Expresso machine purring away; but to either side, the lights on each table very low-powered so that nothing could be clearly seen, within the gloom the shapes of tables and men seemed enveloped in secrecy. Some of the men seated round the tables looked at her – and some went on looking – but there was no lull in the quiet hum of conversation and no one made any move towards her.

So after a few seconds she walked a short way down the aisle, then stepped aside to the right, into the secretive half-light. There were one or two empty tables and she sat down at one by the wall, on its top of plain dark wood two heavy glass ashtrays and, close to the wall, a large brass candlestick converted to electricity but its bulb unlit. She hesitated, then found the switch and turned it on. Feeling suddenly exposed and vulnerable, though the light was very dim, but shrugging that off too, composing herself to wait patiently.

50

He came then. Moving in out of the narrow aisle without warning so that she had no idea from where he had been watching her, only knew that he had been. He stood close by the table looking down at her and she knew at once that he was not just a gun-slinger, this one. More, much more than that. About forty, average height, powerfully built and without softness anywhere in his body, which he held with a kind of taut ease; but authority emanating from him so forcefully that she felt herself momentarily overmatched and, swiftly gathering her defences round her, held his eyes. Then his eyes possessed hers, he was "searching" her and she dared not look away.

It was a thing of seconds only. She felt him release her.

"I am Khaled Namur," he said then, sitting down opposite her across the table.

"Tagarid Kurban – as you already know." His face was dark-skinned, his mouth long and narrow-lipped in a hard jaw; and power resided in his eyes, slate-grey eyes with the dominance quiet now not stabbing into her. She remembered what she had come to this place for. "I have come for the gun."

"Why do you want it?"

Anger moved in her then, that he should question her.

"Surely Ibrahim Selim told you that?" she said.

He leaned back in his chair, and his eyes were cold and indifferent.

"He told me, yes. But I do not give away guns on the strength of stories told me at secondhand."

Her anger mounted, and a chill misery came with it, twisting, tearing the soft parts of the self. Not to let him see that: "You're not giving it away," she said bitterly, "I'm *paying* you good money for it."

His eyes came at her again, diamond-gleaming.

"For your information, I do not *sell* guns. Either I *give* the gun to you or you don't get it . . . Who do you plan to use it against?"

"A Syrian. A Syrian soldier."

"Tell me everything that is behind this."

So she told him. Briefly, but going into it deeply, revealing herself; and the words were simple and true and fast. When she stopped – came back into that lit shadowy place again, leaving Hisham and the mountain night, Hisham and the morning sunlight – there was a cup of coffee on the table in front of her,

51

aromatic black coffee, and a glass of water beside it. She drank the coffee. It was the first time she had told it like *that* to anyone, right out of the inside of herself, not hiding anything; and she felt light and empty.

He asked no questions; merely said out of his quietness, "You shall have the gun on Saturday."

"You mean – you haven't got it here?" She stared at him in disbelief, anger rising again. "Ibrahim said –"

Suddenly, he leaned forward across the table towards her, his right hand making a swift sharp gesture like a knife slicing sideways; and his face close to hers.

"You have entered what is primarily a man's world," he said softly, but his eyes *not* soft, holding hers, and the power in them again. "A world in which guns are given to fighting men with the intention that they be used for the killing of others, where the killing of others is a necessary statement of belief . . . I needed to know whether or not you are a woman capable of handling herself in that world and therefore a woman who, despite a desire for purely personal vengeance, has the *character* to use a gun properly." He leaned back and a faint smile lengthened his mouth. He watched her, still. "We have women in the Group," he said, "but only two of them are, as you are. The others do duties more suited to their gentler natures . . . They do them very well," he added.

Something in him – about him, about the words he used – reached into her and she felt herself aware of him, of the reality of him as a man, as she had not been aware of any individual since the night Hisham had been murdered. Ever since that night she had felt herself separate, shut away from the outside world by an enclosing membrane within which she existed in a newly created one-ness of herself and Hisham-remembered (separate as a foetus is separate, she had thought once, cocooned within its caul, an outside world supporting its life and itself enclosed blind, breathing, living in the shadow of life . . .). Now it was as if that enclosing membrane had split, a thin small slit through which she eyed the outside world again, a world seen narrowly, dimly.

"Shall I come here then, on Saturday? For the gun?" she asked.

"No. There is a restaurant called The Speakeasy, on Mikdassi –"

52

"I know it." Suddenly she was aware of weariness, of a need to be home and by herself.

"Come in the evening," he said. "Around seven o'clock."

She felt understanding in his brevity; and rose to go. As she stepped into the central aisle the light seemed brighter and taped music was in the air, Fairouz throaty and vibrant. How strange, Tagarid thought as she walked towards the door, I did not hear the music begin; I only heard what he and I were saying to each other.

The guard had gone from his place and there were no acolytes lounging outside. She walked away across the court-yard and began to make her way home, keeping close to the housewalls and shopfronts so that their overhanging balconies gave her a darkness to walk within. Near full, the moon stood high in the sky, its brilliance pouring down so that the roadway streamed past in an aura of flat, white light. Her rubber-soled shoes made no sound on the pavement. Walking shadowed and quietly, she set her mind to probe what had just taken place, exploring cautiously the change she had felt in herself and thinking not of the gun and what she planned to do with it but of the man Khaled, the man of authority and "belief".

Walking hidden by the dark, and a new buoyancy in her; met no one, the street hers alone

– heard cars then. Two, in the distance but approaching, driven very fast, the sound of their engines (unsilenced?) ripping the night apart. Coming from the direction of Raouché. She shrank into a dark alleyway because in this city – this year – this time of night – two cars driven like that meant only one thing: violence with guns in it and a shooting at the end. She pressed herself against unseen railings, gripping them tight with her free hand – cold, clammy metal – holding her breath. Listening. About a hundred yards further on Sidani Street crossed the street she was in, and with any luck at all they would turn at the crossroads there, not drive straight across and so come past her . . . ?

They did not turn. She heard the lead car blaring its horn as it came up to the crossroads, but it came straight over without slowing (the driver must think *nothing* can be worse than what will happen if his pursuer catches up with him, she thought, with heart-clenching fear) and roared towards her

– the second car right on its tail swinging out to pass even as it drew level with her hiding place

– frozen, she heard the squeal of brakes, tyres screaming, then the crash of metal against metal and the splintering of glass

– a second of absolute silence.

Then car doors opening, two, one after the other. A thin brittle crackling sound – glass being trodden underfoot, breaking, and across it a shouted command, a man's voice, savage, peremptory.

And suddenly the fear in her succumbed to a swarming excitement. Keyed up, mindlessly intent, she felt the adrenalin coursing through her. And treading with catlike stealth, lips parted for shallow, silent breathing, moved out into the street so that she could see – be part of – what was happening.

Street seen clearly under gleaming moonlight. The two cars were about thirty yards from her, the other side of the road. One, black, forced to swerve sideways as the overtaking car had slashed across the roadway in front of it, had crashed into the metal-mesh frontage of a dress-shop and now was held there, looming curiously misshapen half in moonlight and half in darkness. The other, white, lay athwart the moonlit road, long and powerful, both its front doors open. The two men who had come out of it stood some distance from the crashed car. Gunman fashion: feet apart, arms braced out in front of them, their pistols trained on the driver's door.

"Come out with your hands empty, you bastard!" Arabic, the same command as before. The harsh voice slicing across the quietness.

There was no movement from the wrecked car.

One of the gunmen said something, but it was said so low that she could not hear the words. Only, the other laughed. And at the laugh, Tagarid shivered and stepped back. But continued to watch, as though mesmerized.

Then one of the gunmen ran forward, wrenched open the driver's door, leapt to one side – and crouched covering the open doorway with his gun.

"Out!"

A man emerged. With difficulty, his movements uncertain; he was obviously hurt. One pale hand was lifted to show there was nothing in it but the other, not.

"Get them both up!" The gun jerking, menacing.

54

Tagarid heard no answer. Only saw the injured man slowly straighten up beside the car door, head down. He was tall and slight, his hair quite white. The man with the gun leapt in again and grabbed him with his free hand and – he screamed. But thinly; and the sound quickly suppressed.

"Okay." The gunman stood back, satisfied that the man's other arm was useless. "Now get the girl out of there!"

The old man shook his head.

"Get her *out*!"

The old man's voice quite clear then, coaxing.

"Nisrine. Come out, my child. You've *got* to come out."

She looked very small, a young girl in a white dress, standing in front of the two guns. Maybe fourteen years old.

The second gunman shot her where she stood. Three shots. She crumpled and died without a sound.

It ended quickly after that. The gunmen bundled their captive into the back of their car, got in themselves; and drove away, up the street, tyres squealing as the car was reversed and straightened but driven without haste from then on.

The body of the girl lay as a shapeless huddle in the moon-light.

Tagarid slipped out of her alleyway and ran – lightly and quickly and keeping to the dark – ran away from there. But stopped in a doorway at the crossroads, breathing hard, and looked back: lights were coming on in the flats above the crashed car, people were craning over the railings of their balconies . . . After a time she walked on, at a normal pace. The body of "Nisrine" would soon be taken care of; it was no longer any affair of hers.

At her flat she had just poured herself a brandy when the lights flickered. Usually that heralded a power-cut, so she found candles and placed them ready in the living-room, turned on the central ceiling light and carried her brandy in there. As she set her glass down on the oval-topped table by the window, the light went out.

Instead of lighting the candles, she drew back the curtains. And saw that the power-cut had affected the whole city. Below her, the city lay ghostly in moonlight, embracing the sweet curve of the harbour, running back into the hills beyond; and its spreading distances were not ablaze with lights, were not criss-crossed by the geometric patterns of roadways lined with fluorescent lighting so brilliant that there was only brilliance to be seen: under moonlight the skyscrapers of the city were blocked in in white and black and grey, were jewelled with the soft lights of many homes already burning lamps and candles. It looked very beautiful –

Beautiful? Her eyes found "snipers' tower" and as usual the white glare of a pressure-lamp shone out from the fifteenth floor: the marksmen were in position, up there; from the direction of Caracol el Druze, suddenly, came a fierce exchange of small-arms fire, the crump of an explosion . . . She recalled the body of the girl Nisrine then, lying formless in the roadway, and wondered if the man who had been kidnapped could still see the beauty of the night or hear the sounds of his city.

So she closed the curtains. Sat by candlelight, drinking her brandy and letting her thoughts run free, to Hisham, to the love of Hisham and herself. And the slit that the man Khaled Namur had incised in the membrane enclosing her within her separate world meshed together again swiftly and completely: shut up in there, she considered how to accomplish the killing of a man.

4

"COME IN straight away, will you." Matt Curran's voice over the office intercom clipped and hard, and Tagarid picked up her notepad and went.

He was standing by the window looking out. Cloudless blue skies this day, and the city basking brilliant in the morning sunshine. Streets full of traffic.

"Did you listen to the News this morning?" he asked.

"Yes, Mr Curran."

"My name is Matt."

"All right."

He turned towards her, saw the notepad in her hand and gestured at it impatiently. "You won't need that. Take a seat." And waving her to a chair he sat down behind his glass-topped desk, leaned back and looked across at her. "This kidnapping business last night," he said. "I don't speak enough Arabic for the local News, so I listened to the BBC this morning, but it wasn't mentioned. Tell me what's known."

"Which kidnapping?" she asked slowly.

"How many have there been?" he snapped. Then, "Up in the north. The Group thing. Beyond Byblos."

"Is it so important?"

"Yes." He nodded. "I've just come from the Director. He says that George Salamoun was among those taken –"

"Mr Salamoun!" She knew the man, though not well: Sax-Air's senior representative out at the airport – middle-aged, smooth-faced and (in her opinion) almost too smooth-tongued for comfort. "How does the Director know anything about it?" she asked. "They said on the News there'd been no communication whatsoever from the kidnappers?"

"Apparently Salamoun got through to him on the phone early this morning. They're friends."

57

She smiled thinly. "Yes, so I've heard. Who your friends are can be more important than anything else these days, can't it?"

But he was impatient of her interruption.

"Tell me everything that's been reported," he said.

"It was at a road-block on the coast road running north from Byblos to Tripoli. A 'Group' road-block of some kind. Just before six yesterday evening the militiamen began stopping all cars and then went along the line, taking out all the men and marching them off into the hills."

"How many? All told?"

"No one seems to know, exactly. About a hundred and fifty. It appears the Group – whoever they are – wanted certain men known to be travelling that route at that time every day. Probably those not on their 'list' will be released. Probably. In time."

"What's the background to it? Does anyone know?"

He saw her face change subtly, a momentary tightening of mouth and eyes.

"Revenge, almost certainly," she said levelly. And then her face smooth again, eyes secretary-to-boss impersonal.

He moved in his chair, looked away.

"Go on. Revenge for what?"

"I don't know." She shrugged. "But it's probably a blood-feud between two families, each seeking political domination over a particular area, or town. It happens all the time. Now there's no effective central government and therefore practically nothing in the way of law-enforcement, such things escalate without warning. Perhaps, some time ago, one side attacked the other, killing the opposing leader's son or some other close relative – a 'massacre' it was probably called at the time. So yesterday's kidnappers were out to get even for that, and in exchange will surely kill some of the men they have taken."

"Just – any of them? Whether they were actually involved in the previous killing or not?"

"That is all revenge demands, in the last resort, isn't it: a life for a life?" (He realized his question had surprised her; and felt a definite chill touch him at the realization.) "At the time of the 'massacre'," she continued coolly, "one important man or another of the attacked family was probably taken prisoner. Almost certainly he has never been heard of since until recently,

58

when people began circulating rumours that he is being held in, let us say, Damascus. It is conceivable that yesterday's kidnappers will therefore keep some of their prisoners alive, and barter their lives for the life and freedom of the man they have heard of as being in Syria."

" 'Barter'." He repeated the word quietly, looking down for a moment at the papers on his desk, encompassing with his mind the vast and terrible human desert portrayed by the use of such a word in connection with the lives of men.

"We have always been a trading nation," she said into the silence.

Startled, he looked up at her quickly: almost, she was laughing at him, but at the same time her eyes were very hard, warning him that he had no right to comment.

"So, what of George Salamoun?" he asked presently. Because it was true, he did not have that right. Not as a "visitor" to this country, anyway, only perhaps as a human being.

"Unless he was connected in some way with the original 'massacre', he will almost certainly be freed – since he obviously has effective names to use."

Silent then, she waited for him to question further, or to move on to office affairs. But he did neither.

"Tagarid," he said quietly, "do *you* ever long for revenge?"

"I know it is impossible." Her answer given swiftly and he knew it was an evasion, kicked himself mentally for asking.

She stood up, regarding him impersonally, forcing the talk back into the office strait-jacket, asking, "Do you want me to take any action for the moment about Mr Salamoun?"

He shook his head, already opening a file on his desk.

"Leave it with the Director," he said. "But thank you for filling me in on the situation . . . Is the Accounts clerk back in today?"

"She's not here yet. And there's been nothing more from her sister. I'll try to ring her again, later in the morning."

But she had only just got back to her own office when the Receptionist rang through to say a Miss Dhaibo was asking to see her but refusing to give any reason for her visit.

"Send her along – but don't forget, her hand-bag, or *anything* she's carrying," Tagarid said, reminding the girl of the standard procedures against acts of terrorism.

A tall, slender-waisted creature, Miss Dhaibo, with a drama-

59

tic gypsy face dominated by large brown eyes under tapering black brows.

"My name is Dina Dhaibo and I have come about Siham," she said at once, standing just within the office doorway, her eyes steady on Tagarid.

"I've been trying to contact her," Tagarid said, after introducing herself and pulling forward a chair for the girl. "We're hoping she'll be back soon, we really need her."

But Dina Dhaibo would not sit down. She stood beside the chair, regarding Tagarid narrowly, obviously uncertain about something.

"Didn't her sister ring you?" she asked after a moment.

Tagarid sat down behind her desk, turning her chair so that she faced the girl.

"Ye-es," she said, "she rang yesterday but she wasn't very forthcoming. How is Siham?"

Again the hesitation; then: "She's dead," Dina Dhaibo said abruptly. "I thought you'd know." And in the following silence did sit down, clasping her hands tightly together in her lap. Her eyes did not leave Tagarid for one second.

Who searched them for grief; but discovered only a smouldering anger. And said quietly, "I'm so sorry. I didn't know her well; but I liked her." She was very conscious of Dina Dhaibo's steady regard: it seemed almost as if the girl were *evaluating* her. She wondered why; and then broke the silence.

"Her sister said she was ill," she said, "but she didn't say what was the matter with her."

"She wasn't ill. She was shot."

Every night there is gunfire in some parts of Beirut and the bullets must go somewhere, Tagarid thought. And was marshalling the right words when: "Her brother shot her," Dina Dhaibo said.

For the first time since the murder of her husband, the death of another person really got through to Tagarid Kurban. Suddenly she felt genuine grief for Siham, and horror. Then got a grip on herself, saying coldly, "Her *brother*? I can't believe that."

The girl leaned forward in her chair, still staring Tagarid in the eyes, and the anger flamed in her.

"Of course I have no proof," she said tautly. "But listen. Listen to me . . . Siham was Druze – as I am – she came from a village up in the Shouf not far from mine. Her father is an important man in the hierarchy. And it is – as you probably know – a strict tenet of our Faith that for a Druze girl to marry 'outside' is forbidden. Totally forbidden. The Elders will do – *anything* – to prevent such a thing. Or to 'correct matters' – those are the words they use – if such a marriage takes place . . . Well, Siham married a Christian –"

"She *married* him? She told me –"

"Whatever she told you, never mind! Secretly, here in Beirut, she married him, a month ago . . . Then last week she went up to the village, to visit her family for the first time since her marriage." The girl straightened in her chair and sat back, her hands still locked together in her lap. "Well, two days ago – when she was expected back here – she didn't return. Only, her sister came round to our house yesterday evening and told us she was dead, she'd had a heart attack and died. Up there in the village, she said . . . A heart attack! That has to be a lie. They found out from her, or they had heard, about her marriage – *so they killed her*."

Tagarid shook her head slowly; then asked, "But why should you think – Why do you say it was her brother who shot her?"

"Maybe you do not know," Dina Dhaibo said, "but since the war anything can happen away in the far villages. They are hard people; though I am Druze myself, I tell you – everything about them is hard, barbarous . . . She was frightened, Siham, before she went home last week. They think of a marriage like hers as a betrayal, bringing dishonour to the family, to the clan. Therefore the traitor must be killed by a member of his own family, that is the way of it . . . She was frightened," Dina Dhaibo said again. "The night before she went back she was round at our place, and I think she would have un-made her marriage, if it had been possible to do so."

"Then why did she go back?"

"She said that if she didn't, they would know something was wrong, and come looking for her in Beirut, and if that happened not only she but her husband also would be killed. So she said she had to go, but not tell them . . . But a lie like that is very difficult to keep up with your family around you, especially when you already feel deep guilt inside."

"Can't her *husband* do something about it? If it's as you say, she was murdered. Surely –"

61

A short hard laugh jerked out of Dina Dhaibo, and she tossed her head.

"Him! He is rubbish," she said with fierce contempt. "Handsome, but rubbish. Yesterday, after the visit of Siham's sister, I went round to see him, and gave him the news. I, because I was her closest friend. I told him we should go to someone in authority, he and I together —" She was staring at Tagarid again, and the strong gypsy face was arrogant with her anger. "– And do you know what he did? He started packing. To run away. This morning he took a bus to the South, where he comes from. No one will ever follow him down there!" Her story finished, she sat silent, looking down.

Tagarid saw a proud and bitter girl. And said slowly: "Why have you told me all this? Do you expect *me* to do something? Is that what you came here for?"

Dina Dhaibo looked up, eyes snapping.

"No! I know, really, there is nothing to be done . . . When I came here I didn't know I was going to tell you." The tension was draining out of the girl's face now. "But it was good to tell someone," she said. "Thank you for listening to me."

"Why *did* you come here, then?"

"To ask for Siham's job," Dina Dhaibo answered without embarrassment. "I thought you must know she was dead . . . My training was the same as hers, and I thought perhaps I could get the job before it was advertised."

Tagarid smiled at her, nodded, and rang for coffee. Basically she approved of such straightforwardness; and liked the thought of this girl working with her.

Saturday, and the usual August weather: hot and humid. At midday Tagarid stood at the window of her flat, gazing out at the city and the sea, at the mountains beyond. The air was hazy and overcast, hung heavy and still; no white-caps to break the dull monotony of the sea, buildings all uniform yellow-grey, pallid and lifeless, and across the harbour the mountains characterless, their summits blurred and sombre.

She had woken early to a small breeze blowing in through her open window, a sea breeze; and beyond the curve of the harbour the mountains looming blue-black against a sky suffused with the red glare of the rising sun. The planet Venus blazed brilliant where the red of morning met the blue of night; and Tagarid had watched that brilliance fade and die as the sun came up.

Watching, had thought of Hisham. As dawn moved on the mountains, relived the loving that had been cut – bloodily, entirely and irrevocably – out of her life. And when she came to the end of it, had flung herself face-down on the bed to lie rigid, her eyes clenched shut; one hand was fisted tight against her cheek but the other, open, moved slowly back and forth across the pillow, a small controlled movement, hard, purposeful: she was rubbing the blood off her palm, Hisham's blood that had gathered there as she crawled through it towards his body . . .

She scourged herself free, eventually. And got through Saturday morning mechanically, doing the Saturday morning chores: first organizing Fatmeh's three hours of work, then leaving her to do it and herself going out to shop, to collect some laundry. The streets humming, for although many residents of West Beirut had followed their usual summer-living habit and driven out for the weekend to their chalets in the mountains, many who lived in the predominantly Christian Eastern sector had come across the Green Line to shop for the fresh produce and consumer goods more readily available in the West.

With other purchases completed, she stopped for fruit at a stall on the corner of Sidani Street: she usually bought her fruit there, liking the stall-holder, a tall middle-aged man with a pronounced limp and a pain-ravaged face. He had near-perfect English and once she had asked him where he had learned it. "With the British Army," he had answered shortly; and then had told her the apricots were excellent, just that morning down from the Beka'a . . .

Today, his stall was heaped with peaches and greengages, with big grapefruit whose skins were blushed with pink. As she began to select peaches, he passed her a plastic bag then lifted up a box of fruit from a stack on the ground, ripped it open and set it down beside her.

"These are from my own place, Ja'amshaa," he said, "try these."

She thanked him and did so, half-listening as he went on talking.

"A bad thing, that shooting up the street here the other night, the man and the girl," he said. "So much crime on our streets and none of it punished."

63

Her attention caught, she glanced sideways at him, saw his head down, his hands busy among his fruit.

"Was it a political killing?" she asked.

"Not political, no. The man was in on the 'hash' market and was cheating the big boys. He was a prominent middleman."

"Is it known where he is? Where he was taken?"

"Madame, even his best friends would hope he is dead by this time."

It was said so matter-of-factly that she felt no horror, no sense of involvement. Only asked quietly, "And the girl?"

"No one round here knows anything about her. Not even her name."

"No papers?"

"No papers. Just the body . . . Be careful, Madame," he said softly, his hands unpacking early figs with care, his eyes apparently intent on what he was doing. "Be very careful. Our streets are dangerous at night and when they seem empty they are often at their most dangerous." Then allowing her no time to respond he turned to her briskly, taking the bag of peaches from her hand.

"Just one kilo, Madame?" he asked, moving away round the stall to put the fruit on his scales. They were just under the kilo, and calling to her to bring another peach he concluded the sale with professional dexterity and turned to his next customer.

As she walked away Tagarid had heard them begin to haggle over the price of his "special offer": over-ripe tomatoes . . .

Now, staring out over the harbour, she recalled what he had said – the last part, the personal warning – and considered its significance. Had he warned her because of what she had seen that night, the shooting of the unknown girl, the abduction of the man? Or because of her meeting with Khaled Namur, the known Party-man?

And as her mind moved gradually to a certainty that it was the latter, that through association with Khaled Namur she had moved into a life that had ramifications – connections – far wider than before, she became conscious of an excitement rising within her, flooding her with new vitality, with an awareness that now there was the possibility of her entering for the first time into the mainstream of life in her country. As it was lived in this day and age. She had only to step forward into the world of the man Khaled, do what she had set herself to do, and she

64

would be part of it. Of course there was danger, and killing and death, maybe the death even her own? Yes, that was a real possibility, clearly. But she told herself then that she would accept any risk gladly if in return she were able to feel again that she was contributing – something. Her eyes lifted from the ravaged port-area of the city and travelled to the mountains in the north-east, over which lay Al-Ain; and she thought with elation, *I will have the gun soon.*

But the elation soon gave way to restlessness because of the empty hours between then and now. She had to move, to do – go somewhere, do something – simply to fill up the time of waiting.

Quickly, she stripped and put on a black bikini, belted over it a grey towelling wrap; and then making a flask of coffee put it in her holdall, slung a beach-towel over her shoulder and sped down to her car. And drove out of the city, stopping only to buy a pizza at a shop on Verdun. Working her way slowly across the city, crossed the Green Line at Sodeco, then took the road north, a fast dual-carriageway at first but then, the city fallen away behind, a good two-lane highway running sometimes close to the sea, sometimes through busy villages dry and dusty and drenched in dusty sunlight.

And came to Byblos. Where of old, because the timber-bearing mountains came down near to the coast and because there was a small natural harbour, the pharaohs of the Old Kingdom had sent their sea-going feluccas to tow rafts of cedar-wood along the coasts of the Middle Sea to the harbours of the Nile delta.

Cedar, she thought, once my country's great wealth; and looked up at the treeless, scrub-covered slopes of the mountains. Natural wealth, long squandered.

Parking the Renault down by the harbour, she took out her holdall and set off up the road towards the Land-gate of ancient Byblos. She met no one; and the modern iron gates stood wide open, no tourists now.

For her, Byblos had become a place of dream and dreaming. Since Hisham's murder she had come here many times – always alone – to swim, to sit and stare and simply "be", letting the dream of the ancient site wash over her, into her, making a sort of peace within. Feeling the presence of that long and vivid past around her had seemed to enable her to accept a personal future that until now she had seen stretching before her as a vast and desolate plateau wherein she dwelt in frozen isolation. Now, as she wandered across the site towards the sea, she was conscious that her feelings were different; now, she conceived of that past as leading on into a discernible if turbulent future that contained her own within it. The thought awoke in her an exhilarating, questioning excitement.

She made her way down the rocky cliffs to the narrow beach, and swam; spread her towel on the yielding sand and stretched out in sunlight, the sun drying her skin, the sea singing mermaid songs to her closed eyes, softly; and then ate pizza and drank coffee. No other person came that way; the only sound was that of the sea, and once a bird calling plaintively from among the ruined walls behind her. And dreamily, lazily, her mind recalled the life-history of Byblos, what she knew of it: weaving the threads of knowledge and intuition together and creating a whole that was both sustaining and without end . . .

Neolithic man fishing these blue waters, scratching on pebbles to make the first known idol . . . Jar-burials in the fourth millenium BC, and placed in with the dead the things special to them in life, treasured beads of silver or cornelian, the stone mace-head of a favourite weapon, the dog beloved by its master . . . Move on another thousand years and the people are making stone bases to support the wooden pillars which hold up their roofs, "wisdom has built her house, she has set up her seven pillars"; and now they create a city and within it the Temple of the Lady of Byblos . . .

Their city thrives, it trades with great Egypt and lays the bodies of its Kings in carved sarcophagi, whose inscriptions threaten robbers with death . . . Then – destruction: invading armies burn the city to the ground, and life is circumscribed by fear and death, by rapine and the law of tooth and claw . . .

The city is rebuilt. And over the fire-blackened ruins of the Temple, the people build the Temple of the Obelisks and no one today knows to what gods it was dedicated . . . Slowly, Byblos becomes great again: trades with Egypt once more and grows rich under independent Kings, a coastal city-state . . . Assyria trades with her and does not destroy, the carpenters of Byblos travel to Babylon to supervise the building of Nebuchadnezzar's palace and his marvellous temple (and the prophet Isaiah, predicting that King's death, speaks for the rapt cedars of Phoenicia: "The whole earth is at rest and quiet; they break forth into singing. The cypresses rejoice at you, the cedars of Lebanon saying, 'Since you were laid low, no hewer comes up against us.'") . . .

And the Temple of the Lady of Byblos has great honour from Yehawmilk King of Byblos, an altar of bronze he gives her and an "engraved object of gold with the bird of gold that is set in a precious stone".

Alexander of Macedon is not opposed: Byblos surrenders immediately and – the city lives. But the Phoenician language dies. The city prospers but is Hellenized: those who write, do so in Greek . . .

Robbers raid out of the Beka'a Valley . . . Pompey the Great leads the legions over the mountains . . .

But always the Lady of Byblos is worshipped there, whether she be called Astarte, Aphrodite or Venus.

After 5,000 years, at the order of Theodosius, the final destruction of all pagan temples. The year, 392 A.D. And with the proscribing of her temples, Byblos sinks into centuries of obscurity . . .

Until, in 1108 A.D., the Crusader Baldwin takes the city and builds a church and a formidable Castle. Now, the wars of Christian and Muslim flow back and forth over the city as the years pass. But when the Crusaders are gone, Jebail's importance goes with them. In the Crusader Castle sand lies sifted deep on the stone floors; grasses and small flowering plants flourish in the paved courtyards. The importances of trade, of religion, of political intrigue: all are gone . . .

She returned to herself lying sun-warmed on that silent shore; and getting to her feet scrambled up the rocks and stood looking at the ruins: close in front of her the low eroded walls of the Neolithic settlement of 4,500 B.C.; to their right the necropolis of the 3rd millenium; beyond, across low broken walls and grass-covered courtyards, the Temple of Baalat-Gebal, the city-goddess of Byblos, stood on higher ground and there were pillars there, and trees, it was a place of grace and beauty . . . Her eyes moved on to the Crusader Castle looming beyond, battlemented still, strong and blocky against the barren mountains behind the town . . .

And no people. No tourists, not even any local visitors. At this little point in time, Byblos is nothing . . .

She made her way towards the castle. The bird called again and this time she saw it, hopping angrily about along the top of a grey stone wall. There was a wild fig tree growing beside a broken pillar and she picked ripe figs from it and ate them, they were small and very sweet, warm from the sun.

It was cool within the massive walls of the castle keep. Feet quiet over drifted dust and sand, she climbed the stone steps to the upper floor and ensconced herself within an embrasure there. Two metres deep, the embrasure, shaped like a wedge, broad where she was sitting, narrowing sharply to the arrow-slit facing out towards the enemy . . . No enemies now: before her the site stretched away empty and quiet. A good place for thinking in . . .

There was a sea-change in me this morning, she thought. When Hisham was murdered something in me collapsed and I slid down into a sort of morass, lay unconscious there doing all the interminable things of life like eating, sleeping, working, but *creating* nothing, not part of anything bigger than me. Well, I'm climbing out of that morass now. It will be dangerous out there on the shore of life, threatened by the tides of crises and violence, but that's where I'm going. Like Byblos coming out of its centuries of obscurity, clawing its way back into the lives of the nations of the world; for me it has taken months, for a country it can take hundreds of years. Like Lebanon recently. Collapsing into anarchy and civil war five years ago and then staying down in the muck – For how long? A very long time, perhaps – with something they call peace existing like a skin over the morass of violence and turmoil, and underneath it the people somehow carrying on their existences but not *creating* . . . As if it is necessary, unavoidable, after some disaster, to undergo a time of purgatory: only after you've got through that – as an individual, as a people – are you able to cope once again with the reality of living.

But she did not think long of Lebanon. Returning to her secret world, first savoured the taste of revenge-now-possible; and then bent her mind to consideration of the ways and means to be employed . . .

As she drove back to the city, the sunset was beautiful in the western sky. But she had realized that to achieve the revenge of blood-for-blood, expert advice was necessary. From my meeting with Khaled tonight, my new life will begin, she thought.

He will be my adviser. He is a man of violence, he will give me the methods of violence as well as its tools.

Matt Curran was doing part of this one himself. He did not, usually, for he reckoned his local contacts more suited to "shadow" jobs, for obvious reasons. But the phone call had told him that Mahmoud Al Oud could not take over from Nabil that evening because out in the suburb of Beirut where he lived the Irani Baathists had been throwing bombs at the Iraqi Baathists and one had exploded just outside Mahmoud's house, and now Mahmoud was at the hospital with his three-year-old son, who had been standing by the front window at the time and would never see again even if he lived . . .

So now, at 7 p.m. this Saturday evening, Curran was watching the man who had come out of the café La Paloma a few moments before: the powerfully built Arab stepping out through the glass doors into the pooled yellowish light of the courtyard, and the militiaman sitting there with his gun across his knees leaping to his feet, standing to attention while speaking briefly with him. Curran knew the physical appearance of this man from carefully studied film and photographs; and while knowing of him here in Beirut as "Khaled", knew too that that was only one of the names he went by, for he was "listed" for past terrorist activities in both Britain and Germany (but neither country had ever yet been able to touch him with the finger of its law).

The street lighting was fully on and there were not many people about in the streets since most shops closed at six or earlier for security reasons, and the seekers after the sparse night-life of the city kept later hours. The Arab wore grey trousers and a wind-cheater, and had a small black duffel-bag slung over one shoulder, so he was easily kept in sight.

Curran moved casually along on the opposite side of the street, his blue jeans and sweatshirt suggesting him to be one who fitted somewhere into the ubiquitous life-style of one of the many universities in West Beirut. At the first corner he noticed his second "tail" – Ziad, his name was, a young man, lean and wiry-strong, ambitious – saw Ziad get out of a battered Citroën parked by a florist's and knew he would also follow, ready to take over when the Arab went to ground, or if he tried to take evasive action. At the crossroads beyond, a fruit-stall was still busy (last-minute price-reductions of spoiling stock attracting thrifty housewives, the stall-holder shouting out his bargains), and Curran crossed the street, edged up a little on his quarry.

Who stopped and bought apricots, forcing Curran and his back-up man to do a little careful manoeuvring before the three of them progressed once more in their established pattern of movement.

Halfway down Mikdassi Street the Arab turned into a restaurant called The Speakeasy, going up the broad, shallow steps and in through the double glass doors.

Curran sauntered on past the restaurant without even glancing in as he went by: Ziad would take up the surveillance now, from across the street. Quickening his pace, Curran walked on a little further and after a time found a taxi to take him back to his flat. Letting himself in, he went immediately to the phone and dialled a number. He did not have to wait long; neither did he waste words.

"Handfast," he said, identifying himself. "Speakeasy. You may need a vehicle. Ziad's outside, you go in. Soon as you can, get on a phone and tell me who he's meeting. If you don't know, one of you peel off and follow to find out."

Replacing the receiver, he went into the kitchen and took a cold lager out of the fridge, got a glass. Returning to his sitting-room, he stretched out in one of the luxurious armchairs upholstered in oatmeal-coloured raw silk and drank the lager, thinking about the real job he was in Beirut to do.

5

SHE HAD arrived at The Speakeasy early, eagerness an impatience in her, driving her out of the flat with too much time allowed to make the shortish journey by car, then counselling her to walk, but then again making her walk so fast that she found herself at the restaurant at 6.45.

I am behaving like a girl going to meet her lover: the thought unbidden, sudden and complete. And she was so angry that she annihilated it and walked up the marble steps and in through the double glass doors and sat down at a table at the back of the restaurant. Slender, elegant woman in sleek black linen, sleeveless; taut with anger at herself and the blue eyes clear and cold.

"I shall wait," she told the swarthy, poker-faced waiter, taking out a cigarette. He lit it for her, placed an ashtray before her and withdrew. And after a moment she was able to smile at the anger: it is the gun I have come to meet, she said to it, the gun, not the man. The anger went then; and she relaxed.

Saw him come in through the door, loose-limbed, the physical presence of him tense and controlled, the passion of his commitment in his face. As she looked at him she was not thinking about the gun. Yet although she knew that, the anger did not come again.

"This time, I watched you arrive," she said.

"I am sorry that you had to wait. I apologize if I am late."

"I didn't mean that." But she did not say what she had meant; truly, was not entirely sure of that now the words were said.

He sat down opposite her, slipping the duffel-bag off his shoulder, hooking its strap over his chair; and looked at her as if waiting for her to go on.

She remembered, then; and asked: "You have a weapon for me?"

71

"Yes. But there is something I wish to discuss with you, if you have time."

It was not a question; yet the assumption did not annoy her. She nodded, her eyes not leaving his.

"I have time," she answered. "There are things I wish to ask you, also."

He smiled then, a thing of the eyes mostly, yet his whole face suddenly gentler and giving, surprising her.

"I'm glad." He gestured to the waiter, asking, "What may I offer you? Wine? Or would you prefer coffee?"

She asked for wine; and he ordered from the waiter without looking at the wine-list.

"It's a German wine," he said to her then, "and it comes from a very beautiful place."

"You know Germany, do you?"

"A little, yes."

"I've never been there. Did you like it?" Social chat while they waited for the wine to be served; yet it pleased her to have even this little personal detail to put within the strong, dark outline of his being, for already she was sure he was a very secret man.

"I wasn't there long," he said, the smile again ghosting his eyes. "I think I know the wine better than the people . . . I hope you will find it drinkable," he added.

It came chilled; and was excellent. They put down their glasses and she sat silent for a moment, looking at her glass. Opposite her, he had his forearms on the table and she knew he was studying her face, not inquisitively but because he wanted to discover more about her.

"Tell me now," he said (and she realized he already knew it was not only a matter of questions).

"Since I saw you last I have of course been thinking about *how* to do what I intend to do," she began slowly. "Before" – just the one word to encompass their first meeting, as if it were so clear a landmark in her life that it needed no further definition – "I was so possessed by the, the consuming and terrible *joy* of envisaged revenge that I revelled in it without giving much thought to the physical achievement of the act. I planned for the getting of the gun, and assumed a sort of natural progression from then on, the weapon and the will both being present . . . But afterwards, when I was sure of the gun and

72

tried to plan the act, I realized the enormous difficulties." She looked up at him. "You see, earlier it was entirely unimportant to me whether I lived or died, which of course would make the act much easier to carry out successfully. But I've grown out of that. There's life inside me again and I am no longer careless of whether I lose it or not."

"But you still want the act of revenge?"

"Yes."

"But – you do accept the *possibility* of your dying? If that is what comes out of the achievement of your revenge?"

"Of course. It's only that – now, I *care*."

"So that is what you want to ask me." His voice hardening, but still quiet. "To show you how to plan a killing, a random killing, so that you yourself have a good chance of coming out of it alive." A slow smile touched his lips, but this time found no echo in his eyes. "I can do better than that," he said. "I can give you a man *worth* killing." He saw her eyes widen at the sudden closeness of the reality of a death and added swiftly, "My way, you would give your husband not merely a death, you would give him the death of such a man as he would be glad to see dead."

Their voices murmurous as the voices of lovers. In the soft radiance of low-hanging, silk-shaded lamps, they saw each other's faces clearly; and wove the threads of their lives together in an inner silence, talking of death and other things.

"My way" – She seized exultingly on the words because they committed him to her; and let the rest of the words drop down un-thought-about to the seabed of her consciousness (but she was to recall them later and know then what was behind them – and would not like the knowing).

All she said was: "So you have been thinking about it, also." He nodded; and went on after a moment of quiet.

"I have had the word 'terrorist' used of me," he said, looking down at his hands linked together on the table. "It's a big label, and many people never bother to read the small print. I have indeed planned and carried out acts of destruction, as those who call me 'terrorist' claim; but they were neither wanton nor do I ever strike at random." He drank some wine and when he put down his glass his hands remained clasped loosely round its stem: he had large hands, the fingers long and square-tipped. "When we first met I understood your need and desire for revenge, but I had always despised those who indulged themselves blindly in matters of this kind." He looked up at her, suddenly. "However, I found that I didn't despise you. Then, later, when I thought further about it, it seemed to me possible that, if you did what you had it in your mind to do, a 'blind' killing, you would come to despise *yourself* . . . And I didn't want that to happen."

Suddenly she was afraid that they were making too many words, that whatever it was that was forming between them might be smothered before it began to breathe and grow if too many words were heaped on it.

"Tell me *your* way," she said urgently. "I like the way you talk; the things you've just said make sense to me. But now – *tell me your way.*"

He folded his forearms on the table, leaned towards her, his expression intent.

"You go to London," he said. "For a week, ten days. A visit only, as you have done before, for shopping, for theatre and music – you live the tourist life, so that there is no strangeness in your being there . . . In London you shoot and kill a man. You contact a colleague of mine, secretly, as I shall tell you, and he will provide you with the information you need, and with the weapon you will use . . . And when – afterwards – you have completed your tourist visit, you return home."

Suddenly, it was very big to her. Now, it had moved out of the shadows of the intention in the mind, it was standing custom-built and ready, it only needed the key turned and it would begin to move and progress. She felt her heart tighten.

"Who is the man you want killed?" she asked.

"A Syrian." Watching her to see if she wanted more.

"You said you've never, 'indulged' I think your word was, in 'blind' killing. Why, *this* man?"

"He is an enemy of Lebanon."

Her mouth twisted.

"Whose Lebanon?" she asked in bitterness. "Pierre Gemayel's? Ahmed Choukair's –"

"The answer to that is not yet written." He cut her off swiftly. "But, we intend that *we*, the Lebanese, will do the writing, not the Syrians."

His certainty, the strength of him reached for her, moved into her. She knew she was going to go into his plan with him,

74

understand it and make it her own. But she knew something else, too. And said it: "You're using me, aren't you?"

He smiled and reached one hand across the table, let it rest lightly on her own where it fingered her wineglass. "Yes," he said. Removed his hand and waited for what she would say.

"I don't mind one bit," she said at once, "but I would have minded very much if you had lied to me about it . . . Your plan, will there be much danger in carrying it out? For me, I mean?"

"When you are handling violence there is always the possibility that it may turn on you and rend you. But in this case I think that possibility is very slight. You are totally unknown on the 'scene'. Your reason for being in London, should it ever be questioned, is so simple and ordinary that it will be entirely convincing. And the plan also is, simple. There is little in it that could possibly go wrong, given you and your 'cover' . . . No, I do not believe that you will be in any physical danger."

Again he had surprised her.

"What other kind might there be in this?" she asked.

For a moment they stared at each other in silence. Then he said quite slowly, "Afterwards, an inescapable feeling of guilt. People have been destroyed by remorse before now."

"You must know I have already thought about that."

"And?"

"Are *you* haunted by remorse?" Question to question. And she knowing his answer to hers, but still asking it because there was a little anger in her that he had found it necessary to question her so.

He smiled again; and made no answer. Saying: "We should not meet in a place like this again. May I come to your flat for our next meeting?"

"My house is yours." She gave him the flowery Arabic words of hospitality; but meant them.

As the 9 o'clock News ended Matt Curran switched off his radio and his sitting-room returned to relative quiet, the air-conditioning almost noiseless and the traffic-sound from the street four floors below reduced to a swishing tidal rumble punctuated by the furious blasts, strident tootings and carillons of the musical horns so loved and so over-indulged in by the Beirutis. The room was spacious and furnished with a certain

75

elegance, its colours oatmeal and beige dramatized with a subtle smudged-rose colour, its lighting softly honey-gold. Curran never really "saw" it: it was one in a block of expensive service apartments, and gave him the two things he sought, comfort and the housekeeping chores faultlessly performed by servants he seldom saw. It also gave him one other thing that was necessary to the creation of a credible background to his present job: a suitable place to entertain in, yet with everything done for him by the excellent and highly priced restaurant and bar occupying the first floor of the block.

He leaned back in his armchair, lit a cigarette. And his thoughts revolved for a while round Khaled Namur, this man he had never met yet knew so much about. Two kinds of knowledge he possessed about him. The one kind detailed and penetrating, but secondhand and therefore inevitably coloured by the complex personalities of the informants, because no matter how great a person's self-discipline it was surely difficult – perhaps impossible? – to be totally objective when assessing the qualities of a man who (Curran selected a random example) had shot dead your brother in front of your eyes. The other kind came from his own mind, but again at one remove from the quality of knowledge that grew in you from personal contact because it came from being closely involved in various acts planned and master-minded by Namur but without his actual presence in the field of action. Twice before Curran had opposed Namur's plans: once in Germany, where he had been bloodily defeated; and once in London, where he had cheated Namur of the sought-after assassination but failed to bring him before the courts, though lesser men had been charged and convicted. The time in London had been a bitter blow to Curran: he regarded it as a personal failure, for he had had Namur on British soil and therefore the chance to encompass his legal destruction, but had not achieved it.

This time, if our paths cross at all, I'll get you my friend, he thought now. We're in a Lebanon where practically anything goes and this time I'll not be too particular whether we get you with the law or the gun.

But he knew and accepted that the specific job he was in this country to do must take precedence over his personal desire – need? – to exact payment from Khaled Namur . . .

Suddenly aware of tiredness, wishing the phone call from

76

Pierre would come so that he could go to bed, he stood up, stretching. Sauntering over to the open-fronted bar built into the shelf-and-cupboard rosewood unit covering one wall, he poured himself a long whisky-soda. Sipping his drink, stared moodily for a while at the books ranged along the shelves; and then, failing to find one that made him reach for it, moved on round the room, staring at the pictures. They did not offer him much, either: elegantly framed, modern, they came with the flat and clearly had been selected with an eye to ensuring their inability to offend any tenant whatsoever. Turning from them, he crossed the room to the floor-to-ceiling glass doors, beige-draped, that opened onto the broad balcony, slid one of them open and stepped out, closing the door behind him to shut in the man-made coolness . . . Warm out there, the slight breeze blowing straight in off the sea clammy with summer humidity. At the far end of the balcony the massed shadowiness of a miniature garden flourishing in tubs – rubber plants, hibiscus, three rose bushes and jasmine pale-flowered and fragrant, trailing the length of the balcony on fine wires. He leant on the balcony rail, looking out. Below him, the road ran hugging the inward curve of the coast, on its far side a narrow stretch of rough terrain and then rocks dropping down to the water, water stretching away into the dark and a new crescent moon poised above it. To his right, the night-glow of the city, to his left, the road ribboning on southward along the coast, good fish-restaurants along there, and the night-spots of the Summerland complex, their lights flaring the sky. But beyond again, only darkness: Sidon and Tyre not so many kilometres down that coast, and the ancient enmities warring viciously with modern weapons.

Nearly ten o'clock now, the Saturday-night traffic beginning to diminish. On the pavement below him, a swirl of people gathering round parked cars, customers from the bar on the first floor, he supposed, watching idly as the cars began to move off, cutting out into the fast-moving traffic, their insolence rebuked by screeching tyres and outraged horns . . . As Curran watched, a large figure emerged onto the pavement, accompanied by two big pale dogs on leads, and moved slowly off to the left: Michel Allawi, man of power in one of the Syrian-backed militias. He lived in the block of flats adjoining Curran's, and walked his pair of Salukis every night.

77

Gunfire. Not far off. An explosion, medium strength. Short, sharp bursts of automatic fire, the single shots of repeater-rifles, then the whine of a rocket followed by another explosion.

Curran had moved quickly away from the lit windows behind him to the darker garden-end of the balcony. In the road below cars pulled in to the kerb and drivers switched everything off. Car doors slammed as people got out to take cover in sheltering halls and doorways.

Curran listened to the quiet behind the shooting. It had a special quality, this sudden quiet that gripped the city whenever the guns started. Especially at night. To Curran it had always seemed as if then all the inhabitants of the city suddenly regressed into the savagery of the civil war, and the hatred and terror and cruelty came pouring out of them to infect the very air they breathed. Old memories, old hatreds pouring up out of the dark places of the mind.

The gunfire began again: not static, its intensity ebbed and flowed – street warfare. Then two cars came racing along the coast road, horns blaring, lights flashing, and just beyond the flats turned inland towards the shooting – as the second swung round the corner, Curran glimpsed the mounted machine-gun sticking out of the open hatch-back.

The gunfire intensified; became spasmodic; stopped. In the distance the high-pitched wail of an ambulance siren; loudening as it approached. Then suddenly the fear-soaked silence of the street below was split apart by the crash of a single gunshot fired very close

– and the silence fused together again; total.

Then Curran heard it: a furtive shuffling movement in the road below him. Urgency and desperation in it. A man moving there? Yes, surely? As the sounds moved closer the movements suggested animal stealth and the animal, *man*. Something in the way he moves, though? Wounded. Yes, thought Curran, *that* I recognize, *that*'s got its own hot-line to my memory . . . Below, the shuffling stopped. Very softly, fumblingly, a car door was opened; closed. An engine murmured into life and then the car crept away, its going a whisper across the silence.

And the man inside praying his hunting enemies don't hear it, Curran thought . . .

There were no more shots. And ten minutes later the traffic was flowing once more. Beirut life washes over "incidents", they drop away into a past full of incidents. But for some of those involved, you may be sure, life will never be the same again.

Curran went inside and sat down in the chair by the phone. It was the chair he usually sat in because from there he could enjoy the three objects in this hired sumptuous apartment which were his own: hung on the wall opposite, the silk "runner" from Isfahan, a subtlety of shaded greens, deep red, and black; to his right hand, on the table, a camel two inches high, solid gold, and the man it had belonged to dead now; and beside the camel a fist-sized flint artefact, a skin-scraping tool, pale-brown. He reached out for this now and held it; it fitted neatly into the palm of his hand, and his fingers moved over the stone as he sought for the hand-hold worn into it by the man who had fashioned and used it ten thousand or more years ago. Curran had found it at a Neolithic site near Byblos only three weeks earlier, when Mustafa Bashir had invited him on a visit there arranged by a friend of his, a well-known Lebanese archaeologist. Coveting it as soon as he touched it, Curran had slipped it secretly into his pocket. He liked holding it; the stone seemed to him to have feeling within it, a sort of "life-feel" worked into it by the hands of the generations of men who had used it, and each treasuring the stone as it helped them fight their way inch by inch out of savagery... Grinned at his own imaginings, frequently; but still handled it, as he was doing now, with a sense of an easement of tension within himself.

He picked up the phone as soon as it rang.

"Handfast. Yes?"

"Pierre. A woman. Name Tagarid Salamé Kurban. Address: Flat 923 Mayflower Apartments, Rue Jeanne D'Arc. Want more on her."

Christ, he thought. Answering after a second's pause, "Tomorrow. Drop it now. Thanks. Masalaam."

Gently he replaced the receiver; and leaned back into his chair, his spread hands gripping into the soft upholstery of the arms.

Tagarid? Into something with Khaled Namur?

His mind immediately rejected that; then immediately seized on it again because there *could be* no rejection, no disbelief: Namur was an absolute "loner", he had no purely social activities. Tagarid had met and talked with him: it followed

79

inescapably that she was involved in something Namur planned to pull off. Not necessarily part of the matter that had brought himself, Curran, to the Lebanon, no; but *possibly* so.

He sat a long time, assembling and assessing (again) all he knew about his own mission here, about the men associated with his allies, and his enemies. Enemies of whom Namur was one: the "King" on the "Black" side.

Strange, he thought then, to have Tagarid there beside Namur. And then he felt the anger come: if she were there, Namur must be using her, manipulating her through the murder of her husband? Surely, Tagarid would never willingly be part of the sort of activity Namur engaged in?

Curran answered his own question then: no, *not if she knew the truth of it*. But Namur had such an air of personal integrity that those to whom he talked seldom thought of the possibility that he might be lying . . .

6

THEY WERE driving up to Baalbek for the weekend and had left Beirut at 7 a.m., the morning early-cool and the streets nearly empty. After some discussion they had decided to travel in Curran's Range Rover although Tagarid, who enjoyed driving, had at first wanted to take her Renault 5, arguing that since it was both older and smaller it would be less attractive to the ubiquitous car-thieves. In the end, however, the decision had been mutual: the Range Rover was better for the rough country roads outside Baalbek; and although it would undoubtedly make some mouths up there water at the prospect of a fortune to be made for the taking, second thoughts would surely admit that the right-hand drive would be sure to bring down the re-sale price in Syria.

With no reason for hurrying, they took a side-road climbing southward out of Aley and drove up into the steep surrounding hills; then stopped, and got out to sit on yellow-stone rock, gazing down over the splendid panoramic view of Beirut and the coast while Tagarid talked lazily of the geography and history in the land and cities down there.

"You have a very attractive voice," he said, as she finished telling him the legend of the Spring of Adonis in the hills behind Byblos.

She laughed (which recalled to him that he had seldom heard her laugh).

"Perhaps you really mean I talk too much," she said, rising to her feet and brushing the pale rock-dust from her dark red jeans.

"No. Regrettably, I'm not that subtle." He stood up beside her, looking round at the hills behind them, seeing the trees scattered across the hillside moving softly in a small breeze off the sea; and then his eyes came back to her face. But he did not say any more.

Deciding to fill up with petrol before they got back into the fast-moving traffic on the main Beirut-Damascus highway, he pulled in to a two-pump garage in a small village and got out to check the sale and pay. As he slid back in behind the wheel: "Look," she said, pointing straight ahead.

There was a concrete-faced wall demarcating one side of the garage forecourt, white-washed. And stretching right across it a huge hand-painted mural, many pictures in series, arranged comic-strip fashion, primary colours garishly brilliant and Arabic lettering beneath each one, quite small but heavy and black, telling a story.

"Let's get a bit nearer," she said, "and we'll see what it says."

So he took the car forward, stopped close by.

Deep blue skies, and planes wheeling and turning above green land and the grouped buildings of men. All amateurishly drawn and without proper perspective. But full of strength: the whole thing shouting out the story of the Syrian-Israeli dogfight two weeks earlier, the penultimate picture showing a burning plane (unmarked) hurtling down the sky carrying its fiery ruin inexorably towards the village below . . . To the last picture, bigger than the others: the moment of impact, and the plane explodes in a frenzy of colour; but the village stands intact and its mosque and houses are drawn in strong black outline, the mosque dominant.

"'They fought in the skies and the plane came down. It was aimed at our village but GOD turned it aside. We are his Chosen People. We the Druze nation are the Chosen of God.'" She spoke the words clearly and slowly, translating them from the black script flowing across the white concrete wall.

And as they drove on she told him Dina Dhaibo's theory about the death of Siham Rawdah.

"Does Dina really believe what she told you is the truth?" he asked, finding it hard to equate such fierce imaginings – which was what he took them to be – with the composed gypsy-dark girl who had slid into Siham's place at the office so self-effacingly yet so efficiently.

Beside him, she shrugged.

"Oh yes, she certainly believes it," she answered.

"Do *you*?"

There was a small silence before she replied. Then: "That's a pointless question," she said. "I have no possible points of reference from which to argue belief or disbelief. To be honest, I've hardly given the matter another thought since she told me. There's really no sense in thinking about it. For even if I decided it were true, I wouldn't *do* anything."

"Because you couldn't, or because you wouldn't?" For suddenly she was revealing something of Tagarid Kurban to him and usually she avoided doing this. Now, he had the feeling that really she was discussing her feelings with herself, not telling *him*, hardly aware indeed that she *was* telling him; and he took advantage of her lapse, knowing he was doing so but pushing away the resulting small feeling of guilt.

"Well I know I *couldn't*, such a thing would be utterly beyond the reach of an outsider. But you asked why, and my reason would be, because I *wouldn't*."

"Why not, Tagarid?" And knew at once he should not have used her name, for she looked at him and then away, and he felt her straighten in her seat.

Yet she answered.

"Vengeance belongs to those who have suffered, not to the onlooker, however committed," she said. "Otherwise, it is something different." Then she added at once, "I'd prefer to talk about something else now, if you don't mind . . . Anyway, we're coming into Saoufar. You'd better watch your driving!"

Saoufar of the deep-shaded plane trees, the once-beautiful but now war-shattered hotel, the cool, scented mountain air.

Down through the mountains to the thronging babel of Shtura, market day, and the currency touts already brandishing fistfuls of Syrian money; but beyond, the vineyards reach far and farther still, the fruit hanging heavy on the vines and rustic wine-tasting sheds by the roadside already being refurbished in preparation for the harvest.

And so on to the villages before Zahlé: Zahlé the spring paradise of cherry-orchards, the sweet, rich town climbing up from the main road back into the foothills – and the shops were shuttered and groups of men stood at the roadside, grim-faced, deep in discussion. All variously armed.

"Maybe there's still trouble up ahead," she said then. "Six killed in Zahlé on Thursday, it said on the News last night."

"I heard," he said.

She touched his arm and pointed.

"Road-block, Matt."

It was manned – heavily – by the Syrian army: machine-gun posts either side of the road.

"Baalbek via Zahlé," Curran said to the soldier who waved them down.

Round country-face, very young, machine-pistol across his chest: he stared at Curran, at Tagarid, studied the right-hand drive Range Rover narrowly; and finally shrugged, stepped back and motioned them through.

"Must be okay now, then," Curran said. "They're being careful, that's all." And they drove on, rounded the last corner before the town –

"Stop!" Tagarid cried. "For Chrissake" – her voice rising – "stop *now*! Turn her!"

He braked hard though he saw no reason to do so – the road ahead totally deserted.

"My side!" Her voice brittle and clear. "Tanks. Up the bank." She pressed herself back into her seat.

Bending down and forward, he peered out: up there on his left, a T55 battle-tank with its long gun menacing the road; and beside it machine-gunners dug in behind sand-bags. From the turret of the tank the tank-commander was gesturing furiously at them, making sweeping gestures with his arm.

So he turned the car and drove away from Zahlé, towards Shtura again, to take the long way round to Baalbek, via Rayak.

"The Zahlé business made the BBC News as well," he said. "Two Christian Groups at each other's throats again, so they said, so the APF moved in to sort it out and two Syrian soldiers got killed."

Her laugh was short and bitter.

"Ha! The off-the-record version is different," she said savagely. "Would you like to hear it?"

He glanced across at her but her face was turned from him, she was looking out across the flat sunlit reaches of the Plain. Her hands were fists, clenched in her lap. He thought: *dark*, she feels to me dark and implacable. And remembered that Zahlé was a town in which she had lived a period of childhood happiness.

"Tell me," he said.

"Those given facts you just stated, no one argues them," she said. "But – do you remember the given *cause* of that sudden Christian-versus-Christian flare-up?"

"A top man in one of the Christian Groups was murdered."

"By?"

"Hit men of the rival Group."

"Mmm. Easy, isn't it? That's happened so often in the past that nowadays it's accepted without question."

"And, off-the-record?"

"The Syrians want the Christians out of Zahlé; it's a Christian town, as you know. They want that Zahlé should cease to exist! So they sent in *their own man* to do the first killing, intending it to produce a situation giving them a 'legitimate' reason to go in, and burn and destroy . . . Which it did."

"Mean and very tricky —"

"Syrian!"

Christ how she hates them! he thought. And not having the words to reach her, put his hand over hers where it lay now taut on her knee. After a moment her hand loosened, relaxed, and he felt its light, quick pressure on his own before she withdrew it.

From Shtura they turned east, on to the main Damascus highway again, and so across the Beka'a. Red-earthed Valley of the Fertile Crescent spreading broad between the Lebanon and Anti-Lebanon ranges: in spring the land running with the waters of the melting snows as they are gathered into two rivers, the Orontes flowing north into Syria, the Litani south to empty its waters into the Middle Sea at Tyre. The armies of many famous "men of destiny" (from Sennacherib to Allenby) have marched up or down the Beka'a since the days when, a thousand years before the birth of Christ, the first Babylonian cohorts struck across it to get at the rich Phoenician cities on the coast.

But it was towards the northern end of the valley, where for thousands of years the two springs of Baalbek had provided water for the caravans coming across the deserts from the east to bring silk and spices to the Western world, that the Romans built their magnificent Temples of the Sun.

"Heliopolis." Matt Curran spoke the name of the great acropolis. "Sounds better than 'Baalbek'." They were driving north now, along the main road towards Aleppo.

"But 'Baalbek' is older," she said. "To me it suggests ancient and cruel rites evolved as man tied in his instinctive savagery with his craving for something finer, knowing he had to keep one foot on known ground as he reached upward."

85

Then, looking out as they drove along the last six or seven kilometres before Baalbek itself, she laughed suddenly, pointing out of the window. "In the second century the road between Beirut and Baalbek thronged with the world coming to worship at the stupendous temples; in the nineteenth with archaeologists to dig those temples out of the dust; now in the twentieth it's busy with car-thieves bringing their booty to be processed before re-sale in Syria." For now, every village they passed through had on its outskirts areas of land littered with the skeletons of trucks and cars lying rusting after the removal of every usable spare part for sale across the border.

The town of Baalbek sprawls at the foot of Sheikh Abdullah hill, the lower slopes of the Anti-Lebanon range rising steeply behind and the Plain stretching wide before it to the opposing Lebanon range. Turning off the main road he drove towards the centre of the town – open-fronted shops and garages straggling along the roadside – until suddenly the six mighty columns of the Temple of Jupiter soared up into the sky ahead of them, clear against azure blue . . .

He dragged his attention back to the road and, a little farther on, past an enormous statue of Gamal Abdel Nasser, pulled the car in to the kerb outside the wrought-iron gates of the hotel, which stood facing out over the main concourse of ruins.

His room was on the first floor; and standing on its balcony he looked across at the Roman acropolis and found it truly awe-inspiring . . .

That first morning they spent around the Temple of Jupiter. About twenty years after the birth of Christ, the Romans, seeking a place where they might firmly establish their power and from it disseminate their culture, chose Baalbek and began the construction of the great complex of places of worship, amphitheatres and baths that was to be and remain one of the wonders of all time.

They chose their site well; and built with the intention of showing the world that Rome and the Romans were the greatest power on earth. Already for many centuries a trading-centre, the town was also famous for its temples to the worship of Baal. So Rome sent its colonists there, the veterans of the Legions; and in massive stone quarried nearby built the glory and the power of the Roman gods directly on top of the main altar and precinct of the god Baal-Hadad. Yet within the Great Court of the Temple of Jupiter Heliopolitanus they erected a "high place" so that when the first rays of the rising sun penetrated the temple and the priests sacrificed to Jupiter, a little distance away other worshippers might ascend the steep staircase of the high tower and burn incense, participating thereby, through the propitiation of gods far older, in the ritual worship of the one basic idea . . .

"Jupiter, Venus, Mercury, Bacchus." Matt Curran spoke the names of the Roman gods softly, the gods to whom the Romans had given pride of place in this metropolis of the ancient world. As he did so he stood gazing up at the six huge columns of Jupiter's temple reaching skywards to – nothing, any more. "The great male god for the generative forces of nature; his consort, the goddess of fertility; and the young god, incorrigible and profane . . . Strange, isn't it, how gods seem to move down human history in trinities?"

She sat down on a fallen block of rose marble, once part of a great column.

"Tell me about this place," she said. "I think you know more about it than I do. Of which I am ashamed. From which I should like to profit."

So he told her what he knew. Of the three great pagan temples of the Romans, of their closure by Constantine, and their destruction by Theodosius, who raised up a Christian basilica to cover most of the area of the Great Court.

"His basilica is gone now," he said. "Nothing left of it but that." He pointed to a squat monolith of carved limestone lying not far away, between where they were sitting and the partly restored Temple of Bacchus. "You can see Christianity carved into that, the cross and the Greek alpha and omega."

"The Word of God," she said. "I am the beginning and the end."

He nodded. "But the Christians didn't have an easy time of it at Heliopolis," he said. "The place was too old, and had too many far earlier memories. Besides, it had always stood on the very edge of 'civilization'. There was a host of martyrs, even before Julian the Apostate. And even during his time, all over greater Syria the Christians kept on destroying graven images while the pagans threw down the churches, here and elsewhere . . . Then around 526 came earthquake and fire. And in the wings, the Arab tribes gathering, biding their time . . ."

87

As the sun rose higher, he went on to tell her of the Omayyad Caliphs turning the acropolis of Jupiter's temple into a fortress, using the temple-stone of the Romans; of the armies that marched into the Beka'a, plundering and ravaging, during the time of the Crusades; of the sacking of the city by the Mongol hordes of Hulagu Khan in the second half of the thirteenth century; and of a time of comparative peace under the Mamelukes . . .

"It doesn't really 'belong' to any country or time, does it; it's simply a great monument to the aspirations – and fears – of mankind," she said as they walked back to the hotel. "In its high days Baalbek took on a shape the remains of which we see today; but it was always there and always will be . . ."

They lunched off "mazzé" followed by fresh trout from the local rivers. Then as they ate apricots, he recounted the story of the eleventh-century Fatimite Caliph Al-Aziz in Cairo, who one day observed to one of his ministers that he had never tasted the famous cherries of Baalbek. At that time a relay service of carrier pigeons was maintained between the great cities of the Eastern world and, by good luck, pigeons from Damascus were in Cairo that day. Therefore, the Minister at once ordered one despatched to Damascus carrying urgent instructions that bunches of cherries should be attached to the legs of all carrier pigeons available in the city and flown to Cairo without delay.

"So in less than twenty-four hours the Caliph had all the cherries he could eat," he ended, watching her face open to him, smiling; and the blue eyes unshadowed. "Your eyes are like sapphires," he said.

She laughed. "Did you know that sapphires can be orange?" she said.

So he joined in her laughter and they talked of gems.

But as he showered that evening, on their return from a walk through the crowded but tourist-less town to the spring at Ras-el-Ain, he thought about the difference he had sensed in her recently. Slight, subtle, it was nevertheless an unmistakable change. So far she had always kept him at a distance (allowing him, as it were, the freedom of the courtyard but not of the inner "keep" wherein she dwelt with her private grief); and he had accepted this without too much difficulty because he had felt an untroubled certainty that the rest of the world was out there in the courtyard with him. But recently, that sureness was no longer so complete: its surface was occasionally fretted by unformulated doubts as a coming squall flicks catspaws across calm water . . . She *has* changed, he thought as he dressed; and seeking possible catalysts, numbered amongst them the terrorist Khaled Namur. That was the element which most worried him, for although he knew she had met Khaled once at The Speakeasy, and that Khaled had been once to her flat, he had no way of knowing *why* they had met: there was a possibility that in some way their meetings tied in with local pressure to force the authorities to take some sort of action over the murder of Hisham Kurban; there was also the possibility – given Namur's past history, and was Tagarid aware of that? – that she was personally involved in some operation of Khaled's particular group. If the latter were the truth, by any chance, then Tagarid was in deep and bloody waters; and he, Matt Curran, was her enemy.

After dinner they played chess, sitting out on the vine-covered balcony of the second floor of the hotel. It faced out over the ruins, beyond which the Plain stretched silvery dark under the high moon to the tremendous sweep of the Lebanon mountains. Tagarid was wearing a long sheath-dress of grey silk jersey, and her shoulders were bare except for the narrow shoe-string straps banding her smooth, pale brown skin; her only jewellery was a bracelet of jade and double-linked gold. She was very beautiful to him . . . They did not talk much; made their moves and a little small-talk: not strangers, but by no means close either. Again he felt strongly aware of her new separateness; and it awoke in him a restlessness and a sense of frustration, because she was there with him and he could reach out and lay his hand upon her arm (though he did not), and yet he knew that in some indefinable way she was gone out of his reach.

"Would you like a brandy?" he asked, when the game had ended and she had complimented him on his victory. She said she would and he went down to the bar. A cool, dark-panelled room, discreetly lit: Mohammed the barman stood behind his high counter, polishing glasses; and the only other customers were a Syrian Army captain (presumably from the barracks up on Sheikh Abdullah hill) and a local girl drinking together at a candle-lit table at the back of the room.

"Will the Zahlé road be open tomorrow, d'you think?"

Curran asked quietly, leaning on the bar as he watched Mohammed preparing the tray of drinks.

"Who can tell? When the Syrians say we may pass through Zahlé, we will pass through Zahlé." Mohammed was an old man, grey-faced and sick; but he had twelve children – the youngest just five – and would go on working at the hotel as long as they would employ him.

"What's going on there now?"

"They say it is quiet." He polished the already gleaming bottle of Corvoisier with his cloth and set it on the tray beside the glasses and water, and then leaned across the counter towards Curran. "It is only the Syrians who make the trouble," he said softly, bitterly. "Last night they position their guns up in the mountains and start shelling the town. One shell every five minutes, all night. No fighting was taking place, the town was quiet. Still they drop their shells down on the houses, from the heights, out of the dark."

"To make sure the people of Zahlé have learned their lesson?" Curran, too, kept his voice very low, although he could hear the Syrian officer behind him engrossed in chatting up his girl. "To make it clear to everyone who the real bosses are in Lebanon?"

For a second or two the old man stared him in the eye; and then suddenly he looked away, reached down to move things about (minutely) on the tray before him. (As if the touch of the familiar things eased a little the pain inside him: his knowledge of lost courage, perhaps, Curran thought, his terrifying awareness with him again that to keep his job was truly – though the conversation had made him forget it for a moment – the most desperately important thing in the world?)

"Allah kerim," Mohammed said quietly. He picked up the tray then. "Room twenty-eight, sir?"

"I'll take it," Curran said; and did so. As he went out of the bar he heard the Syrian summoning Mohammed over to serve him.

When he rejoined Tagarid she had turned out the lights, the balcony was full of moonlight, lace-patterned with the shadows of vine-leaves.

"So on Tuesday you will leave for London," he said, as they sat with their drinks beside them. "A whole week. I shall miss you."

"Dina Dhaibo can do everything that's necessary. She's highly efficient, that girl."

"I'm sure she is. I didn't mean that."

"I know." She sipped her brandy; and then setting down the glass got up and went to stand, leaning on the wrought-iron rail of the balcony.

After a moment, he joined her. Stood close, but not too close.

"On a night like this, they shot Hisham," she said quietly into the quiet.

His hands tightened on the cold metal as for a blinding instant a total comprehension of the breaking of her hit him. It passed, leaving him chilled and empty. It is like a brand upon her living being, he thought; she is scarred perhaps for ever. And he could make no words.

"Have you ever seen anyone shot? Purposely shot?" she demanded suddenly; her head turning towards him and her voice hard with challenge (and with her personal desolation, he knew).

"Why d'you ask that?" He made his own voice as hard, and was glad she had not asked him if he had ever shot anyone.

She thought for a moment; then: "I think those who have must be different from those who haven't," she said. "*Have* you?"

"Yes."

"Friend or enemy?"

"Both." And he saw the implication of the word hit her.

"Tell me," she said.

He reached out and put his hand over hers where it gripped the balcony rail. Because he knew that in some strange way she was open to him now – a little.

"No. Not now. Under sunlight, not now." Turned her face to him and kissed her. On the mouth and gently.

She neither drew away nor returned the kiss. It was he who drew away; and spoke without looking at her.

"I love you, Tagarid," he said. "It's there if you need it." Almost, then, he asked her about Khaled Namur. But not quite; saying instead, "Use it, if at any time you want to . . . Or need to."

Heard her laugh her surprise –

"*Need* to? Why should I?"

– and instantly wondered if her surprise were assumed. So they were where they had been before: apart.

"Lebanon, Beirut. They are both strange and cruel places to live in these days, especially the city," he answered sombrely, considering for the first time the possibility that she knew more about him than he supposed (as he did, of her!). But only briefly; realizing after an instant's thought that that was *not* a possibility: his cover, his security unbreached, he was a hundred per cent sure of that.

"Thank you," she said, and meaning it. "I'll remember."

Baalbek stands nearly 4,000 feet above sea level and the early morning of a summer day is beautiful there, the air cool and clear, sunlit.

They drove out of the town just after eight o'clock. Having decided to spend the morning exploring the other side of the Beka'a, they went a little way back along the main road then turned off westward. The Plain was about twenty kilometres wide at this point and their map showed the road they were now on cutting straight across it – only one village marked, named Badari, a few miles along it – before working its way through the lower reaches of the Lebanon range into the long, narrow valley where the town of Yamouné gathered about the foot of the waters which, bursting out of solid rock high above, rushed wild and splendid down the mountainside before being tamed to irrigate the cherry orchards below. Also the fields of hashish, doubtless – for which Yamouné was renowned – but those were not shown on their map.

They met no traffic; and smiled at each other, joking at these upcountry lie-abeds and watching the shapes of the mountains ahead changing subtly as morning moved along slopes and summits, the grass up there summer-parched now, bare scree showing through, the outcrops of rock sharp-fanged and inhospitable. The surface of the road deteriorated fast, Tarmac thinning away to nothing, so that after two or three kilometres they were driving on packed foundation stones, skirting cautiously round great holes and runnels that had been ground down into the cracked and dusty roadway. On either side of the road the land stretched away ungrazed and uncultivated, tall weeds rank and matted where water lay underground, dusty and dry-dead where that was denied them as soon as the rains ceased. Ahead, some three kilometres perhaps, the low buildings of Badari straddled the road, lay as a dark mass across the otherwise featureless expanse of plain.

He had to stop the car at one point and get out and walk a little way along the road to plot out their best route round a sort of chasm where the roadway seemed to have collapsed entirely: as he stood staring down into this "trench" he could see the red earth waterlogged beneath the scattered rubbish and rubble. It looked as though the roadway had been deliberately destroyed at this point.

"Listen to the birds," she said, coming up beside him. "There aren't usually so many anywhere near a village. They all get killed and eaten."

He heard then: myriad twitterings and tweetings from amongst the high-grown riot of weeds on either side of the road; and saw a flight of larks rise suddenly and fly off, low, skimming the tops of the greenery.

Side by side, silent, they looked around them at the good arable land stretching away into the distance, the hand of man withdrawn from it. Beside him, she moved suddenly, a shiver jerking through her body. Under the sun.

"It feels – so desolate here," she said. "I don't like it. There's something . . . The air seems, *chill*." And turning, she began to walk rapidly back towards the car.

They drove on, negotiating the "trench" in low ratio. The road surface deteriorated yet further. As they drew near to the village they passed a small and slummy Bedouin encampment, two low tents of old matting and plastic sheeting, some sheeppens, a litter of the impedimenta of living scattered about them; a tall woman robed in black appeared at the open front of one of the tents as they passed by, but although Tagarid raised her hand in greeting the woman made no answering gesture.

So eventually they came to Badari; and found a dead village. It was a small place: one church and one mosque, and about thirty houses, some close to the road some standing back from it. The two places of worship were both fire-gutted, blackened shells; some of the houses had burnt also, but most had been blown apart and the walls that still stood were pitted by gunfire.

They got out of the car and stood for a while taking in that desolation, looking round them but not moving far from the car. The air heavy, brooding; and the silence more the presence of death than merely the absence of life.

"It feels, *godforsaken*," Tagarid said. But left it there, turning suddenly back to the car. "Let's get on," she said, getting in.

They drove on across the Plain, not talking much and not referring again to Badari. Where the foothills began there was a checkpoint manned by two young men of some local militia, strongly built fellows with cheerful country faces, who waved them on without even halting them; and a short distance beyond it came to a petrol station and a shop with oranges piled outside in wooden boxes. While Curran got petrol, Tagarid went to buy fruit.

"I asked about Badari," she said as they drove on. "I had to know, else it would have haunted me all day . . . It is better to lay ghosts, I think."

"What happened there, then?"

"It was back in '76, apparently. Until then the village had been a united community: roughly half and half, Muslim and Christian. Then, because of the war, an old squabble between two families over land was raised again – one family was Christian, the other Muslim, but religion wasn't involved in it, to begin with . . . There was a fight, though, between two of the young men, and one was killed. *Immediately*, the community split down the middle into its two separate halves. They burnt and bombed and shot each other to death . . . The woman in the shop said ninety per cent of the villagers died in one night."

"Will they build again? What's left of them. Eventually?"

"It would have to be one side or the other, now. But I don't think anyone from round here would go near the place any more, not for many years." She paused; then said, "Let's forget it, may we: it's a village on the Plain and we're going to the mountains now . . . That's how we live, here in Lebanon nowadays, isn't it," she added, her voice suddenly harsh. "In one breath 'Oh how tragic!'; in the next 'so glad it wasn't me'."

"Come off it," he said. "That's not just Lebanon and you know it. That's the way the world lives with itself. That's only commonsense."

"But if carried to excess –" she said; and turned away.

They threaded their way through the hills, stopping once to scramble up a rock-strewn slope to where conifers stood grouped round cropped grass starred with tiny yellow flowers. Sitting in the shade, they ate oranges and listened to the quiet; which was soon broken by the brassy "clonking" of a goat-bell, and they watched the herd pass across the hillside below them, the animals widely scattered and moving on quite fast because in the summer even goats cannot win much from these arid slopes.

"It's good to feel alive again," Curran said. "That village got into my bones."

"You come from Britain and Britain is an island, your battles have usually been your own . . . Our bit of the Fertile Crescent has been tramped across by the armies of innumerable conquerors often heading for other countries but nevertheless mostly leaving death and destruction in their wake. Sometimes I think that nowadays we are born with an acceptance of brutality and violence already in our blood. It 'excites' us and if it doesn't happen of its own accord, we create it."

He stood up and stretched; then reached down a helping hand to pull her to her feet.

"I've seen it happen, elsewhere," he said, his voice quiet. "The South American countries, the Far East, but never quite so close to Europe . . . But you – the Lebanese – you're a very resilient people. It will – sometime – come good again. You will make it come good."

She brushed her hands through her shining black hair and lifted her face to the sun.

"Thank you for that, anyway. Maybe every individual who believes that is helping to make it come good again, eventually." And she went running down the slope towards the car.

When he got there she was waiting at the driver's side, smiling at him.

"May I drive for a bit?" she asked. "I've never driven one of these, I'd like to."

Going on through the hills, they came down into Yamouné and threaded their way through its narrow streets, heading for the waterfall. Many of the houses were new, big, ultra-modern in style, often ostentatiously so.

"Must cost a fortune, to build like this out here," he said.

"Holiday villas for hash-barons, most of them. Our 'tea'-trade has been growing and flourishing since the civil war. No one bothers to keep it under wraps any longer . . . You'll soon see," she added, swinging the car left, out of the little town again, along a tree-lined avenue. At the end of the avenue she drew up in the heavy shade of a huge and ancient willow much larger than the rest and rooted at the edge of a wide expanse of marsh.

And what she had said was true. He soon saw: to the inhabitants of Yamouné, visitors to their town could have come with only one purpose in mind – to buy hashish.

They walked along a track beside the marsh, passing the remaining walls of the once-imposing Roman administrative centre which once-upon-a-time had stood beside a beautiful and sacred mere; paused to look at the broken "throne" nearby in which the mighty statue of a god had once been seated; and were trailed all the time by a constantly changing retinue of youths, who chattered on to them without cease, in broken English, French, German, inviting "You come to my house, take tea, very nice tea, you come, oh yes, welcome" – and the like. Then, for the moment leaving their escort behind, climbed up the steep and rocky hillside by a narrow sandy path towards the source of the spring high above, so close to the rushing torrent of the waterfall that its cascading roar numbed the mind and set the senses reeling. Halfway up, as they paused to rest, their followers caught up with them again, laughing, pointing down to the town, "You come down now, what you look for up here? – in my house the *tea* very good, you know, 'tea'."

So climbing on they reached the source of the falls: out of a cave in the solid wall of rock the water shot forth to pour down into a long pool, the water foaming white as it fell but then quietening to lie rippled but clear; and at the bottom of the pool you could just make out the ruined stone-work of the temple of Minerva that once had spanned the water. They stood marvelling, sound-dazed; and then noticed on their left a youth lying full-length on a flat rock beside the water, a book in his hands. He looked up and saw them, scrambled to his feet and approached. "Hello, good morning," he said, smiling. Then held out the book to them, proudly. "I am reading Shakespeare," he said, "it is very interesting. I am going to the village now. You come with me. There are many things in my house, and we will have some tea . . ."

Defeated, they left Yamouné. And spent the rest of the morning in the hills, driving, stopping at places that attracted them, walking the slopes as the spirit moved them. She drove all the time.

"Shall I take over?" he asked once.

But she smiled and shook her head. They were on a relatively good road and she was doing well over a hundred.

"You drive her well," he said. Then grinned, adding, "But too fast."

She laughed.

"I like driving fast. But I do realize that as it's your car I ought perhaps to go more slowly. Shall I?"

"No. Go ahead and enjoy it. What are a few broken 'shocks' between friends."

Looking at her covertly, he saw her smile; saw her whole body easy and relaxed, her hair windswept and her hands on the wheel grubby from scrambling over rocks and hillside. He had never seen her like this before; and he wanted her very much.

"Will you do any driving in Britain?" he asked, looking away from the curve of her neck.

"I don't suppose so." She laughed again then, adding with light self-mockery, "I'm Lebanese – London is for shopping!"

"And when the shops close? Or are you too exhausted by then to do anything but plan the next day's expedition?"

Momentarily, her mouth tightened.

"I've never been there alone before," she said. "We used to go to concerts in the evenings."

He was silent, frowning, searching desperately for something to say that would take the conversation away from places known to Tagarid-and-Hisham.

But she did that herself, saying, "I shan't go to concerts. I'll go to the theatre."

"What sort of play?" To keep it going now the dangerous corner had been rounded.

"Shakespeare." As he turned to her in surprise, she laughed at him. "Remember, I was educated in an English-medium school," she said. "I've read all the big ones, but never seen any – except on film, and that's surely not the same thing at all."

"Then you should go to Stratford."

"I know. I'd like to." She hesitated, then added softly, "Another time, perhaps. Not this trip."

"Too much shopping to do?"

She smiled. "Of course . . . Anyway, *Richard III* and *As You*

Like It are on at the Aldwych. For the rest, I shall content myself with the moderns. My tickets are already booked . . ."

They did not take the Badari road back across the Plain. Travelled instead the road that came over the Lebanon mountains from Tripoli and Becharré, further north, and ran straight as a survey-line to Baalbek. Straight as the Romans built roads; and two-thirds of the way across the Plain, about two hundred metres off the road, a single Roman column of grey stone reached skywards, and there was no sign or trace of any other building of any kind for many miles.

And after they had marvelled, stood for a while in the shadow of this, some conqueror's celebration of some triumph long forgotten, they drove on, homewards, the hashish on their right and on their left, an uninterrupted sea of green stretching away into green distances. The tall spike of yellow flowers, the deep green of the feathery foliage, very beautiful; it is in its natural state a lovely plant.

They left Baalbek after a late lunch, speeding along the Beka'a and then up into the mountains. But after Shtura the flow of traffic increased twenty-fold as the Beirutis who – like themselves – had sought relief from the coastal heat for the weekend headed back towards the city: cars and trucks travelling nose-to-tail except for the numerous maniacs who, horns blaring and headlights flashing, overtook in near-impossible circumstances – it was surely a kind of game to them, the equivalent of Russian roulette – and progressed in frenetic leaps and bounds.

At one of the checkpoints on the outskirts of Bhamdoun, the military – Lebanese Army this time – were stopping all vehicles travelling into or out of Beirut. Curran was driving, taking the Range Rover forward about three car-lengths every five minutes or so; and there was a long line of traffic ahead of them.

She glanced at her watch, asking impatiently.

"D'you think we'll make it by six o'clock?"

He shrugged.

"God knows. Sorry –" for she had said earlier that she wanted to be back by six "– but I hadn't reckoned on this. Must be something on."

"Probably merely showing their faces," she said bitterly. "To remind people that we do possess a so-called army, sometimes."

They moved forward again. And this time as they came to a halt a man got out of a red Buick ahead and prowled back along the line of cars, pausing from time to time to talk to people in them. He stopped by the Range Rover and, leaning in through the window, greeted Curran in Arabic; then spoke to Tagarid, who listened, questioned, and listened again.

"It's pretty bad," she said as the stranger went on his way. The sunlight of the day gone out of her.

"What's happened?"

"In Beirut, this morning. They tried to get one of the big Falangist leaders – Bechara – but they killed his baby daughter and his driver instead . . . *By mistake*, as it were," she added.

"How was it done?"

"They exploded a bomb by radio-control as his car went by, in Ashrafieh somewhere. He – the big man – was supposed to be in it but he was travelling in the car behind. He was unhurt."

He thought about her voice, how it sounded – what? Lifeless? No, he decided, not lifeless. Old. Yes, her voice sounded, *old*. As if the appalling things she was talking about were acceptable, and only minimally relevant to herself and life as *she* saw and comprehended it. And, therefore, to the best of her ability, ordered it so that it conformed to her own desires? . . . Now, for the first time, he accepted as a serious possibility the premise that Tagarid Kurban was involved in Khaled Namur's political activities. For that way of thinking was often typical of terrorists, he had found; being of course the only way they could live with the things they had done and planned yet to do.

"Was there any particular motive, do you suppose?" he asked. "Or was it plain terrorism?" Questioning now not simply as Tagarid's friend wanting to know about her because she was Tagarid; but as the man Curran who was doing a job and needed to possess any knowledge about her that might ever be used to attack her and discover – and therefore possibly thwart – any action she might be involved in.

"Oh there was a personal motive almost certainly. Something between the Becharas and the Zaccas who've been rivals for power and position for years now. A year ago, the man they missed today, Fuad Bechara, masterminded a more successful assault on the Zacca people, killing several of Hamid Zacca's family including a son . . . Today would have been adequate

99

revenge, if it had succeeded." Her voice reasoning coolly, apportioning no blame and revealing no emotion. "They're looking at everyone's papers," she went on after a small silence. "Permis de Sejour, work permit, etcetera, everything to show the car's yours, too . . . Pulling quite a few cars off the road for the full search, too, but we've so little with us that I shouldn't think they'll bother . . ."

They did not. The soldiers came, one to each side window, and demanded and closely inspected every paper that should be carried by an individual of whatever nationality, in Lebanon; this done, they stepped back and waved them on, the man on his side smiling briefly at Curran.

"Lebanese Army," he remarked as he drove on. "One wishes there were many more of them, and better led."

She made no reply, slipping her papers back into her bag and then settling back into her seat, staring out. The hillside rose up sharply on their left, and she jerked her head in that direction.

"Look up there," she said.

He looked. And saw the little nests of machine-gunners sited up above, well-positioned to command the road.

"Not Lebanese up there," she said. "Syrian."

As they came down the steeply curving road towards the city, daylight was already fading from the sky, the sea gleamed darkly blue. She reached out and touched his hand, briefly.

"It was good up there," she said. "Thank you."

"Remember what I said, Tagarid. I love you. Many things change, but that will not."

"Not?" The word came out of her stillness, softly; and then she questioned again: "*Whatever* else changes?"

"That will not," he repeated. And was secretly glad that she had sought the re-statement.

She phoned as soon as she got back to her flat, anxious because she was nearly an hour late and he might have left.

"Khaled!" she said, her throat tightening as she recognized his voice stating the number. And she apologized for her lateness and then told him she would be leaving on the Tuesday morning plane, she had checked her reservation. He asked her if she had questions to ask him, if there was anything she was unsure about; but there was nothing, all had been planned and thoroughly discussed at their last two meetings.

100

"Good luck," he said then. "We are with you. Remember that."

"Remember": for the second time that day the word used to instil into her memory something of great importance to the speaker. But when she put down the phone the words that Matt Curran had so gladly repeated had gone entirely from her mind.

"We are with you." This, she remembered.

7

THE FEELING of "lift" as the plane left the ground, the greenish-brown airfield and the grouped airport buildings rushing into view as the plane banked, turning away from the mountains; then, as it held the curve of flight, the sea sliding into view, and, briefly, the long northward reach of the coastline, the brown spine of the Lebanon range striking down to the sea at Byblos.

And then only the blue of the sea, below. Looking through the cabin window, Tagarid smiled. She was free. Beirut, the Lebanon, was left behind and (perhaps?) a way of life was also left behind and forever. I shall never be quite the same person after the doing of this thing which is beginning now, she thought. But corrected herself immediately: *has begun*.

And leaning back into her seat stared out at the unchanging blue of the sky and deliberately set her mind to move into and become part of the plan Khaled had laid out for her in meticulous detail. The plan of action was direct and simple; the investigations behind and the preparations leading up to it, complicated. She had total confidence that the operation would progress exactly as Khaled had foretold, to culminate in the final achievement so that the whole had been created and carried out by Khaled and herself, together.

After a while, when she had thought herself fully into the part she was to play, knew she could *be* it and *live* it, she thought about the man she was going to London to kill.

A total stranger to her, and she to him: that was one of the particular strengths of the plan. A Syrian; one who (Khaled had told her) had been an agent provocateur working under the cover of Diplomatic privilege during and after the civil war, whose job, among others, had been to inflame from within the rivalries of the warring "Groups"; one of his special responsibilities during that time – early on, when he was still "on his way up" – being to encourage and facilitate the use of hashish by the

102

fighting men (of *all* sides) so that their moral restraints dissolved
. . . Tagarid had studied well the photographs of the man,
given her by Khaled; had been given reports to read on some of
the bestial things done by those hopped-up gunmen, and had
known that she would kill the man not only for Hisham's
sake . . .

In London the afternoon was grey and cool. She was possessed by this feeling of newness that had come into her so
suddenly as her plane had taken off from Beirut. She felt as if
she were living a dream she had always desired to dream ever
since she could remember; but now dream and life seemed to
her to have merged and become one so that life simply flowed
forward along lines that had always been there, waiting for the
woman called Tagarid Kurban to arrive and live them.

The taxis looked dark inside, and earthbound. She travelled
towards the heart of the city on the upper deck of a London
Transport bus, sitting in the front seat and looking out and
down at the remembered Englishnesses: traffic streaming its
separate ways, following as a matter of course the dictates of
road-signs and the law; herds of boys playing football on a
school playing-field, yellow jerseys versus red surging over
green grass, and in the distance white-clad tennis-players on
grey asphalt; the gardens of suburbia green-lawned and pat-
terned with the colours of autumn, the colours subtle and
warm, repeated everywhere in hedges and trees; High-street
shops, windows lit because the greyness was running down out
of the sky and darkening the air, but the grey a quietness, soft
and filmy; and now gradually the pattern of the life of the city
changing –

Pattern? The word (in her mind) halted the smooth drift of
her thoughts. She considered the word again and told herself: in
Lebanon now the pattern of life is broken and we do not know
how to put it together again. But although this thought seemed
important as it occurred to her, it faded again immediately,
away into nothingness. And she looked out and watched once
more the city that for ten days would be hers.

At Victoria, milling crowds of day-trippers, and the adver-
tisements beside the Underground escalators all new and amus-
ing since last seen; on the train the faces of other passengers
certainly the faces of strangers, you will never know them, she
thought, and they *cannot* know you.

103

She felt this anonymity like a cloak around her. And it was a cloak of some voluptuously beautiful material so that she drew it close, delighting in the feel of it. Looking quickly at the faces of her fellow-travellers, these strangers who were for these moments of time her companions, she saw how ordinary they all looked and yet how individually unique, and liked them all very much . . .

When she walked out of the Underground station into the streets again the sky was clear pale blue and the air gleamed with thin autumn sunshine. The hotel was nearby and as she walked there, carrying her case, a small wind sprang up and the brown leaves scattered on the pavement were whisked into small, whispering whirlpools and then, as the breeze died, left lying in the gutters or against garden-walls, silent.

Big, modern, a place of glass and acres of carpet, of elegant flower-arrangements: the hotel welcomed her with professional solicitude and she smiled, knowing that in such a place she would live and move as one silvery fish among its shoal in a huge glass aquarium, observed, cared for, and personally unre-marked. It did not take her long to unpack; and then she changed into a grey trouser-suit and went out to walk on the nearby Common.

Incredibly green, the grass; and springy under the feet, the feel that you are walking *on the earth* coming right up into your blood. Huge chestnut trees massy with the tired green leaves of autumn, boys playing with the shiny brown nuts, yes, I remem-ber, "conkers". People walking dogs or taking a short cut home; cutting hedges, tinkering in garages; and teenagers clustered round gleaming motorbikes, the groups esoteric, giving the raw self its protection and demanding in exchange the bended knee of fealty . . . Walking within this pattern of London life she felt light and happy; and infinitely secure in her purpose.

After dining in the hotel, she returned to her room and lay down on the bed and read *Richard III*. It was a play she knew well and she was absorbed swiftly into the intricacies of plot and counter-plot, the past reaching out its strong fingers and wrap-ping them round the throats of the living, holding their life or death, their honour or dishonour, within its grasp . . . Later, put down her paperback copy and turned out the light. And lying in the dark, recalled Khaled's words the second time he had visited her at her flat, the second and last time.

"Think through and round and *into* our plan until the undertaking of it is worked into the fabric of your brain," he had said, his dark face intent upon hers. "Then work that undertaking into the larger pattern of the day-to-day realities of your visitor-to-London life. So that when the time comes you will live *that* day as if everything you are doing is entirely commonplace." Now, she did that; and when the operation was "complete" in her mind, slipped away gradually into sleep . . .

"Did you have a good day, madam?" the receptionist asked when she returned to the hotel the next evening and went over to the desk.

"Marvellous. Truly marvellous. I love Knightsbridge." Tagarid smiled at the girl, a red-head, very attractive. "But your London prices are not so kind to visitors as they used to be!"

"I suppose now that we have North Sea oil we feel we have to punish ourselves for our good fortune!"

Tagarid laughed.

"You could make a charge for the weather if you produced more days like today," she said. "It's been glorious . . . I came to tell you that tomorrow a messenger will deliver a parcel for me, from one of the shops. I don't know whether it will be in the morning or afternoon, but I shan't be back till late in the evening so would you please take it in for me?"

"Of course, madam." The girl's surprise in her face and voice. "Naturally."

"I thought I'd better mention it," Tagarid said quietly. "I know that packages addressed to Arabs aren't always so welcome nowadays."

And in spite of the red-head's protestations, knew she had been right to make the accusatory statement herself and thus put the matter out in the open . . . "It is the *unexpected* that arouses suspicion," Khaled had said. "That, and to conceal or mask in any way what you are doing . . . Live an open life, be frank and even a bit talkative. And only hide what it is absolutely essential to keep hidden."

So that morning she had dressed in clothes that were obviously expensive but not ostentatiously so, and the colours quiet;

and taking with her a nondescript canvas holdall bought the day before had gone by bus to Knightsbridge. It had been a day of cool golden sunshine and she had lived it taking pleasure in the hundreds of little things that – for her – made London a place where she felt the pulse of the city beating in rhythm with her own.

She went on living her dream; and the second day was like the first, golden and blue. She spent the morning on the Common; the afternoon in the West End; and the evening at the theatre: *Richard III*. When she got back to the hotel at about 11.30, the parcel had been delivered.

"What a marvellous day it's been again, I feel we should thank you for coming to London, Mrs Kurban," the red-haired receptionist said. "The sun came out the evening you arrived, and it hasn't stopped shining since!"

Taking the parcel from her, feeling its weight (yes, it feels right, she thought), Tagarid laughed.

"Oh I have friends in high places, you see . . . Thank you for taking this in for me."

She opened it as soon as she was in her room and set its contents out on the dressing-table: an automatic, and a silencer, separately wrapped; a sheet of foolscap with typed notes on it; and two keys, each with a tag. The make and type of weapon was entirely familiar to her: under Khaled's instruction, she had practised with an identical gun in Beirut, both the assembling and the firing of it, in a long narrow cellar-room beneath La Paloma; and now she put this one together, wrapped it in a yellow plastic bag and placed it in her holdall.

It had seemed right to get the gun packed away out of sight immediately. But when that was done she relaxed, had a leisurely bath and made ready for sleep. Then she carried the sheet of foolscap, the keys and a copy of *London A to Z* over to the bed, set them all down on the paisley bedspread and made herself comfortable, piling pillows against the bedhead and leaning back into their softness, slipping her bare feet under the covers.

Picking up the keys first, she read the tags. One said simply, FRONT DOOR; the other, ROOM 8 (Second Floor). She studied the notes, then. First, the name: Tarek Fakhoury; underneath that, the address: Room 8, 27 Nelson Road, Earls Court; underneath again, the time: 10–11.00 a.m. A neatly ruled line confined that information to the upper half of the page, and below it was printed another name: Miss Jane Edgeworth, Room 14 (Third Floor). That, too, was confined to its own place by a ruled line, beneath which were supplied detailed instructions for travelling from the bus-stop near her hotel, via Marble Arch tube station, to Nelson Road. And so taking up the copy of *London A to Z* she traced the journey she would make to her destination, checking it with her instructions, committing everything to memory.

No part of what she would do was complicated. And briefly, then, she was reminded again of Khaled: "Always the *action* should be as simple as possible," he had said; and then had smiled at her, sharing with her his silent laughter as he added, "The *people* in it are invariably so complicated that this simplicity is essential to success."

Slipping off the bed she put the two keys in her handbag; and got rid of the page of notes then, burning it over a big glass ashtray so that it flamed and shrivelled, flushing the charred detritus away down the lavatory, washing the ashtray clean again. When she turned off the light and drew back the curtains, moonlight streamed in through the open window; and the sounds of the late-night city ran softly along the cool night air.

Lying in bed, head pillowed on her clasped hands, she watched the moonlight slide smoothly slowly across the walls of her room; and inside her head, thought and pictured the doing of every single move she would make the next day, "seeing" the numbers on buses and doors, her back-up man in the fawn-coloured wind-cheater, the face of the man who would open to her the door of Room 8 . . .

Morning clear and sunny under bright blue sky: looking out at it from the window of her room, Tagarid smiled, seeing the dream-day waiting for her so bright and lovely. As on previous days, she had toast and coffee in her room before dressing. It was just before 9.30 when she left the hotel and walked away along the street towards the bus-stop, a vital, svelte-moving figure in well-fitting black jeans and a loose white overblouse wide-necked over a white polo.

On the bus she climbed to the upper deck and was childishly pleased to find the front seat empty, anticipating the fun of sitting poised high above mere earthbound creatures as her bus cleaved its way through the press of traffic. Settling down there, her holdall wedged safely between her feet and the side of the bus, she looked out through the glass of her dream.

As she paid for her ticket, the conductor remarked that it was a lovely day, that at this rate his chrysanths would last another week.

"Whole front garden's full of 'em," he said, the middle-aged pleasant face telling her he was visualizing his flowers as he spoke of them. "Every colour there is, I reckon. The wife plans the colour scheme, see." He grinned, adding, "But it's me makes 'em grow!"

When she got off the bus he was standing at the bottom of the stairs to the top deck. "Have a good day," he said; and as the bus gathered speed and passed her as she walked along the pavement, waved to her.

The ride by Underground was totally uneventful. In any case only three stops.

"Left at The Rose in June, then first right . . ." The instructions clicking out smoothly in her brain, and she followed them, working her way through the streets of London suburbia: small groups of shops here and there, the houses quite big, doubtless medium-range residences once but each divided and subdivided now, the area a colony of bed-sitters and small flats. Therefore very few people about: Monday to Friday, from 9 to 5, the "colonists" are at work . . .

Nearly there now: the next turn left would be Nelson Road. She glanced at her watch and it was ten past ten. That was good, for she could carry straight on with the plan, for the notes had told her that between 10 and 11 o'clock was the safest period, the period when Tarek Fakhoury was invariably in and the other lodgers invariably out (though that pattern *could* of course change unexpectedly – which was one of the reasons why the man in the fawn wind-cheater was needed).

Turning into Nelson Road she observed the houses continuing of the same kind, though perhaps a shade smaller and with an indefinable air of raffishness now (suggesting that perhaps owners and tenants here were careful not to evince too much curiosity about their neighbours' personal affairs and activities?). She smiled momentarily at the thought, walking along the pavement not too fast, not too slow, checking the numbers on the house-doors without turning her head, only her eyes moving.

Soon, now: Number 19, the other side of the street; and as she paused on the edge of the pavement, looking right then left before stepping out into the roadway, she saw the man in the wind-cheater. He was standing by the Request bus-stop across the road from her and a little further along it, hands in pockets, looking towards her. As she crossed the road he turned away, idly pacing a few steps along the kerb, gazing up the street (waiting for the bus, obviously!). As she approached she heard him whistling softly, and then he turned so that he would face her as she went by. A burly young man, plenty of strength latent in that indolent strolling walk; his face as she passed him fair-skinned and unremarkable. She knew that after she had gone by he would turn to follow her with his eyes until she had entered Number 27 (naturally, for he is bored and she is young and attractive, it passes the time pleasantly, any watcher-behind-curtains would think). She knew, too, that he would not get on a bus until she had come out of the house again and walked away.

If he had not been there she would not have gone into Number 27; she would have waited at the bus-stop herself and boarded the next bus that came along; to return the next day. Now, she felt her heart lift a little because everything was progressing according to expectations and the operation could continue to be unfolded and lived.

Going up the four shallow steps to the blue-painted door of Number 27, she took the key out of her handbag and let herself in. As she closed the door quietly behind her she was suddenly aware of sunlight shut out; then, of herself in a hallway dimly lit by the daylight coming in through a heavily glassed window above the door. For a second her consciousness lurched out of the confines of the imposed dream and she was gripped by a sense of unreality and an urge to advance by stealth into this hostile territory. But the dream re-cast its strong nets swiftly, gave her back her confidence.

I live here, she told herself. Room 8 is on the second floor. That is "my" room. And resting the holdall on a narrow table with some letters on it she drew the gun out of its plastic bag, smoothed the bag down into the bottom of the holdall and carefully laid the gun on top of it, ready.

Went up the stairs then, no stealth in her movements; an eagerness, rather. On the second floor there were four numbered rooms, the figures black on white-painted wood. Number 8 was close by the stairs, and as she stood at the door she could hear music inside, pop-music playing quite quietly, a radio perhaps.

She knocked and waited. After a slight pause the door was opened, held ajar: he stood holding the door-knob with one hand, the other against the jamb.

"Yes?" Tarek Fakhoury: the heavy brows, the full-lipped, sensual mouth and the white scar across one brown cheek where in '76 someone had gone for his eyes with a knife.

"Hi!" And she was smiling and casual, her eyes just slightly inviting. "Sorry to bother you but I wonder if you'd help me?"

He relaxed visibly; grinned.

"Why not? I always help pretty girls if they ask me."

"Well, you see, I just dropped in to see my friend Jane – Jane Edgeworth, she lives upstairs, Room 14 – but she's out, and there's a message I *must* get to her, it's about tonight. Could I please borrow a pen and a bit of paper to write on, and leave it with you to give her later on?"

"Sure." He dropped his hand from the door jamb, standing back and pulling the door a little further open. "Come on in." As she did so he closed the door to behind her, grinned again. "Wait here for her yourself, if you like. She's usually back around eleven and I'm not busy. We could listen to some music, or have a drink or something." The invitation obviously implying more.

"I'll write the note anyway, if you don't mind." She giggled. "First things first."

"Okay. Why don't you sit down?" He waved an arm at a chair and turned, walking away from her towards a table near the window, plates and a coffee cup over there, a jumble of books and papers, his chair pushed back when he had got up to answer her knock.

Behind him, she took out the gun and let the holdall fall to the floor. Quietly. Was ready then.

He turned round towards her, an exercise book in one hand and a biro in the other, asking.

"You're not English, are you –?" but then his face in shock

110

knowing that he had been too careless and that death was *now* and
— she fired twice.

The bullets took him in the chest and smashed him backwards: he fell sprawled against the table, one hand scrabbling convulsively there for a second, knocking the cup over but then sliding away loosely dyingly as his body tumbled heavily to the floor.

She stood still. There was no thought in her; only an emptiness, a sudden and total quiet. She was looking at his face; after a moment blood began to flow slowly from his mouth and from his nose. Not very much; when it had stopped, she went closer and carefully and steadily shot him for the last time, in the forehead.

Then she wrapped the gun in its plastic bag, stowed it away in the holdall. And let herself out of Room 8, out of house Number 27, closing the two doors quietly upon what she had done.

Outside, she stood on the top step and looked up for a moment at the blue sky and the sunshine streaming down out of it: like the wild high joy of lovers, the sunshine, she thought, that sheens for them everything it touches. Then she went down the steps and away down Nelson Road; as she passed the man in the wind-cheater he winked at her (though that was not in his instructions), but she looked straight through him (and he wondered whether that was because she was in shock or whether it was because she had not noticed him, and decided ruefully that it was more likely the latter). But he was wrong: it was because she was in a state of exaltation.

As the rest of the day passed the exaltation quietened into tranquillity; she walked in a park whose name she did not know, ate delicious roast beef for lunch, then took a bus to Trafalgar Square and spent the afternoon in the National Gallery.

That evening she had dinner at the hotel. And later, in her room, took the two keys out of her handbag, tore off their tags and destroyed them as she had destroyed the page of notes the night before.

Moonlight bright in the room as she lay in bed. Tarek Fakhoury is dead, she thought; and with a great peace in her, fell asleep.

8

O N THE Saturday morning after Tagarid left for London,
Matt Curran drove alone up into the Beka'a. He went in
the Range Rover, taking drinking water and coffee, and a
Thermos bag with a couple of beers, some cold chicken and
sandwiches in it so that if he decided to stay out the whole day,
he could. Born with a good sense of direction, he had developed
the ability to retain mentally the details of a route previously
taken; and set himself now to return to the place where he and
Tagarid had had their picnic together, weeks before. But he
made one mistake, and realized this when, the other side of the
mountains and soon after passing through a small village, he
noticed on the right-hand side of the road a massy ruin of cut
grey stone, an orchard of cherry trees beside it in heavy leaf. He
knew he had never seen this before, and turned the car around.
As he drove back the way he had come, he recognized the T-
junction where he had taken the wrong turning and got onto the
right road then; and soon came to the big tree in whose shade
they had lunched before. The place was as quiet as on the
previous occasion; and the beauty of the lonely lands lay in the
long, sweeping lines of mountain and valley, in the colours of
late summer on heights bright and stark under the sun – but
always greenness where the water flowed, and in the Beka'a there
are many tributaries to the two great rivers.

Pulling the car in off the road he got out and stood looking,
breathing the cool mountain air in deep. Then reaching into the
car, took out the flask of coffee and poured himself a cup, stood
leaning against the bonnet while he drank it. The sunlight was
very bright and he tipped the khaki-drill digger-hat forward to
shield his eyes from the glare. He decided that when he had
finished his coffee he would explore downhill, towards the
valley.

But as he was stowing the flask away he heard and then saw a car coming along the road, travelling in the same direction as he had done: a battered Land Rover, its original blue paint weathered and aged to a dull grey and worn right through in many places to rusting metal below. He straightened; and stood watching it approach. Nothing wrong with the sound of its engine, he noticed; and as it slowed down and then pulled up almost opposite him he had already half-sensed who would be driving it.

Ibrahim Selim. Who advanced across the road with the remembered swing to his powerful body; whose strong-featured and handsome face had no softness in it anywhere. And no friendliness, either.

"You remembered the way here," he said, not offering either the hand or the words of greeting; simply the statement spoken harshly in simple Arabic and his grey eyes cold and watchful, slitted against the sunlight.

"I have a good memory for places," Curran answered, keeping his Arabic well-schooled. And since no friendship had been shown, offered none; asking with equal directness, "How did you know I was here?"

"You were seen at Al-Ain," Ibrahim Selim said. The anger in him a bitter power hardly controlled. "Round here every stranger is watched from the moment he enters a village until the moment he leaves it."

Al-Ain: the name was enough. Tagarid's village-by-marriage. The village where she and her husband had lived, and in which her husband had been murdered. The little place with the ruin and the cherry trees that he had passed through when he had taken the wrong turning.

"I didn't know," Curran said quite softly, holding the other man's eyes. "Believe that."

Briefly, their eyes held. Then Ibrahim Selim looked away out over the valley.

"It is believed," he said. And Curran knew himself accepted.

He offered coffee then; and they drank it sitting cross-legged in the shade of the big tree, smoking cigarettes.

"You have learnt a lot of Arabic," Ibrahim Selim said; and although it was presented as a compliment Curran knew there was suspicion behind it.

113

"I study with an Arab teacher," he said. "Also, I have a fair ear for languages, I learn them quickly."

"What is your opinion of the Lebanon?" It was not the sort of question most Arabs asked these days of anyone who was a stranger to them.

Or would answer were it put to themselves, Curran thought. And, first, answered evasively, "My opinion would be without value because I can touch only the surface of life here." Then, turned the question back, saying, "But *your* opinion would be of value to me." Waited then, half-expecting a refusal – not an evasion, this man surely a facer of issues, not an evader, he felt sure of that, but a refusal because to answer could be to give hostages to fortune.

Ibrahim Selim finished his cigarette in silence, scrubbed the butt dead in the hard brown earth. Looked out over the land, then; and spoke thoughtfully, slowly.

"We, the people who live on the land, the country people – we are nothing to Beirut. We know this. We are the very source of their ability to live, because we win for them the produce of the earth; but still to them we are ignorant peasants. And *kept* that way because although the importance of the land is known, it is made little of, sometimes denied, so that the wealth continually being created from it may be pocketed by the city-men, the city-lovers." As he went on speaking his right hand, resting on the ground where he had put out his cigarette, began to move about, the strong stubby-nailed fingers sifting the yellow-brown dust of the dry earth, stroking the coarse grass. "The Government in Beirut, saying with pride that it represents us all because the President is Maronite, the Prime Minister Sunni and the Speaker of the House of Representatives Shi'a – *they* do not govern. The Groups are the law in the land, under the eye of the Syrians. Only some of us pay our taxes to the Government; but all pay their dues to one Group or another. Not necessarily in money; but all *pay* because they have seen what happens to those who do not . . . But we who live on the land" – the repeated phrase separating them from lesser men – "will not beg from the city the things that truly are ours by right. Our loyalties are admittedly feudal, but very strong because of that. Baalbek and Zahlé, the villages of the Beka'a and the mountains – their allegiance to Beirut is a single strand of new wool. Easy to break." Then his voice altered subtly. (And Curran heard – or thought he heard? or simply sensed? – threat in his words. Veiled but – there.) "Even the flame of a village-made candle might burn through such a strand," Ibrahim Selim said.

Curran listening to the careful simple Arabic; and the knowledge growing in him that this was a lonely man who treasured and guarded his loneliness. It is easier for him to talk of such things to a stranger, he thought. Or was Ibrahim Selim testing him, to some purpose sounding him out? He sat silent, hoping that this man-of-the-land would go on talking of his people and of himself.

He did. His hand now resting quietly on the earth.

"Men have farmed the Beka'a and the narrow valleys of the foothills for thousands of years," he said. "Conquering armies, Government tax-men, brigands, all have robbed us. It is an old story, for us. Now, we are going through a 'low' time. But it is only – a time. It will pass as it has always passed." He was silent for a while; and then said quietly, his eyes moving over the barren slopes of the hills, "A true leader will come; or Lebanon will die: one of these two things will happen. *But the villages will never die.*"

Then suddenly Curran remembered the fire-blackened walls; the bomb-blasted places of worship.

"Some do," he said sharply. "I've seen one, a place called –"

"Badari. Madame told me." Ibrahim Selim turned and looked at him, suddenly and completely of the present and the grey eyes slightly mocking. "Study your Arabic, Mr Curran," he said, "my words were 'the villages', not 'a village'."

Curran grinned.

"I wouldn't mind a teacher like you," he said. And then, holding the other man's eyes, the decision already taken and the grin entirely gone from his face, continued, "I have a great deal to learn, in places like this. I'd very much like to learn some of it from someone like you."

And the air tautening between them. The Arab tense and aware as an animal of the wild scenting a new thing and searching it out for hint of threat.

"You mean?" he said softly (and Curran knew his own danger).

"That what you said is of interest to me. That we serve the

same *beliefs*. That later we may find mutual profit in discussing them further."

"Perhaps." The Arab looked away.

But Curran knew they had established contact of a sort. It was, of course, a contact that might never be used, he knew that too; but he was a man who usually played his hunches, and this one that had prompted the sudden "opening" he had offered just then had been strong and sure, he had spoken the "lead"-words, hardly considering their import.

"Madame has returned from London?" Words into the sunlight. Neutrally spoken.

Curran shook his head; and followed the change of subject.

"She will come back on Tuesday, I think. That is what she said before she went."

The silence returned then. It sat easily between them for a little while and then Curran spoke again.

"What is happening at Al-Ain?" he asked. "Has anyone been arrested?"

There was no immediate answer. After a pause, the question was parried.

"Did you not ask Madame?"

And Curran wondered if Ibrahim Selim was smiling, but he did not look to see.

"No," he answered evenly. Gave him what he wanted, then, "One would need to be a close friend to ask questions like that."

The Arab made a curious gesture of the hand, small, suggesting perhaps acceptance of a gift. Spoke at once after that.

"The Syrians say they are continuing their enquiries," he said, "but there have been no arrests."

"But he was a well-known man, a respected doctor. Surely there are people with the necessary influence to take the matter up with Government officials in Beirut, officials sufficiently highly placed to bring pressure to bear where it would produce results? Especially as he was known to have absolutely no political attachments, so there'd be no risk of stirring up even bigger trouble."

"None of those things are relevant. Not to stand against the wishes of the Syrian Army." Ibrahim Selim turned to Curran, his face wiped clean of all expression. "That is a fact that has to be accepted," he said blandly.

Curran could not accept it.

"But surely *something* will have to happen?" he demanded angrily. "For heaven's sake, *murder* was done, *rape* was committed. Surely the Syrians at least want justice to be *seen* to be done, even if they *undo* it later, in the privacy of their own country?"

"They do not appear to want this."

"But – the people? *You*, men like you? Even if it was only *seen* to be done, well at least that would be a sort of admission of guilt, which would be something!"

Ibrahim Selim got easily to his feet, stood looking down at the ground.

"*'Seen* to be done'." He repeated the words as though wondering exactly what they meant, as though perhaps seeking in them (or giving *to* them?) some hidden meaning. "*We* are not concerned that it is *seen* to be done," he said. And, without saying anything further, turned and strode away up the slope towards the road and the two parked cars.

As Curran followed him, taking his time, he was conscious of a strange and inexplicable feeling that in some indefinable way, underneath the words, the Arab had been laughing at him . . .

The next morning being Sunday, Curran played tennis as he often did, with three other men, meeting them at the Club courts at 9 o'clock, playing first an hour's singles and then ending up with a couple of sets of doubles. The humidity was still high and, apart from loving the game, Curran found it a relief to use up some energy in outdoor activity, to get really hot and sweaty. Afterwards they took water and salt tablets, showered, then settled down to cold lager in the shade of trees at the side of the Club's private pool. Usually the four of them swam and lunched there, too; but this week Curran's Sunday followed a different pattern because there was one thing he wanted to do, and one thing he had to do.

The thing he wanted to do was to be done first because the timing of the second was dictated by outside events. Leaving the Club after drinking a single beer, he walked through West Beirut, working his way towards Tagarid's block of flats. He felt very good, his body well-used now, springy and vital; but the city air was already thick with heat, rank with the smell of the rotting rubbish piled in the streets, and then as a small breeze blew up from the South the stink of burning rubber, "they" (some Group) had been burning tyres not far away, someone protesting about something. But better that than letting fly with a Kalashnikov at anything that happened at that moment to bring your bottled-up frustration/rage/hatred seething up past boiling point, he thought.

He stopped at a shop he knew, to buy flowers. Fresh in on Sundays here, he knew; and could smell them fifty yards away, the perfume clean and lovely on the air and then the flowers seen cascading out of the shop on to the pavement, banked high on tall, shelved stands, massed and clustered in huge pots – cheaper ones in great buckets – and the inside of the shop gorgeous with massy arrangements of exotic blooms, with drifts of roses. Dazed with colour, he bought a dozen roses and a sheaf of white flowers, whose name he did not know, knew only that they smelt lovely and reminded him of tall hyacinths.

When he rang the bell of Tagarid's flat it was answered almost at once. The door opened and Fatmeh stood there looking up at him: thin and dark, everything about her dark; and the brown eyes so curiously blank, yes, he felt again the slight cold shock those eyes had given him the first time he had seen her, that momentary sense of disorientation *in himself* because her eyes said that the world outside was too hostile for her to admit its existence.

"Fatmeh." He said her name gently. "Good afternoon."

At her name spoken gently, she frowned.

"Good afternoon," she said; and he felt she was actually seeing him now.

"I have brought some flowers for Madame. Would you please put them in water so that they will be here to greet her on Tuesday?" He held out the flowers.

But she made no move to take them. Only stood waiting, staring up at him, and frowning.

"What shall I put them in?" she asked at length, quietly, unhappily, the burden of decision too big. "Where shall I put them?"

"I'll come inside, then, and we'll do it together." But she did not move, regarding him doubtfully. "May I do that, Fatmeh?" he asked after a moment.

She said nothing; only opened the door a little wider, stepped aside as he made to enter and then closed the door behind him.

In the kitchen, he unwrapped the flowers and spread them out on the breakfast table. The girl hesitated by the door for a moment, watching him; and then came and stood staring down at the flowers. After a moment she looked up at him and her eyes, her face, were subtly different: the blankness had been smoothed away, leaving a softness there.

"I will get the vases," she said almost eagerly. And did so, filling them with water and setting them on the table; stood back then, hands loosely clasped in front of her, looking at him.

"You do them," he said.

"Oh I can't. I never do the flowers." Her face closed in on itself and she looked down. "Madame does the flowers," she said.

He caught something in her voice. It made him look at her sharply; but he could not see her eyes, only the whole of her in this submissive pose, as if she were denying the very existence of herself. But there was something else in her: he had caught it in the tone of her voice just then, and now as he looked at her he realized suddenly that the submissive pose was not in any way an abasement of herself, it was a cover for the essential secrecy of herself. The realization disturbed him.

"I'd like you to do them, Fatmeh," he said. "You'll make them look prettier than I can." Still she looked down. "But I'll tell Madame that I did them," he added.

She put the flowers into the vases then.

Standing leaning back against the stainless steel sink, Curran watched her.

"Do you like working for Madame?" he asked.

"Yes." The word came out at once and he knew it was a lie, her mouth tightening, her hands suddenly ripping leaves cruelly off slender elegant stems.

He said no more. And as she arranged the flowers her whole body relaxed and quietened. Her hands were strong and rather beautiful, he noticed; as she worked, the grey headscarf slipped back and curls of black gleaming hair escaped; she looked terribly vulnerable, and her face lost its stubborn bony look in response to the pleasure she was finding in what she was doing.

They carried the vases of flowers into the sitting-room and placed them carefully to catch the eye as one entered, welcoming. In that room, a personal room, Curran felt a strangeness at being in Tagarid's flat alone, uninvited by her.

"They look very nice," he said, beginning to move towards

119

the door, wanting suddenly to get out of there. "Thank you, Fatmeh."

"Monsieur!" The word harsh from behind him.

He stopped, turning to her. "Yes?"

"I want to tell you. There is something I want to tell you." The words tumbling out and then the girl was silent, staring at him, tense; and her eyes, bright and hard, seemed to him to have got smaller.

"What is it, Fatmeh? I'll help if I can, just tell me."

Her head moved in a sharp gesture of negation; her hands gripped the stuff of her full skirt as she fought whatever it was inside her that was trying to stop the words getting out.

"Madame is —" She broke off, staring at him out of the maelstrom of her personal battle.

Madame? – Instantly, he was as tense as the girl. But he could control it better.

"Tell me, Fatmeh" – very gently – "tell me now. What you want to tell me."

"She has a gun." It was said; and the girl stood trembling.

"Many people in Beirut keep guns in their houses nowadays." Calming her. But he wanted to know it all, now. "*Where* does she keep it?"

"It is not an ordinary gun. It is a very good gun and it has a silencer. It has not been here very long."

You seem to know a lot about guns for a girl of eighteen, he thought; and asked again, "Where does she keep it?"

Suddenly, without answering, Fatmeh turned and went out through another door into a room beyond. In a minute she was back and there was a small ornate key in her hand; walking past him to the bureau near the window she bent down and put the key into the lock of the bottom drawer, turned it. Then stood back and looked across the room at him.

He went and stood beside her. The drawer was still closed, and tension came out of the girl like a silent scream. Getting down on one knee, he pulled the drawer open: the gun lay there on a bed of folded cloth, a Weber 7 mm, clean and gleaming, the dull metallic sheen; its silencer lay beside it.

He heard the breath hiss through her teeth. His eyes went to her face but saw only her profile. She was leaning forward staring down wide-eyed at the gun; and the whole of her stone-still.

120

After a moment he got to his feet; and she straightened, turned to him. Now he could see her face properly he knew at once the driving-force behind what she had just done: it was hatred. The deep hatred running in the blood. Having seen it before, he recognized it. As before, it knocked him off balance for a second; and he reached down and closed the drawer (his hands a little clumsy), locked it and withdrew the key.

"Thank you for showing me, Fatmeh," he said then, handing her back the key. "It is good to know such things, these days." He walked away towards the outside door and she followed him, sandalled feet whispering over the carpet. And the whole of her quiet now, he saw as he turned with one hand on the door handle, saying, "Goodbye."

The servant-mask was back in place, out of it the brown eyes secure in their blankness; and the thin body without youth, submissiveness in every line of it as if she had lived a thousand years of servitude and there was nothing else in her, *nothing*.

But he knew now that there was, and he knew its names: anger, fear, loathing. Fatmeh hated: but *which* did she hate, the gun, or Tagarid? As he walked back to his own flat he thought about this; and concluded that in some way the gun and Tagarid were meshed together in Fatmeh's mind, somehow they made an entity and upon that entity her hatred was focused . . . He thought about Tagarid then; and saw her surrounded by two concentric circles of danger. She owned a gun; not the sort of gun a woman living alone in a lawless city might be expected to have, but the sort of gun intended for planned and secret violence: that was the inner circle, ringing her tightly with danger. Also, she was hated by a person who had total access to her place of living, to her way of living, to (if that were what was sought) – her *life*: that was the outer circle; and as well as threatening Tagarid with its own danger it crowded close against the inner ring and the two together surely compounding the threat to her a hundredfold . . . By the time he was letting himself into his flat, Curran had decided that it would be wise to find out more about Fatmeh; and that this should be done without wasting any time.

The fat brown envelope lay waiting in the top drawer of the desk by the window of the small back room he had set up as his office: as usual on Sundays, Ziad had let himself into the flat with his own key and delivered the mail – the desk had an electronic guarding-device with Ziad on its guest-list, and the drawer a rather nasty self-destruct attachment if touched by unauthorized hands. It was reasonably secure.

Curran opened the envelope and checked to see if any of the papers in it were headed with the "Emergency" cypher. None was, so for the moment he shut them away again: there appeared to be no rush on, and he was hungry. So he treated himself to a lager and a curry lunch, sent up from the restaurant below, before setting to work.

It was nearly 7 o'clock by the time he had finished decoding the four pages of information contained in the envelope. Then, picking out one of the sheets of paper covered with the neat, printed capitals of his own decoding, he set it on top of the others under the light of his desk lamp and read it through again.

It told him that on the morning of 12 September an Arab male with papers in the name of Tarek Fakhoury had been shot dead in a rooming-house in the Earl's Court district of London; that Fakhoury had entered Britain illegally; that it was suspected he had been a Syrian agent in the Lebanon from 1974 to late 1977, but that there was no evidence of his present involvement in any terrorist activity in his host country; and that to date there were absolutely no pointers as to the identity of his assassin(s).

When Curran had finished reading he locked the papers away again, mixed a long whisky and water and took it out onto the balcony, stretched himself out in a yellow canvas sun-chair . . .

Tagarid? She has a gun, here. She also has had meetings – here – with Khaled Namur. Who is, by his own lights, a Lebanese "patriot".

And she is in London now. She was in London on 12 September.

Yet, as he thought round it and through it there appeared to be nothing at all to be built out of those disparate facts.

But: *Tagarid?*

His instinct needled him, forcing into his consciousness its own certainties: there's something going on – in London, in Lebanon, or in both – and she is involved in it . . . Oblivious to the noise of the traffic below, drinking a second whisky and then a third, he fought against his instinct.

But neither of them won.

And he realized that if he found out that she was involved in

122

some serious act of terrorism – was involved without doubt and provably and *still stoppably*, though that would reveal her guilt and therefore expose her to punishment – *he did not know whether he would be able to move against her or not*.

Which appalled him.

9

SOON AFTER eleven the next morning, Curran took an hour off and drove across the city to the offices of the organization called "Back-up". It had been formed after the civil war to help unskilled workers – especially young women – find work where they would not be exploited: unemployment ran high in the devastated, shocked and stagnant city and often such people, vulnerable to the blackmail of "those are the terms, take it or leave it – if you don't want the job there are plenty others who do", were forced to accept slavey's hours for very little money. Four years after the uneasy "peace" had been imposed and held relatively steady by the APF, the city was still stagnant and it was still a buyer's market as far as jobs went: so Back-up was still very much in business, with hundreds on its lists, some with life-stories that were merely sad, others seeking to rebuild lives scarred by the most violent and fearful tragedies. It functioned with a nucleus of full-time staff, some trained, some not, assisted by voluntary part-time workers. When Curran had phoned earlier to make an appointment he had been put through to a woman who – speaking English that was fluent but heavily accented – had assured him that she would give him all available information providing his enquiries were aimed at helping a person they had recommended for employment. So he had given her Fatmeh's name to look up in her books, and made this appointment.

The offices occupied the third and top floor of what before the war had been a somewhat pretentious private house, a yellow-plastered building with large ornate balconies overlooking the road. Clearly, the first two floors had been taken over by squatters: lines of drying washing festooned the balconies, and as he climbed the stairs Curran glimpsed through open doorways large, high-ceilinged rooms divided up by sagging curtains hung on ropes, mattresses in serried ranks on uncarpeted

124

floors, and battered furniture that had once been elegant and expensive.

The office he was shown into was clean and sparsely furnished. The woman behind the desk was about forty, a dark-eyed blonde, immaculately coiffured and made-up, but dressed in a beige shirt-waister of heavy cotton. Very workmanlike, thought Curran; and imagined her at home, diplomatic circles, probably . . .

She was good at her job. Having checked Curran's credentials and established that Mrs Tagarid Kurban, Fatmeh's employer, worked for his company, she opened a drawer in her grey-steel office desk, took out a file with a plain blue cover and placed it before her. She did not need to open it yet, Curran noticed; and respected her for that.

"What exactly is it that you wish to know about the girl?" she asked.

"The story behind her. What you know of it."

"But, Mr Curran, that's just the thing we try to free our people from. We want to give them the confidence of knowing that for them the past will stay in the past, so that they can go out and make a new life for themselves – which is a thing that's very difficult to do at all here, nowadays, even without a psychological millstone round your neck."

"But – if perhaps there's some *danger*? Danger to others?"

The dark eyes challenged him.

"You are saying that, in this case, there *is*?"

He sat forward, accepting the challenge and momentarily obscurely glad that Fatmeh was so well guarded.

"Madame," he began carefully, "please do not think that I am in any way *against* the girl. Very much the reverse . . . I got a strong impression that under that shut exterior there's a violence, that it's building up inside her and quite likely to explode quite soon. If that should happen, some outside person could get hurt. And then, *so would Fatmeh*: anything like that would surely put Fatmeh back where even you could *never* help her."

Relaxing then, he sat back in his chair and waited.

She regarded him in silence for a few moments, obviously weighing things up; and then got up and came round the desk to stand leaning back against it, facing him.

"It's not a long story," she said; and went on to tell it in a quiet, almost expressionless voice. "She came here, to Beirut,

125

with her family in '76, one of the thousands of refugees who poured over the borders when the war was on, and settled in the Lebanon. Her parents; and three sisters and one brother, all younger than she. They lived in one of those shanty-towns the refugees built for themselves out of packing-cases and bits of wood or corrugated iron, even cardboard sometimes. This one is out beside the road to the airport. Such places have coagulated into fiercely – *ferociously* – independent living units: no law applies there but their own, neither the Lebanese Army nor the police go in, not even the Syrians. The shanty-town where Fatmeh's family lived was big, five or six hundred people, and mostly on the borderline of starvation . . . I met Fatmeh's mother, she was a fine big woman, vivid, she must have been very handsome once; and Fatmeh loved her. *Adored* her.

"The summer of '79 was a long one and water grew scarce. There were only two stand-pipes giving water to Fatmeh's 'town'; one of these was close to the family's house, right by the road. Like lots of other places in and around the city, they could only get water at certain times of day, and even then the supply was severely limited. They never had enough; not even though they rationed themselves strictly. But because their stand-pipe was close to the road, outsiders in cars used to stop by it and take water. Steal it. Apparently there was one man in particular, a Beiruti businessman who lived in a biggish house in the foothills nearby: he appeared regularly with water cans, and filled them up there. The shanty-town people dared not oppose him because he had influential contacts within the Amal."

She paused a moment, as if surprised at what a long time it was taking her to tell the story, after all.

"I said it wasn't a long story," she said, "but it is, isn't it. And I'm not telling you even a quarter of what there is to tell about life in the refugee shanty-towns."

He nodded. "I realize that. You couldn't, not in a million words. No one could. I know that. Just tell me about Fatmeh."

"Yes . . . Well, this man flaunted his untouchability, encouraged others to do the same as he was doing. The people of the 'town' put up warning notices, stating that the water from that stand-pipe was theirs, not just for anyone, and that there wasn't enough for outsiders. But it made no difference. Finally, they put up a notice saying, 'Any person from outside who takes this water will die.' Yes, I'm quoting verbatim. Those were the

126

words used, Fatmeh told me. And, after that, most of the water-thieves took heed and left well alone, knowing those people had indeed reached the end of their patience.

"This one man, though, the one who had begun it all, he came by one day and drove his car close to the stand-pipe and began to wash his car with the 'town's' water, using a hose and the water running off his car onto the ground. One of the shanty-town people – an old man, there aren't many young men in such places – this man tried to stop him, tried to turn off the water. They began to fight, the old man was knocked down and the other turned away and went back to washing his car.

"That was when Fatmeh's mother, who had been watching, took up an axe and attacked the man from behind. She didn't stop hewing into him even after he was dead . . . And Fatmeh saw it happen. At the time she was sixteen years old."

"Christ." Curran, softly. Tagarid was forgotten; in his mind there was only this sixteen-year-old girl watching, screaming – watching the blood spurt out of a man as her mother swung an axe into him and cut him to death; and he put his hand up to his face in a curious smearing movement as if to wipe something off the skin of his cheek, his jaw.

"I don't know what Fatmeh was like before," the blonde woman went on. "When the Red Crescent referred her to us she was as you know her now, psychologically maimed. But it was, and is, the psychiatrist's view that she is not likely to harm anyone."

Curran forced his mind back to the reason why he had wanted to learn more about the girl.

"I formed the impression that she has a kind of *hatred* for Mrs Kurban," he said. "The sort of hatred that might, as I said earlier, lead to violence of some sort."

"What were your reasons for that impression, Mr Curran?" The woman's voice rather cold now, her manner altogether more distant; and as he made no immediate answer she turned away and went and sat down in her chair behind the desk again. "It is extremely difficult for us to find jobs for young and untrained girls," she continued. "If Fatmeh were to lose this job for what you are hinting at, we couldn't possibly recommend her to anyone else."

When she threw it back at him like that, his "reasons" seemed unforgivably frail: his "intuitions," the girl's eyes, her

127

agitated hands, the presence of a gun – any gun – in Tagarid's flat? On account of those things, to cause to be taken from Fatmeh the one thing that might give her wounds the chance – the *time* – to heal: her job?

Sensing his sudden unease and taking advantage of it, the woman said quickly, a warmth in her voice again, "Perhaps if you ask Mrs Kurban to show Fatmeh extra kindness, that would help. And you also, Mr Curran, talk with the girl sometimes, compliment her perhaps on some aspect of her work."

Fatmeh's story like an inescapable pain in his head, he got to his feet. And left then, making the right words of thanks for information received. But he knew that what he had been told had immeasurably increased his disquiet that such a girl, with such a history, should be anywhere in the vicinity of the woman he loved.

The afternoon of the next day he drove out to the airport to meet her (seeing the linked shanty-towns as he had always seen them when he drove that way, acres of squalid huts, a chaos of sun-faded browns with here and there the thin green of a stunted tree planted perhaps by someone who had once loved his own land, to help him remember that love when everything else in his life as now lived instructed him only in hate). "Fatmeh's town", that one, perhaps, Curran thought now, glancing across the road at one such place as he drove by: and he wondered if her family – the father, the three sisters and the brother – if they still lived there . . .

Watching the passengers come out through the low wicket-gates that released them from the grille-protected desks where officials had checked their travel-documents, he did not see her until she was close in front of him, smiling. And then he stood staring at her: he was seeing a different person, there was colour in her clothes – peacock greens patterning a white silky shimmer of a dress – and she was wearing lipstick, eye make-up –

"I'm Tagarid Kurban," she said gravely to his silence. "I believe a Mr Curran is meeting me –"

Then they were laughing together in greetings, and as they walked across the big hall to wait for her luggage he said, unable to keep his eyes off her, "You look entirely different, I'm sorry –"

"Good different, or bad?"

"Oh good. Very good." But as they stopped by the revolving turntable that had already begun delivering passengers' luggage his face sobered, and he stared at her searchingly. "Why, though, Tagarid?" he asked. "Is it – can you leave it in the past now?"

She met his eyes easily; but she did not answer his question decisively, and he knew himself held at a distance.

"Perhaps," she said. "I'm not sure. But for clothes and social things – yes it is in the past, now." Then she smiled, moving smoothly away from the closeness he sought, evading it. "Mostly it's that one *feels* different and life has sorted itself out again . . . London was marvellous. Sane. No gunmen on the streets, no shootings. The dark hours are for sleeping, beautiful untroubled sleep. And the people, they walk about without death and violence written on their faces . . ." And as they collected her luggage, as they drove back to the city and then through it to her flat, she told him about the things she had bought, about the plays, the films, the restaurants she had been to.

"You had a pretty good time, didn't you?" he said once.

She laughed, and for a second was suddenly quiet, her face turned away from him as she looked out of the window of the car at the close blue sea.

"Yes I did," she said then, with a quick intensity that startled him because it was so different from the easy ebb and flow of "What-did-you-do? Where-did-you-go?" that had gone before – and which she went back to at once thereafter, the vivid face turning to him again, sapphire eyes enormous and brilliant within the mystery of their subtle make-up, long, full lips telling him of her delight in *As You Like It.*

Stranger face, he thought as he drove away from her flat (she had not asked him to stay, only thanked him for meeting her and carrying up her three suitcases, for the flowers that awaited her). But the stranger-face as fascinating to him as the sober one of Tagarid-in-mourning, and he knew himself in danger of moving into a new dimension of loving.

Fatmeh had made coffee and set it on a tray, with a small plate of the sesame biscuits that she made so well. Tagarid thanked her and, opening one of her cases, gave her the presents she had

129

bought for her: a headscarf of Liberty silk, a chunky cardigan of pure Arran wool, and a pair of sheepskin gloves.

"One thing from each part of Britain," she said as she passed the unwrapped gifts to the girl.

Fatmeh took them, her hands and eyes moving over them with a sort of frightened reverence.

"Thank you, Madame," she said, standing with the gifts spilling over her arms and she stroking the materials, the strong hands (Tagarid had never noticed the beauty of their strength) luxuriating in the feel of silk and wool. Then – with a controlled impatience – Tagarid fetched a large plastic carrier bag and took the gifts back and thrust them into it, then handed it to the girl and told her she could leave, she need not stay to prepare dinner.

"Thank you, Madame," Fatmeh said again. And as she walked away through the darkening streets was wishing fiercely that it would happen that, sometimes, *she herself* could do the giving. It is easy to give when you have so much, she thought, as much as Madame has. And then after a little while came consolation: but I do possess one thing that Madame doesn't realize I have. I possess a secret. I know *Madame has a gun . . .* Fatmeh discovered a strange warming pleasure in this thought, a sense of importance in possessing such knowledge. Madame doesn't know I know this secret thing about her, she said to herself, *but I know it.* And gradually a small feeling of power began to rise and grow in the young girl.

Alone in her flat, Tagarid went to the window and looked out: evening was darkening the air, but over to the north-east the mountains stood clear against a saffron afterglow.

A man is dead, Hisham, she thought steadily, thinking the words black against the yellow sky. I killed him and I wish he had been the man who killed you but I had no way of finding *him.* I have made the death of a Syrian, Hisham. For you and me . . . Then for a blinding instant of inner sexual ecstasy she *lived* Hisham and herself again.

– The moment was gone; and she felt light and quiet. Closing the curtains, she turned on lights and drank coffee, ate sesame biscuits. Then, to fill in the time, unpacked.

Khaled telephoned at seven o'clock, as he had said he would before she went to London. She asked him to come round to her flat at once.

She changed into a jump-suit of scarlet silk jersey. With the passing of that quiet mood, an excitement, a blood-warming exultation had gradually possessed her. As she sat at her dressing-table brushing her hair she saw her face in the mirror and it was smiling – not only the newly glossed lips but the *whole* of her face, eyes and skin, the smile was from inside her and expressed *through* her face, not merely *on* it. Her hand stopped moving then, suddenly, and moved quietly downwards to rest (still holding the forgotten brush) on the glass top of the dressing-table; she leaned forward and stared at the reflection of her own face and her breathing was soft and even. Hisham and Tagarid; Tagarid and Khaled: *Hisham-Tagarid-Khaled belong together*, she thought. And savoured the new knowledge with wonder for a moment, knowing that she was back in the mainstream of life again, the thing she had done in London (a gift from Khaled) had set her free . . . Then she shook her gleaming hair, making it swing loose and free, and went back to brushing it.

He came soon, then. She opened the door to him and he was just as she remembered him, strong and dark, his eyes immediately conveying the drive of his will; she watched him move across the room and sit down in the armchair by the onyx table, and knew she did not want him to go out of her life.

"Let me tell you all that happened in London," she said when they had greeted each other and she had poured Almaza for them both, setting one of the tall, cold glasses beside him and taking her own across the room to the dining-table. Sitting down there, in one of the upright chairs, she put her glass on the smooth, varnished wood of the table top. "First I want to tell you every single thing," she said. "Just as it happened. If there are any questions, please ask them afterwards."

"I know from others that you did what you went there to do." Under the ceiling light his face was hard, its strong bones clearly defined. "Tell it to me as it was to *you*." His smile moved into his eyes, she felt he was smiling *to* her. "Then I shall know not only what happened, which was a killing, but also *what happened to you in the doing of it*."

So she told him. It was well told, concise yet detailed. She knew that as she talked she was revealing to him a great deal about herself; and knowing this made her search into herself as

131

she talked so that *every*thing was true, not only the facts.

He had no questions. Simply said, when she had finished, "It was well done." And then, "You have changed very much, do you know?"

"Yes. I know." Suddenly, she knew what she wanted to say to him now and her mouth went dry with the excitement of it. But she held the words back; only looked at him, willing him to take the words out of her mind and use them himself so that she did not have to *ask*, she could move into it because he wanted her there.

"Tagarid." He said her name quietly and their eyes met and held. "I understand what has happened to you. I've seen it happen to men and women before. After you have once killed another person, with the intention of violence and a reason for it, you accept – totally, positively – the need for violence in the living of life. And a different world opens to you after that, a world where you can use this strange new strength that is suddenly yours."

"You understand because that's what happened to you." She said it as a statement, not a question; and neither of them thought that an answer was needed.

"So, you want to join us," he went on. "You want to be part of what's going on in Lebanon now."

"Yes. You see, I know nothing about politics. Myself, I don't know enough to know *what* to join . . . So I would like to go with you. Not to escape the responsibility of making up my own mind but because you are Lebanese and because I trust you. *You* know why you do the things that you do."

He did not disclaim the position of "leader", nor did he appear in any way to feel pride in it or to show modesty about it; he simply accepted it.

"We all have reasons," he said; and the platitude was edged with bitterness.

Which she was too self-absorbed to notice; asking, "I may join you, then?"

"Yes." "You": it was already clear to him that she was committing herself to him personally, not to the larger entity of the Group except in so far as he was part of that. And he went on, carefully. "I considered that possibility as far back as when I gave you the gun, but I knew no decision could be made about it until I saw what the London assignment brought out in you,

132

until I understood *you in action*. Which I do, now; and would like to use – now."

Silent, she sat staring at him, not seeing him, seeking to assimilate the enormity of what had happened, what was happening. But after a moment she moved impatiently, and looked down: to think she could do that was a stupidity, such understanding could only come with time, she supposed – she had to live and act her way into it, it would never come by merely thinking about it. As she surfaced again, the implications of the last word he had spoken suddenly struck her: "and would like to use – *now*". Recalling the slight but intentional pause before that last word, the stress his voice had laid upon it, she straightened where she sat, and stared at him again.

"There is already something planned," she said with certainty, "and *I am to be part of it*."

His face suddenly grim, forbidding.

"Listen," he said harshly. "What we do is for men and women, not for little girls. There is one paramount thing about joining me that you have to know and accept."

"I already know it," she flared back angrily. "It is that *I* might be the one who gets killed." Stating it plain and ugly for them both.

He leaned back in his chair, looking away from her. When he spoke again his voice had a remote quality, as though he were speaking to her from somewhere else.

– *Somewhere I have never been yet*, she thought suddenly; and shivered.

"'Expendability'" – he spoke the word as a synonym for death, with a chill reverence – "It is a principle that has to be accepted if you desire to influence, if you declare yourself ready to take *action* to influence the direction events in your country are going to take during your own lifetime – especially if your country is at a cross-roads period in its history, as surely the Lebanon is now."

There was a small silence; and then she said softly, "Give me the credit for thinking that through before I made my decision, before I got round to hoping *you* might use me." She smiled then, adding, "Give me that credit, and I will give you credit for putting into words something I'd already accepted but never expressed – even to myself – so tidily!"

He turned back to her, the smile flickering in his eyes again.

133

And began to weave her into the plan he had prepared; knowing she was capable of doing what would be required.

"First, I want to tell you that this 'action' is not the Group's; it is *mine*. For this reason – and others – there are only four of us: myself, my right-hand man, Ali, and his brother, Tallal; and now – you. These are the central and pivotal figures. Of course, other men are involved in the mere mechanics of the plan."

"*Why* not the Group?"

"It is a personal revenge . . . Like yours," he added smoothly.

"Revenge? A killing, then?"

"Abduction. Then killing."

Her mouth dried. "Why the delay?"

"There are questions we have to ask." He answered without hesitation and she accepted that he now regarded her as a sort of extension of himself, to be used totally and trusted totally. "Also," he said, "before the woman dies I want her to know the reason for her dying . . . As you, had you had in your own hand the killing of the Syrian who murdered your husband, would have wanted that man to know the reason for his death."

Her thoughts moved swiftly, linking the names again: Hisham-Tagarid-Khaled.

"I understand," she said.

"It will be secret from the Group in its execution," he went on levelly, "but after it is done there is bound to be speculation about the possibility of the Group's involvement. For it is a killing many of them will be happy to learn of."

After a small silence she asked quietly, "Who is she?"

"There was an incident during the civil war when a deliberate action of hers – a betrayal – caused many deaths. Deaths of other women and young people . . . It has not been forgotten."

So Tagarid realized that he did not intend to give her names. Probably better so, she thought then; and almost certainly, the name would mean nothing to her.

"And – my part?" she asked.

"You will drive one of the cars. You will not be involved in anything beyond that. But if you believe that that will be easy, think again. Your part will require cool nerves and exact timing." His lips moved in a tight smile: she realized the violence in him and it meshed into her own. "You will bring the

134

car back to the city after the abduction is complete. After that, the woman, she is for us."

She sat back, breathing deeply; but asked simply, "When will it be?"

"The exact day is not yet certain. I expect it to be in about two weeks' time. As the day approaches and arrangements become definite, we will plan in detail."

It was finished. He got to his feet.

"I am glad you are with me," he said rather formally. "I will contact you again when it is necessary, in the way we used before." Then, as he walked towards the door, "The flowers are beautiful," he said, stopping suddenly, facing her and his eyes narrowed, searching hers. "Who sent them to welcome you home?"

She smiled. "Matthew Curran. My employer – remember, you asked me about him before? He is a little in love with me."

He left it at that and took his leave. But as he walked away along the street he had already decided that the routine investigation he had had carried out on Curran – as on all Tagarid's close associates, when she had contacted him about the gun – needed to be taken further: Curran as Tagarid's boss was one thing, but Curran establishing himself (or seeking to establish himself) as Tagarid's lover suggested a possibility of other interests, other motives . . .

She tidied the room that he had left, and then turned out the lights and drew back the curtains: under the moon, the lit city half-circling the deep-dark water of the harbour; and the mountains to the north-east hazed with mist.

She thought: he asked me about the flowers because, being entirely committed to what he is doing in his life, he is continually alert to protect that and to probe even trivia for what may lie behind. He did not ask from jealousy, as another man might – as Matt might, were things the other way round? . . . Jealousy could never exist between Khaled and me: we are together in a way jealousy can never touch.

So we make the perfect whole: Hisham – Tagarid – Khaled.

And she knew herself prepared to do *anything* to preserve that whole. Which made it possible to accept dying, if that was the way things turned out.

10

THE FOLLOWING Thursday morning, the streets of West Beirut were unusually quiet. The hundreds of people who usually came across from the Eastern sector for work, study or shopping, kept to their own side of the Green Line. For soon after nightfall the previous day, street-fighting had broken out in Ashrafieh (East Beirut) between the rival Christian Groups of Gemayel and Chamoun, and during the night had escalated into full-scale battles so that the next morning the citizens, white-tired and frightened, mostly kept to their own homes. The gunmen of the Groups collected their dead; or, hate-motivated, sniped from high windows and roof-tops at anything that moved, uncaring if the head in the gunsight were merely that of an old man sidling along close to the housewalls to try to get some bread from the local baker; or else gathered behind bullet-scarred walls to stoke the fires of revenge with stories of the old martyrs – and the new. The heavily manned barriers at the two main crossing-points on the dividing line between East and West stayed down.

At La Paloma a guard sat as usual in his chair beside the door, bored, sub-machine-gun across his knees. Occasionally he would exchange gossip and pleasantries with the four or five young men hanging around in the courtyard: two of them were playing backgammon with the rapidity of experts while the others lounged at their ease, sauntering out from time to time on to the pavement to cast a professionally watchful eye on any activity in the street.

Inside the café, a few of the tables were occupied by men having coffee, reading newspapers or talking. It was a place that came to life twice a day: at lunchtime, and in the evenings, after seven o'clock.

That morning, just before ten, one of the waiters went behind

136

the bar, prepared a small cup of Turkish coffee and carried it out through a narrow door opening into the back-quarters. There was only one small room there, windowless, an air-conditioner set into its one outside wall, which gave onto a blind alley.

This secluded back-room was comfortably furnished and well-lit. At a large grey-metal desk, Khaled Namur sat writing. The waiter set the coffee down in front of him and turned to go out.

"Samir." Khaled spoke without looking up, and the other checked, looked round. "Tallal should be here soon. Tell him to come straight in."

"No one else?"

"No one else. Tell Habib I'll need the car at eleven."

When the waiter had left, Khaled wrote for a few more minutes and then put down his pen and sat back, pushing the file away, drawing the coffee cup in front of him. He drank with pleasure, slowly, savouring each sip, and thought about the man named Matthew Curran.

Two days earlier, having decided that Curran's background and reasons for being in Lebanon needed to be investigated further (as a purely precautionary measure – there seemed no overt grounds for suspicion, but he was a foreigner, a European, and, therefore, in Khaled's world, a non-friend to be regarded with suspicion until and unless proved otherwise), he had given orders for that to be done. The Group had informers in every relevant Government department; at a relatively shallow level such investigations could be carried out quite simply by them, were merely a matter of the passing of money and the subsequent provision of confidential information from official records. If anything even faintly disquieting were revealed about Curran by that method, bigger guns would be needed; but that would prove no problem either, for Khaled had such on call in many parts of the world if and when they were required. He might expect to receive preliminary information about Curran any minute now –

There came a muffled knock on the door, but the man came in without waiting for permission because that was what he had been told to do. A young man, and tall. Shutting the door behind him he came to stand before the desk. He held himself straight: broad-shouldered, blue jeans belted with broad

137

leather slung low on his hips, blue-and-white check shirt open-necked and casual, sleeves rolled up loosely to just above the elbow, forearms sinewy and well-muscled. He was fair-complexioned for an Arab, and his straight, short-cut hair was brown.

"Sit down and make your report," Khaled ordered, staring into Tallal's face. It was a handsome and virile face, but the brown-flecked hazel eyes, long and heavy-lashed, were cold and curiously forbidding. Khaled knew what lay hidden behind those eyes: it was cruelty. That he had known for a long time now; had used more than once; and planned to use again soon.

The younger man sat upright on the straight-backed chair, his arms folded. He looked to be what he was, Khaled thought: restless for action, dangerous; and hard to handle unless you understood what was in him that needed to be assuaged. Ride Tallal on a tight rein, but give him the one thing he craved and he was your man; deny him that one thing, and he would turn and rend *you* if the opportunity arose.

"The investigation of the foreigner is complete," the young man said, his eyes fixed on his leader. "I used the Department of Immigration, working through his Permis de Séjour; also his application to obtain a Work Permit here. For the job side of things – his knowledge of procedure, previous experience and so on – SaxAir's confidential reports on employees were made available to me after pressure was brought to bear." For an instant the long, mobile mouth grinned. "I discovered that the Director's Personal Secretary there is extremely vulnerable," he said. "I will remember her."

"Your findings?" Khaled asked coldly, allowing an edge of contempt to sharpen his voice and seeing the grin wiped off the young man's face immediately.

"Nothing to support any suspicion was discovered," Tallal said. "The man is clean so far as it is possible to determine in this country. But – on my own initiative – I photocopied the photograph of him held by Immigration; and delivered three copies to Asif Jammal. As you suggested might be necessary."

"I see." Khaled glared at his protégé for a moment – to approach the man Jammal had by no means been included in his instructions – but then decided to let the matter rest. You could not be too careful in a business like this, and he himself would very likely have taken the same step. Jammal would, as usual, treat the matter as top-priority and would have the copies of Curran's photograph in London, Paris and Bonn within a day, requests for information about Curran sent to contacts in those cities within a few hours. The name Matthew Curran would soon be spoken, the photographs of him would soon be shown, in some strange places, and by or to some strange people . . .

"And – the other thing?" Tallal asked quietly, watching Khaled intently.

"The day has been advanced. It will be Monday afternoon. Hold yourself in readiness, be available all that day. You'll be told when to come for the final briefing." And with a gesture Khaled sent him away.

Tallal striding loose-limbed to the door; smiling as he went.

Matt Curran had taken to walking to and from work because he was not getting as much physical exercise as he liked: fencing and karate were fine in the UK, but although there were clubs for the latter here he had not joined one because it would not be possible to feign mediocrity, and in this agent-ridden city of present violence high competence in such potentially lethal skills would be sure to attract unwelcome attention, which would certainly be closely followed by suspicion, and suspicion would inevitably lead to enquiries being made –

Which must not happen. To jeopardise his cover was the last thing he wanted to do. And he had soon discovered that this half-hour walk relaxed his mind, gave it both the time and the chance to break free of an office job that did not really interest him yet had to be done with a convincing degree of efficiency if – again! – suspicions were not to be aroused. He needed to break free: the *real* job would be waiting as soon as he got back to his flat.

This Thursday, though, as he walked home through the known streets, he was already thinking himself into the real job again because he could not avoid it, the city and its people were tense with the "feel" of the violence of the previous night. Even here in West Beirut, you could see the knowledge in people's eyes, in the way they moved, softly and wearily, about their daily tasks: "the fighting and the killing; dear God, not *again*". And if you listened to the quietness you could hear it there too, an echo only, perhaps, but there: "not *again*".

The previous night's eruptions of large-scale violence would put Curran straight into action once more. Not his usual kind of action, he thought now with a certain regret: this one was practically an Admin. job, a routine thing he had been put on because he'd had a fair amount of experience in the Arab world, and because when the opening had been successfully engineered and set up he had not been engaged in any active assignment, and "urban guerrilla" affairs were his forte. So at home they had done a rush job on him and despatched him to Beirut (with how many others? he wondered) to discover and report to London – for cross-fertilization London-Paris-Bonn – on the connections already built up between the larger Groups in the Lebanon and the urban guerrilla cadres in Europe . . . Today, as soon as he had decoded the ex-London messages Ziad would again have delivered to his flat, he would activate the lines of communication he had already established in the city and seek to keep in touch with recent developments behind the scenes.

But he did not do that quite so soon as he had anticipated.

The "URGENT" message was on top of the pile in the drawer, where Ziad had put it. When he had decoded it he sat back and thought about it.

Rawa Laudi. The Lebanese journalist and Editor who had dared, as no one else had dared, to speak out against the way the Groups were destroying the Lebanese entity, destroying *down to the roots* its very chances of survival, by their feuding and their unending struggle for personal power; who had spoken out against the Syrians for their ruthless and cynical duplicity; who had castigated the corrupt men in government assiduously tending and increasing the flow of corruption, and thus denying the Lebanon its chance to re-build and re-establish itself once more.

Who, therefore, had made powerful enemies. Powerful men, powerful families and rich ones too: several times they had tried to buy her death, and finally she had exiled herself to France because a dead woman lacks eloquence once the days of her martyrdom have been celebrated. In France, closely guarded, she was still working for what she believed in; and her enemies were still, doubtless, waiting for their chance.

And now, this coming Saturday, Rawa Laudi would be arriving in Beirut. The date for a planned secret meeting between her and an (unnamed) politician had been advanced: her aged mother, who had remained in the city when she left, had died; and she was coming to attend the funeral. The planned meetings had been re-scheduled for Sunday; the funeral would take place on Monday morning; and then the journalist would fly out again on Monday afternoon. Throughout that time, naturally, Security organizations of several nationalities would be watching like hawks over Laudi's safety – but they would have to do so discreetly, for it would be the sort of job (Curran thought grimly) where over-manning would have the counter-productive result of drawing attention to the very events it was essential to keep secret.

Curran knew a great deal about Rawa Laudi: in France, the journalist had been a long-time target for assassination, and ripples from numerous plots against her had worked their way into his contingent spheres of activity, resulting in a useful two-way flow of information.

Therefore: URGENT. Curran to maintain a parallel but long-distance surveillance, a watching brief only on Laudi during the three days she would be in Beirut. But it was the hedges his London instructions put round his freedom of action that infuriated Curran, the way they ordered him to do one thing and then issued categorical instructions which made it almost impossible for him to do that one thing realistically or to any purpose. IMPERATIVE NO PERSONAL INVOLVE-MENT REPEAT NO PERSONAL INVOLVEMENT: the words burned themselves into his mind, inescapable –

Christ! he thought, what the hell did they expect him to do, then, if while he was "standing by" someone got to and had a go at Laudi? Simply let it happen, then go home and compile his nice, concise report? . . . Doubtless they had their reasons, he told himself: his people in London were not fools. Yet, in this instance, to put him in the picture would surely have given him some idea of just how far, on Rawa Laudi's behalf, he ought to permit himself to go –

Laudi: yes, Curran knew a lot about her, information gleaned from other men. And now he recalled one particular thing about the woman: she would accept "protection" only in buildings in which she lived or was visiting, and at airfields, against sabotage or hijacking; she refused absolutely to travel through built-up areas with anyone "riding shot-gun" on her because she held

141

that a person going around the streets of a city accompanied by armed heavies might easily provoke a gun-battle and so put innocent passers-by at risk. "She is a woman of the highest principles" Curran remembered one agent commenting; others, however, had phrased their opinions rather differently . . .

"Shall I leave the milk in the refrigerator, Madame, or put it on the tray?" Timidly, Fatmeh made her enquiry, hovering uncertainly by the door between the living-room and the kitchen.

"It can stay in the fridge," Tagarid answered shortly; thinking with exasperation, the girl gives the impression of perpetually apologizing for her own existence. "You can go now," she added, impatient for Fatmeh to leave. "Don't forget to buy bread as you come in tomorrow. Goodnight."

"Goodnight, Madame." And the door closed softly.

Tagarid got up from the settee to draw the curtains: outside, it was not yet quite dark, light still lingered in the hazed sky, was caught and held on the long crest of Mount Lebanon sheening it pale as skimmed milk. She gazed for a moment at the beauty of her view; then shut it out and forgot it. Khaled would be arriving any minute now. When he had phoned half an hour earlier his voice had been hard, his words brooking no refusal; the urgency in him had immediately communicated itself to her. Now, she awaited his arrival with rising excitement: clearly, something was happening, or going to happen soon.

As always, his vitality, the sense of unshakeable purpose in him seemed to her to charge the atmosphere of the room with brilliant life the moment he arrived. But this evening there was a new quality in him, he stood hard and bright within her softly lit room and she thought – suddenly and with knowledge – he is prepared for action, he is like a sword newly burnished for battle. Swiftly dismissed her own fancifulness, saying tightly, "It's begun, hasn't it? I can feel it in you."

He nodded and, brusquely refusing the offered drink, sat down where he usually sat, in the armchair by the onyx table.

"There has been a change in the timing," he said. "We shall carry out the planned abduction on Monday. Monday afternoon. Four days from now."

For a second her world swung wild: it is one thing to accept a part in a planned and violent action against another person, and you with no *personal* debt to repay, and say "I will do it"; it is quite another, she suddenly realized, when the undertaking of that act suddenly stares you in the face, so close in time that very soon it will reach out to touch and then engulf you –

"I will tell you now what you will do."

His voice cool and quiet. Khaled's voice: and at once her world steadied and was at rest within the buoyant stillness he commanded into existence at will. She relaxed, leaned back against the soft cushions scattered on the settee.

"There will be a grey Mercedes parked outside La Paloma. It will be unlocked and the keys will be in the ignition. At three p.m. you will get in it and drive out of the city along the airport road. About two kilometres along the road there's a big horticultural shop called Jardin Araman. Do you know it?"

"No" – she shook her head impatiently – "Never mind, I'll go out that way, today, and have a look. Go on."

But he did not do that. Regarding her steadily, asked, "Are you in a hurry now? Perhaps you have another appointment?"

"Why, no –"

"Then *listen* to me, Tagarid." He sat forward and linked his hands between his knees; looking down at them, he went on quietly, "This is a big thing. It is not at all like what you did in London, it is not simply a matter of an individual walking in, committing a simple act of retribution, then walking away again. This is complicated, difficult, and highly dangerous. There is an overall pattern, and there are smaller and separate patterns which, woven together, make the whole –"

"I remember." Her interruption softly spoken but he stopped at once, although he did not look up. "And I'm sorry, truly sorry . . . It was true, what you told me before I went to London, that if I think myself right into the part I have to play, then – it happens. When the time comes, it happens easily, *naturally*."

"There's a big open space in front of the Jardin Araman," he went on at once, looking up at her now, using his hands in small descriptive gestures as he continued speaking. "They fill it with pot-plants and garden furniture. You will park the Mercedes outside the shop and wait."

"What if there's no parking place?"

"There *will* be . . . Make sure all four doors of the car are unlocked. Wait in the car, ready to drive off – the time for that

143

will be around three-thirty, I cannot be exact to the minute, but it will be a matter of two or three minutes only.

"Watch *behind* you in the driving mirror so that you're with the situation as it develops. There'll be an incident in the road, not more than fifty metres behind you. During it, I shall come up to your Mercedes, from there, with the woman. She will be at gunpoint but you won't see the gun. We'll both get into the Mercedes, the *back* of the Mercedes, and you drive off immediately."

She sat still, absorbing it silently. Then: "This woman – she won't resist?"

"No."

"How can you be sure?"

"Her husband will still be in the car we took her out of. It will be behind us, held up by the 'incident'. There will be two gunmen with him – not looking like gunmen, that goes without saying – and if there's any gunfire from me, he dies at once. She will know that, we shall have told her." For a second a smile touched his lips to an arrogance of known power. "They will be hostages for each other," he added simply.

"What happens to him, afterwards?"

"We have no quarrel with *him*. After ten minutes, the 'incident' will have been resolved amicably and the traffic will be flowing freely again: he will be driven farther on and then to a safe house, held for about an hour there. They'll let him go after that."

"And us? The Mercedes?"

"You continue along the airport road. I'll direct you as we go along."

"Do I come far with you?"

His face sharpened suddenly. He did not answer at once; and when he did it was to question her.

"Why do you ask that?"

She stared at him, a stillness in her; and said after a moment: "Don't you trust me?" Her voice was steady but rather high.

He saw her aloneness then, and realized that a moment ago and in some way he had almost broken something she had built up in her own mind. He did not know what it was, but he knew that she needed it intact, knew he must – for the time being – keep it that way.

"You don't come far with us, Tagarid," he said. "There's a

144

car-switch arranged. You'll be back in Beirut by six o'clock or before . . . Is there anything else you want to know?"

"The number of the Mercedes?" And then, when he had told her that, "What's the best way for me to dress?"

"Jeans or trousers and a blouse; keep it ordinary and wear a headscarf. All dark colours."

"Shall I bring the gun?"

"No. This time, no gun, for you." And he waited then for the question he had left unanswered when she had asked it earlier, the previous time they had met. The name of the woman. But she did not ask it. Only asked if he would prefer to drink tea or lager; and when he chose tea, went out into the kitchen and made it, brought it in on the tray Fatmeh had set ready.

And sitting drinking tea in the softly lit room high above the city, she told back to him the part Tagarid Kurban would play in the abduction of the woman whose name she had schooled herself not to ask again.

145

11

O N FRIDAY night the darkness of the city resounded not with
gunfire but with thunder: the storm-clouds came rolling in
from the south-west and the mountains denied them passage;
then the temperature changes in the sea created a very special
havoc in the trapped cloud masses so that lightning gashed the
black, dark power-house up there and thunder crashed, rolled
and rumbled until the whole sky seemed on the move. And the
rain streamed down out of that heaving dark.

The next morning dawned grey and still. The air of the city
had been washed clean but the untended drains had blocked up
completely and the streets were foul with sodden rubbish, the
gutters were stagnant canals.

In his office behind the bar at La Paloma, Khaled Namur put
down the phone. The man he had been speaking with had told
him to come in person and at once to be given important
information just received from sources in London; but Khaled
had no intention of complying because to do so would reveal his
eagerness and therefore inevitably send the price up – and this
operation was being financed with money from his own pocket,
not that of the Group. So now he rang for a waiter, one of his
own men, and told him to send in the driver-messenger.

Who slouched in almost immediately, a short, balding man
with the beginnings of a paunch and dark, angry eyes set deep
beneath thick brows. His name was Ahmed Zayroun. When
younger, he had been a very tough character indeed. Now, in
early middle-age, the toughness was beginning to lose its edge
and, therefore, his hard world was inclined to show him less
respect; resenting this, he compensated for it by an increased
readiness to take offence and by the use of greater brutality
when meting out punishment if offence were given: at present

146

this was proving effective, but it was swiftly making him a lot of enemies. However, since he possessed a relative quite highly placed in the Group hierarchy, these enemies kept quiet. Khaled loathed him but found him very useful; and now gave him written instructions to hand to the information-broker, Asif Jammal, and told him he must bring back a written answer with all possible speed.

"I'll take the car," Zayroun said, hot-eyed, looking for an argument.

But Khaled agreed at once: it was not worth exerting his authority about, and it was a debatable point whether, after such a storm, a man travelled about the city faster by car or on foot . . . When Zayroun had gone, he returned to his deskwork.

Zayroun was back within the hour, and dropped the buff envelope on the desk in front of Khaled with a triumphant grin.

"Made it in the fastest time yet," he boasted. "All these one-way streets – they're for the boys, not the men. I drive the way I want to go, the others can get out of my way . . . They do," he added, still grinning.

Khaled dismissed him; and then, alone, opened the envelope. The single sheet of paper within looked rather like a bill, and informed him that much time-consuming use – by *numerous* agents, naturally – of the photograph of the man known in Beirut as Matthew Curran had revealed that the said Matthew Curran was certainly using a false identity; that there was a possibility that he was, in fact, an undercover agent working on a political assignment; that various leads were being followed up with all speed with a view to more definite information being obtained; and that any further definite and pertinent *facts* would be communicated to Beirut as soon as possible, in the event – which was to be expected – that such were discovered.

Asif Jammal playing the thing along, skilfully. As usual. On the other hand he had never yet been caught out in supplying unverified material. Which was why so many people continued to use him.

Khaled placed the paper down on the desk in front of him, sat back and considered the situation and what action he should take, in the very limited time available to him, now that Curran stood pinpointed as – at the very least, surely – a man who was in

147

Beirut for some ulterior purpose. But the city was full of such men these days; always there was money available to buy the services of the clandestine sellers of information or weapons or contraband, to pay agents-provocateurs or hit-men of one kind of another. The city drew such people like a magnet . . . However, there was nothing yet that connected Curran directly with the woman Khaled would hold at gunpoint on Monday afternoon; and would later kill. So was it worthwhile to detail men to watch him? The men available to Khaled for the carrying out of the abduction were limited in number, and men already tired from surveillance work would be no good to him for Monday's action, those men *had to be* fast-thinking and fast-acting, their minds and bodies hair-trigger alert yet totally disciplined. So if he put men to shadow Curran's movements, they would have to be outsiders, paid help. And in Beirut, where there was a great demand for such work, you had to pay pretty high to get good quality . . .

Khaled made his decision. But though he finally ordered the surveillance, he contented himself with buying men of the middle rank; for it seemed an outside chance that, of all the rich political (or otherwise) pickings to be had by an undercover agent in Beirut, Curran should be involved in the affairs of *this one woman* (who assuredly already had her contacts and protection, when she wanted it, long established).

Matt Curran did not like to feel unsure of anything when he was on the brink of action. But this time, in this sideline job so suddenly thrust upon him, he felt unsure, uneasy; and as a swimmer drowning in a quiet sea strikes out in the hope of touching something, anything, solid to grab on to, his mind felt about in every direction searching for hard facts. But found none: found only suppositions; and all the time his sixth sense warning him that behind the apparent security of "nothing-is-going-on", something *was* going on. He felt as if he were looking in the right direction for something he knew was there and needed to discover and act on, but that he was getting the *focus* wrong. All the time the one thing central to total understanding was being obscured by blurred images that would not go away.

He had checked on other people's security arrangements for Laudi and found them prepared in depth, though as usual the

148

journalist was refusing the armed protection offered for the journeys – few in number – which she would make within the city. Late in the afternoon of this day, Saturday, Curran had ascertained that Laudi had already arrived at the airport as planned, on a plane from Riyadh, and then had been whisked from the airport through the city safely and without attracting attention and was now ensconced in the house of the friend with whom she would stay throughout her brief time in Beirut . . . Curran had also learnt one unexpected fact: Rawa Laudi's husband, a lawyer of some distinction, was with her.

In his flat now, Curran switched off the BBC News and stared moodily at his beautiful carpet. It was twenty past six, and this Saturday evening stretched out before him and he saw it long and empty, for he had not made any social arrangements for the next few hours in case something happened during or after the time of Laudi's arrival and he had to move in closer. But now, the journalist was – for the present – home and dry: she would not leave her friend's house until she attended her mother's funeral on Monday morning, and the safety of that house was in other and very experienced hands; Curran neither could nor would play any part in that . . . But when he rang Tagarid a little later to suggest that they might have dinner together, it was only partly because she was the person he would prefer to spend the evening with: it was also because she seemed in some way always to come into his thoughts when he was considering the Laudi visit. Without substance, the "feel" of Tagarid would come into him then, as if his sixth sense were whispering her name in his mind. Unease, uncertainty drifting through him, and that shadowy awareness of the being of Tagarid, awareness without any understanding of why it should be there . . .

But although he rang her number several times, he got no answer. And was not really surprised by that, having half-expected she would have some other engagement, the Tagarid-who-had-returned-from-London having begun to re-establish her social contacts: when he had dropped her at her flat after work that morning, her car being off the road for the fitting of a new silencer, she had spoken of a lunch-date.

So he put the phone back in its cradle, but as he was getting up to mix himself a drink it rang. It was Fatmeh.

"I'm listening, Fatmeh," he said in carefully slow Arabic, and using her name to send his human warmth to the girl. "Yes, if you speak slowly I will understand. Speak now, I am listening to you."

"Sir, when I left the flat this afternoon at two o'clock, a man stopped me in the street. He offered me money and asked me about *you*."

They – who? – must be watching me, he thought. They saw me drop Tagarid home and decided to check up.

"What questions did the man ask, Fatmeh?"

"He asked how often you come to see Madame. He asked if you spoke Arabic. And then he asked if . . . if . . . He asked if . . ." Her voice trailed away into silence.

"I understand, Fatmeh, don't worry –"

"But, sir! I answered them. I was afraid!" The desolation of betraying someone who had been kind to her – her voice crying with it.

"Fatmeh! Listen! It's all right. You were right to answer . . . That last question, the one you did not finish. You wanted to tell me that he asked you if Madame and I sleep together, I think. Was that it?"

"Yes. He asked that." Her voice small and tight: a very human misery across a long long distance.

"Fatmeh, you were absolutely right to answer and I am very sorry the man made you afraid. I want you to know that I am very sorry about that . . . Now, one more thing, please. Can you tell me what this man looked like?"

The description she gave him was quite detailed but it meant nothing to him; however, he stowed away in his mind the picture her words had enabled him to create, because he knew that in his job to be able to recognize a face as that of an enemy might make the difference between his – or someone else's – life or death.

He thanked the girl then, and rang off. And as he went on from where he had left off five minutes earlier, pouring himself a whisky and going onto the balcony to drink it, he pledged his gratitude to the young girl; for now, some of his uncertainty was gone. He *knew* he was being watched; and it was fairly safe to assume it was Khaled Namur who had ordered the surveillance, because he knew Khaled had visited Tagarid on Thursday evening and from there it all flowed on in a definable pattern . . .

At this point he grinned suddenly, remembering the two

150

things that had made him, to and for Fatmeh, a real and thought-about person: sesame biscuits and roses! Sesame biscuits he had always complimented her on, roses he had given into her hands though he had bought them for someone else. Strange, he thought, strange how things work out . . .

And *knowing* himself watched by Khaled's men meant that he could be certain that Khaled considered him a possible danger; therefore he must *be* a possible threat to something Khaled planned to do – and the doing of it surely not too far into the future!

Laudi? – A possibility, no more.

But – *now*, yes, a possibility.

And somewhere in all this was Tagarid. Suddenly, Matt Curran found in himself a sickening sureness of that. Which sureness hounded real sleep out of his mind and body that night.

He came out of a half-waking doze soon after six the next morning. Sunday morning, no office and the sun already strong through the lined yellow curtains so that his room was full of a sort of thick radiance –

Tagarid. She stood there in his mind as she had in the thin hours of the night before the semblance of sleep had slid in over his restless weariness: Tagarid beautiful, vivid, loved; for him, the suspicions surrounding her clouded none of those things that were hers and hers alone; if anything they seemed to cause them to gleam more brightly, especially the loving.

But it was Laudi's *life*. Deliberately, Curran forced himself to a discipline of priorities: Laudi's *life* might be at stake here. That came first.

He showered and cooked himself a breakfast of eggs and bacon, brewed himself a pot of coffee; and as he ate and drank, listened to the Arabic news. But there was no mention of Laudi's visit, so either they really had managed to keep it quiet or for once a severe degree of hush had been clamped on the media . . . More likely the latter, he decided; and went out for a walk.

Down on the Corniche a small morning-cool breeze was blowing in off the sea. Close on his left, the railings edging the broad pavement gave on to yellow-brown rock dropping steeply down to the water, the blue calm of the open sea edged in the

151

eastern distance by the dark line of the horizon. To his right, a splendid line of huge palm trees growing on broad green lawns divided the two roadways of the dual-carriageway banding the coast. Cool, and very quiet: the jet-set hotels and restaurants, the blocks of once-opulent apartments attract no tourists now, no wealthy Arabs out of the oil-lands come here any more to enjoy the things that no amount of money can buy in traditional Islam.

Curran breathed the salt air and felt himself coming alive again. Later, the Beirutis would stream down to the Corniche and it would resemble a warmer and more highly coloured Blackpool promenade; now, it was his. The only other person he saw was the khaki-uniformed guard standing on the pavement outside the huge hotel taken over by one of the Groups, its once-famous gardens a desert of churned earth now, efficiently fenced-in with barbed-wire and sandbags.

When he got back to his flat he rang Tagarid and asked her if she would go out for a drive with him.

"This morning or this afternoon?" she asked.

"Whichever you like."

"That sounds as if your day is empty –"

"It is. And I'd like it very much if you'd fill a bit of it up for me."

She laughed (she too had woken early, excitement building a restlessness in her so that before he rang she had been wondering what to do to make this day pass quickly so that Monday would come).

"Me, I'd like to take a picnic lunch and go to a place I know where we can swim without crowds." But she would not tell him where; and as soon as they had arranged about time and food and drink, rang off, saying she had to wash her hair before he called for her at 11.30.

It was a day he was always to remember. One of those watershed days passed in the company of another person when neither one does or says anything of particular impact or decision but, nevertheless, by the end of the time spent together each knows that – in some way indefinable at the time – a new course of feeling and living has been determined on (or an old one channelled deeper).

They went to Byblos. He had been once before, but that had been with a small group of historians and archaeologists, an expedition organized by his boss, Mustafa Bashir: Curran had absorbed an enormous amount of erudite and fascinating information, but had had little opportunity to browse around and get the feel of the place – just enough to know that he would like to go there again.

And now, that was what they did: browsed through the day. First, on the beach: they had parked the Range Rover and walked up from the harbour and, leaving the Crusader castle on their left hand, strolled away across the grassed-over expanse of the ruins; and where the land met the sea, scrambled down a narrow, rocky ravine into a small cove of golden sand. There was no one else there. The water was green-blue and clear and warm; and after the first cooling plunge they stretched out on towels spread on the sand and basked awhile in the sun. Not talking much; but each aware of the pleasure it gave them to be together.

Then, thirsty, they gathered up their belongings and moved up from the beach, settling in the shade of a small grove of pine trees. As they drank cold lager, "Tagarid," he said, "I know that in some way you're happier since you came back from London. It must be *because of* something." He left a little silence for her then, in case she wanted to close that particular door in his face; it would not break their present closeness if she did that, he simply hoped that she would not.

She leaned back against the trunk of the tree behind her, sea-sleek and beautiful, a towelling wrap loosely belted over her bikini, a small smile lengthening her lips as she looked at him; and said nothing.

"Is it perhaps because the men who killed your husband have been caught?" he asked. And was surprised at how easy it was to say that.

"No, not that," she said after a moment, looking away towards the sea.

Her smile was gone. The sadness in her reached him but it had not got the hard, dead feel to it that it had possessed before. For a moment he could not name what he *did* feel within her sadness, but then the word for it came in his mind: excitement. Which surprised him very much –

"No, no arrests," she said (and he switched his thoughts away from that word so strange in its observed context, and listened to her). "The last news I had from Al-Ain was that the

153

Syrians are continuing their enquiries. But the feelings of the villagers still run high. They say *they* will persevere until they finally get justice."

"And, *you?*" he persisted gently. "Would it help you, to know that the men responsible had been punished?"

"There would be only one punishment that meant anything to me at all," she answered at once.

He did not ask her what punishment that would be: it was obvious. But as he thought about it he wondered if it were some planned act of bloody revenge on the Syrians for her husband's death that was the thing linking her to Khaled Namur; some ferocious act of terrorism such as Khaled had master-minded and taken part in before, in other countries. Surely, though, *not?* The Syrian Army? Khaled wasn't that good: his targets had always been civilian, not military . . . Yet, the doubt remained. Covertly, he looked at the woman beside him. Beautiful, vivid, *loved*: he remembered how she had come into his mind as the dawn sunlight had woken him; and as he looked at her now the same feelings were aroused. Tagarid – linked in planned violence with a man like Khaled, a known terrorist, and killer? He wanted desperately to ask her if that were true; but knew he dare not because he was sure that at this moment she would not lie to him – and then the answer might destroy them both. *Dare* not: he admitted it and then stared at the words in disbelief, for only once before in his life had he been faced with something he *dare not* do . . . And even that he had eventually done, almost – but, thank God, not quite – too late . . .

"Matt, where were you before you came to the Lebanon?" She had put down her beer and was unpacking lunch, laying the food out on the cloth spread between them over the big rush mat they were sitting on: he had ordered the whole meal from the restaurant on the first floor of his block of flats, and she seemed absorbed in what she was doing, looking with hungry interest at each delicacy she uncovered.

"What, you want the story of my life?" he joked, grinning across at her. "Pretty dull, I'm afraid. I'm just a businessman, on the Admin side."

"Tell me, anyway. I'm interested."

So as they ate, he did that, producing in all its dove-tailed smoothness the carefully researched cover story of the life to date of Matthew Curran. And he had no way of knowing that (as

154

he talked) she was "listening" on a deeper level than the hearing of the ears alone: she had a good brain and was using it, probing, searching, sifting through everything he said, alert for anything that might reveal that Khaled had been right in his suspicions about this man with whom she had chosen to spend her day.

But there was nothing: no unaccounted-for gaps in time, no hesitations, and a total ease in the telling; no sudden absence of candour in the answering of her questions artfully put to break the flow. Until, right at the end: "How long do you expect to be in this country?" she asked. And saw him for a second at a loss for words.

He covered it quickly, reaching for her glass to pour her more wine, saying "At least two years. More, maybe." Cursing himself for behaving like some love-sick teenager, for he knew that his hesitation had simply been because, on the asking of the question, he had thought at once: *Christ, I'll probably have finished what I came here to do in another eight weeks, leave Beirut then and never see her again.*

She knew he was lying.

"That's not true, is it," she said, taking her wineglass from his hand. "Why the untruth?"

"Because – as you already know – I love you and therefore wish we had all the time in the world."

That, she knew for the truth; and questioned no further, following quickly when he changed the subject (a small bitterness in him that she had used the reality of his love to hide behind) and began talking about ancient Byblos.

After they had eaten they wandered round the site. There was no one else about; the quietness that brooded over that place moved into them and they were careful not to disturb it, moving with the slowness of dream, talking in hushed voices. At length they went down to the sea and swam again, then beach-combed their leisurely way along the coast.

"They say people often find old coins here," she said, stopping at a place where the rocks held back from a long stretch of golden sand. "There were many ships sunk at anchor in the great earthquake of 1891, they went to the bottom and still the movement of the tides throws the sand from deeper water up onto this beach; so people sometimes dig here, sometimes even find a coin lying clear on the top of the sand."

"Have you ever tried your luck?"

"Yes; but I never found anything."

"Try again now. Let's dig." He was grinning, running up the beach to the low cliffs then returning with a piece of driftwood in each hand. The soft sand brought him to his knees when he was half-way back to her and she laughed and ran to him, taking one of the wooden "spades" from his hand and kneeling down beside him where he lay propped on one elbow, watching her, making no move to get up.

"Look!" she cried, "I'm going to dig in your last three footprints!" And she started in at once on the nearest.

He scrambled to his knees and joined her, and the sand went flying through the sunlight and they found an old chicken-bone in the first scoop of sand from the middle footprint.

"Chicken-bones always bring me luck," she said laughing – she had laughed a lot, that day, and to her even the serious things had not seemed sad, only what they were, *serious* – and went on digging.

From the third and last footprint she scooped out loose sand, let it trickle through her spread fingers – and then felt the small rounded hardness touch her skin. She held it and rubbed away the last of the warm sand: the circle of metal lay in her palm, heavy for its size, so encrusted with verdigris that it was impossible to make out the details of the markings upon it.

Quietened, a little awed, by this finger from the past reaching out to brush against their lives, they dug no more, but dressed and walked away from the shore. And inside the Castle keep, climbed the wide stone stairways to the upper floor, Tagarid leading the way. Dust lay drifted upon each step and the soft sounds of their passing found no echo within the massy stone walls. She sat down within an embrasure, her back against its wall and her hands clasped round her drawn-up knees.

"I love this place," she said, looking out through the arrow-slit, green and blue out there, and grey stone rich with age. "All of it, I mean; not only the Castle, the earlier parts as well . . . Do you like to go to old places, in Britain? Be in them, 'feel' them?"

"It's not so easy to do that, nowadays. Too many people . . . But there's one place I know." Abruptly, he fell silent: suddenly aware that the quality of the light was changing, that the afternoon was dying away into evening.

"Tell me," she prompted.

"It's a place up in the Marches, the border country between

England and Wales. The Cistercians built an Abbey there, sometime in the ninth century. A place called Abbeycwmhir. They sited it in a soft, rich valley, hidden and narrow among the hills . . . There's hardly anything left now, only shapes marked out by grass-covered stones, mounds . . ." But he was speaking with conscious effort now. The desire he had felt when he began – the desire to communicate to her the feeling he got from that place – that had suddenly shrivelled up and died when he had noticed the sunlight fading where it lay on the old pale stone, and had thought with foreboding: tomorrow is Monday, outside life begins again then and Khaled Namur is in it and *Tagarid is with him.*

"Tagarid," he said.

"Mm?" She turned to face him.

"Can I ask you something? Not about the past. About now. About the Lebanon, now."

Her face tightened a little; but then she gave a small, hard laugh and looked out of the arrow-slit again.

"Why not?" she said. "It's running away, isn't it, really, the way I love to soak myself in places like this. I know that . . . Ask, and it shall be given unto you."

He smiled; then said, "I was going to ask you in what direction you think the Lebanon will move."

After a moment she answered slowly, "It doesn't seem to me to be likely to move anywhere at all in the forseeable future. Everyone appears to be solely interested in keeping going the present static balancing act which some call 'government'. There's nobody capable of actually *governing*, so it seems . . . And look at the Christians, they fight *each other*." She turned on him, saying with anger, "Just before you came out there was a three-day 'war' in the Christian sector: Chamoun's men against Gemayel's, Christian versus Christian; officially, there were about sixty killed but that's not the figure the people who live there give . . . And it's real hatred. You know these apartment blocks, ten, twelve storeys high? In some of those, men fought to the top floor by floor, and as they battled their way up *they threw the wounded off the balconies, however many floors up it might be, down into the street* . . . That's not *us*, that's not the people of Lebanon." She let the silence return to the ancient walls that had surely seen many deaths in their day. And then straightening where she sat, said strongly, "What the Lebanon

157

needs now is people big enough and brave enough to speak out against those who keep us divided; and clever enough to do it with words that cannot – either at the time, or later – be twisted or denied."

Her passion gave him the opening he sought, through which he might conceivably discover if she were involved with Khaled in the way he most greatly feared.

"The trouble about that, so far," he said, moving into the opening carefully, "seems to be that anyone who has tried it either gets intimidated, or hounded out of the country . . . Take Eddé, or Rawa Laudi. All right, she went to France of her own free will but she hadn't much choice, had she, if she wanted to stay alive."

"Laudi." She repeated the name and he felt at once that she must be clean of any involvement in violence planned against the journalist. Her face told him so; and then her words. "Yes, Laudi could do it. She has all the gifts required. She could become this country's conscience."

"It would be a thing that took time, and she would need powerful support here, which she already has . . . Might it be possible, do you think?" He did not want to talk about it any more because he *knew* now and he felt light with the relief that knowledge gave him; but the thing needed to be rounded off, he could not just drop it.

"Possible, of course," she said after thought. "But if she were to try it, it would have to be kept severely under wraps. She may have powerful friends here; but her enemies are just as powerful – and a great deal more ruthless . . . I met her once," she went on, "when I was a schoolgirl, many years ago. I remember being terribly impressed. Don't suppose I'd even recognize her now."

They fell silent again. Watching the shadows darken in the Castle keep. And soon left that place, treading softly and carefully down the old and broken stairways. Outside, the air was golden with the radiance of the afterglow; the grey-stone ruins of ancient Byblos ran down to the empty sea; behind the town the long spine of the Lebanon range stood dark against the sky and no trees grew there, no cedars to bring the trading-ships of all the known world to the ports of Phoenicia.

12

O<small>N MONDAY</small>, Curran left the office at midday, telling Tagarid that he was going out on a business call and did not
expect to return that day, instructing her to deal with matters
that arose, everything should be fairly routine . . .

But he went straight to his flat. He had driven to work that
morning, and now, as he made his way patiently through the
heavy traffic of lunch-time, kept a practised eye on the following stream of cars: observation through the rear-view mirror
soon pinpointed a grey Volvo that was working hard at following the same route as himself . . . When he turned off Rue
Gen. Gamelin into the forecourt of his block of flats the Volvo
drove on past but found a parking space a little further on.
Curran eased his Range Rover down the steep incline to the
underground parking area below and put his car in its reserved
place, then took the lift up to his flat.

Changing his light-weight business suit for grey slacks and a
fawn open-necked shirt, he went down to the restaurant and
had lunch, sitting at a table in a corner by the windows, the fine
muslin curtaining ensuring that he remained unseen from
outside while able to observe what was going on in the circumscribed world of the street immediately below him. Eating
shish-kebab and Baba Gannoush, tabouli and fresh salad, he
observed the grey Volvo: it was parked on the other side of the
street, facing away from him, but still close (it was outside
another block of flats, so perhaps its driver was innocent after
all? Perhaps – it was something to bear in mind, anyway!). By
the time he was enjoying delicious fresh peaches straight from
the Beka'a, he had reluctantly decided that it was not possible to
isolate any particular one of the many idlers and passers-by
outside and declare him an enemy: there were too many of

them, and none gave him any reason to suspect him. Over coffee he made his decision. His was strictly a watching brief; London's "imperative no involvement" was as near an absolute as you could get; other brains and guns here in Beirut had Laudi's safety under their protection: so he decided merely to drive out to the airport and be on the spot during the afternoon. There were two afternoon flights scheduled, at 4.30 and at 5.25 – the last before the airport put itself to bed for the night: no after-dark take-offs being allowed lest the guns in the commanding hills above mistake friend for enemy (or pretend to?) and let loose. Of course, there would be others at the airport, doubtless many of them; but an outsider might come in useful, you could never tell in a situation like this.

However, he did not want a follower, if one were around. Going up to his flat again, he rang Ziad and told him to drive round in the white Volkswagen, leave it in the underground parking area and come up.

Ziad got there fast, coming in lithe and eager as always; and grinned when he was told what to do.

"Okay. Hope you're wrong, though," he said, as he flipped Curran's "digger" hat on to his head, pulled it forward low over his eyes and examined the effect in the mirror by the door in the square, well-lit hall of the flat. "Shame to take it out on a car like yours."

But Curran hadn't been wrong. As Ziad edged the Range Rover out of the forecourt into the stream of city-bound traffic, a nondescript black Renault parked nearby, its engine running, surged out into the traffic and rammed him – quite gently, but with a plentiful breaking of glass as various lights on both cars disintegrated.

Curran, watching covertly from his balcony, saw the two drivers get out and begin the furious argument customary on such occasions, and a crowd gather . . .

Taking the lift down to the parking area, he got into the white Volkswagen and drove up into the forecourt and away, heading first for the city but then turning south onto the dual-carriageway leading out to the airport. He got there a little before three o'clock. After careful observation of the Terminal building, both inside and out, he came to the conclusion that there did not appear to be any unusually heavy security cover in position, at least not yet, and decided therefore that he would sit

160

it out until he had seen Rawa Laudi arrive and board her plane, and that plane safely airborne.

At this time, Curran was merely uneasy: the fact that there had been an attempt to immobilize him – rather amateurish though it had been – suggested the possibility that *some*one had *some*thing on; but, that "something" did not necessarily have to be directed against Laudi, there were many other possibilities, once "they" had begun (for whatever reason) to suspect him, Matt Curran. However, the feeling of unease did not leave him; renewed doubts about Tagarid wove themselves into it and he grew more and more anxious to see Laudi get on that plane and safely away, out of her homeland with a whole skin. To see Rawa Laudi live to fight another day.

Tagarid eased the Mercedes to a halt, close in to the kerb and a little distance before the entrance to the Jardin Araman, people coming and going in the street, cars, not many but enough for her to see the sense of this parking-place having been kept free for her. As she switched off, she noticed the man who had been working nearby, among pot-plants massed in the open space in front of the shop, move away from the kerbside and into the shop, still working.

She sat unmoving for a moment: a girl in a rather old grey Mercedes parked outside a shop which sold pot-plants and garden-furniture. She had dressed as Khaled had instructed her, and was wearing black jeans and a loose-fitting navy sweatshirt; a plain black headscarf bound her hair tightly, and the driving-gloves on her hands were of soft black leather.

After a while, she turned in her seat and slid across the catches to unlock the two rear doors; checked that both front doors were also unlocked, that all windows except her own were fully closed; glanced at her watch and saw it was 3.15. Settling back in her seat, she relaxed deliberately, controlling the excitement rising in her; and then set herself to register with eyes and mind the feel and the features of this piece of world surrounding her so that when things began to happen in it she would be at home here, would be moving and functioning within a known context and therefore with confidence.

At 3.20 she adjusted the driving-mirror with meticulous care to ensure as clear and broad a view as possible behind her; and checked that everything in the car – *and in herself* – was ready for instant action. Her eyes and mind were working in a purposeful and tightly disciplined assessment of the situation outside the car as it changed minute by minute, traffic and people going about their own business, but what they were doing would possibly – and soon now – dictate what she had to do.

The road was fairly busy but the afternoon rush-hour had not begun yet; it would be easy to swing the Mercedes out and away. In the driving-mirror she saw that, behind her and about fifty metres distant, the yellow-painted tanker-truck which had been pumping water into somebody's roof-tank had finished that task, its crew were at work round the cylindrical body of the truck, turning off taps, stowing away the grey prehensile tubing, and the driver leaning out of his cab high off the ground, gesticulating at his mates, probably shouting though she could not hear what.

And it was 3.25. She took the driving-glove off her right hand and brushed away the sweat beading her forehead; flexed her body into driving-readiness and put the glove on again.

Heard the siren begin, then. The wailing sound whirling up from nothing to full power, sustained now and loudening – an ambulance approaching fast. She saw the traffic behind her edging reluctantly in towards the side of the road and then the white vehicle (no flashing blue lights, just the siren) come up fast close to the central reservation, past the water-truck – then it was gone by and speeding on along the main road ahead.

But her eyes had left it. Behind her, it had begun. In her mirror she saw the water-truck immediately back out into the roadway (as though seizing this god-sent opportunity to turn and get into the stream of traffic) but when it was completely blocking the road, it stopped. She saw the driver swing down out of his cab and, gesticulating a defiant helplessness at the furious hootings that greeted him, open up the bonnet of his huge truck; his crew gathered round him –

Except for one man. Her eyes caught the movement that did not conform to the pattern: one of the crew peeled off and ran back along the road, keeping close to the kerb. She lost sight of him then, the unremarkable figure quickly absorbed into the coming-and-going of the people back there. But she was entirely sure that it was Khaled. Drew a deep breath; and grinned tightly at the simplicity of it.

From that moment it developed so fast that there was no time for thinking, only for action. She saw a man and a woman walking along the roadside towards her, close together as friends walk, and fast as though they had some common purpose in view. One was Khaled, the known look of him, the known spring to his walk. The other was a woman of medium height, rather squarely built and wearing a pale two-piece suit and a broad-brimmed hat. They stopped as they drew level with the rear door of the Mercedes; and she heard Khaled say, "Open the door this side. Sit well back from the window."

The stranger did as she was ordered at once. Then Khaled followed her into the car and sat down beside her, closing the door behind him. Tagarid saw the gun then, just for an instant, as Khaled drew it out of his pocket and held it across his lap – then his other hand covered it, and he said quietly, to her but without speaking her name, "Drive on, through Shi'a. Turn on to the main Beirut-Damascus highway at the road-junction. Keep your speed normal and approach the checkpoints with the usual care."

She had already adjusted the rear-view mirror; and now pulled out into the roadway, and drove off. Behind her, the yellow water-truck still lay athwart the traffic, a crowd of onlookers about it now. There was very little on the road ahead of her.

Two checkpoints before the turn-off, one Lebanese, one Syrian: the soldiers on duty searched the car with their eyes from a distance, then gestured them on with small movements of their automatic weapons.

The road-junction then, the main road joining the one from the Christian sector and striking inland. Tagarid took the Mercedes up into the hills smoothly and fast, through Aley and beyond: the car's age and somewhat shabby appearance deliberately deceptive, for under the bonnet lurked a superb engine lovingly and proudly maintained to the highest pitch of perfection. It was a joy to handle, a car you *felt* as well as drove.

But her eyes continually flicked to Khaled who, seen in her mirror, sat looking out of the window beyond his captive. She could see his face in profile and knew him to be tense but calm, full of the sure confidence that was always his. The woman, she could not see. And was obscurely glad of that.

Heard her voice, though: "What about my husband?" she

163

asked, after some while. Quietly, impersonally as someone making conversation about a stranger.

She got no answer for a minute. Then Khaled said, "He will not be harmed unless the provocation comes from himself."

"You will free him?"

Khaled smiled with his mouth. And answered the question behind the words.

"We need no hostages, now. It is *you* we want. And, we *have you!*"

And on the words, for a second, Tagarid sensed an intense upsurge of feeling invade the atmosphere of the car. But it was gone before she could identify it. Alert, puzzled, she probed the memory of it: relief? A very brave woman, then . . . But the one word alone did not satisfy her: relief, yes, that; but there had been something else –

"*When* will you release him?" the quiet voice continued. A French-educated voice, though the words were Arabic –

Answered at once, and brutally, "When you are dead. Keep your mouth shut!"

That was not true, Tagarid knew: Khaled had told her his men would release the husband –

"Driver!" His voice cut into her thoughts and immediately there was nothing and no one but Khaled to speak and Tagarid to listen. "About a kilometre beyond the next village we pass through, there is a big lay-by on our side of the road. Pull in to it. You'll see a blue Datsun already parked there. Put the Mercedes beside it."

She caught his eye in the mirror then; and smiled briefly. Silence returned to the interior of the car.

Automatically, the eye of her mind registered the name painted on the small metal sign up on a post at the approach to the village: Talia, white letters against a blue background. It was a small place; she had been through it many times before. They passed a car-repair shop with a beaten-earth forecourt where a few men were at work on some farm machinery, a bread shop, a little general store with wooden boxes full of garden-produce ranged outside it, and there were a few women about in the street, sombre in dark long-skirted clothes and their hair hidden away under closely bound head-scarves tied beneath the chin, no brilliance anywhere. They were quickly through it, and the country opened out into a world of hills and valleys

164

spreading far and wide, and sometimes the heights of the Lebanon Range were lined against the sky, sometimes those of the Anti-Lebanon across the Beka'a. The towns and villages are gathered at intervals along the metalled road linking Syria with the Mediterranean ports; but from those, other roads and dirt tracks lead off to smaller hamlets far away in narrow valleys or ledged into rocky hillsides, and those tracks are often only cart-wide and stony . . .

Coming to the lay-by, she saw the Datsun parked there and ran the Mercedes up close beside it, switched off. Like the Mercedes, it was not new, looked rather uncared-for. The right-hand rear door was open and a young man leaned in the opening, drinking Pepsi out of a can. As the Mercedes approached he had raised a hand in greeting, but made no other move. Tagarid looked at her watch and it was 4.10. To her right cars and trucks went by from time to time on the main road, fast.

"We go in the other car now," Khaled said, behind her. "We drive off first. You drive on, towards Shtura. About six kilometres from here there's a garage, just beyond a village called Nabaya; it's on the right, set back from the road, three pumps. It's the only garage you'll come to. Drive the Mercedes straight round to the back, get out and lock it. There'll be a taxi parked there. Get in it and wait; in a few minutes a man will come out to you. He'll drive you back to Beirut. Got it? Understood?"

"Yes." She nodded. Then asked, "When will you be back?"

But he had already turned away. The gun was in his right hand now, held low, pointing at the woman.

"You and I get out now," he said softly. "Maybe you're thinking you'd prefer that I shot you right away, but don't try anything like that — remember, *we still have your husband* . . . Get out before me, and do not do anything at all to attract attention. Stand still, facing the blue car."

Tagarid did not watch them get out. Only heard the door slammed shut. And then saw the young man toss his Pepsi can away over the roof of the Datsun into the bushes, and come round the bonnet of the Mercedes towards her side. He was tall, lithe and narrow-hipped; hardly Arab-looking at all, she noticed, straight, short brown hair, fair-complexioned; and his thumbs hooked into the pockets of tight-fitting jeans.

165

Cars still passed at speed along the main road to her right, and she thought with detachment: it must look like a rendezvous, friends travelling in two cars but with a common destination . . .

Then the young man was leaning down to her, his face close. He nodded, smiled at her, ran his eyes over her; then straightened again. For some reason, something in his eyes, she had found it very difficult to face him.

"Everything ready?" Khaled asked, from the other side of the car.

"*I* am ready," the young man said – and she heard the cruel mockery in his voice, and in a moment of blinding comprehension a cold horror gripped her heart, her mouth dried. "And we've enough gas to get to Lamarés and back to Beirut without filling up. Okay?"

"Okay," Khaled said. "Don't get into the car until the woman and I are both inside. Wait for me to close the rear door."

So, one after the other the three of them got into the Datsun, the woman, Khaled, and then this chilling young man who, she was quite certain, would do the eventual killing. And, if necessary, much else besides.

The blue Datsun moved off fast, showering the Mercedes with gravel, rear indicator-light winking as the young man gunned it hard out of the lay-by into the main stream of traffic.

She switched on and followed. After five minutes the Datsun turned off to the left, onto a side-road narrow and stony-pale, little more than a track, heading off into the hinterland, un-metalled, used to bring the produce of the valleys in to the towns, but it would soon be evening and there was no traffic on it now. Only the blue Datsun with three people in it.

Tagarid drove on along the highway. She went quite slowly and the countryside looked very beautiful to her, and very remote. She felt a tremendous sense of relief that the thing, for her, was over.

Laudi would most likely fly out on the 4.30 MEA flight to Paris, Curran thought, though you could never tell, and he had been given no definite information, it could be the 5.25 to Karachi. Around 3 o'clock, therefore, he stationed himself in the main entrance hall of the Terminal building, near the huge glass doors giving out on to the main parking lot, so that he could keep in touch with events both inside and out. The main hall was lively and noisy with the excitement of travellers and their well-wishers, was littered with baggage and children, but he quickly became aware that suddenly the security men were there, both Lebanese and others, some standing out like sore thumbs, purposely (to discourage), others – and how many of these could he actually identify? – very unobtrusive indeed: the hand-picked men, as hard and ruthless as their adversaries. Actually he knew two of them, he thought, both posing as departing passengers, and with one of these he exchanged the merest flicker of a glance of recognition. Outside, the pattern was the same, only there the Lebanese Army was in control, but again picked men from one élite battalion, the first nucleus, it was hoped, of the force which would one day re-assume responsibility for the destiny of their strife-ravaged country. Curran was very pleased to see them employed on an occasion like this.

There seemed little reason for him to remain down in the entrance hall so, after a final prowl around, he showed his pass to the heavily armed soldiers on duty at the bottom of the broad, carpeted stairway and went up to the departure lounge.

There, there was relative peace, and lots of room to move about: the bonafide passengers (if that was what they all were), freed of heavy baggage and relations, were filling in the remaining time before departure in the usual ways of those who travel by air, sitting reading or gazing quietly into space, looking into or buying from the duty-free shops, drinking yet another unwanted cup of coffee because it passed the time, occupied the hands . . . The smell of coffee on the air but, being no addict, Curran bought himself a Seven-up at the long counter down one side of the room and carried it away to a low table nearby. In the room the indirect lighting was reflected off tinted glass of pearly-white and Persian blue, and that suggestion of sea-calm and clear skies was harboured and echoed in the smooth sculptured curves of an ornamental pool. Covertly, sipping his Seven-up, he studied the faces of the "passengers" scheduled to leave Beirut on the Paris flight.

And at once recognized a man standing side-on to him by the pool, a folded newspaper under his arm. And taking out cigarettes, selected one and felt in his pockets for matches; then got up and went over in that direction.

"Buy you a coffee?" he said, having lit his cigarette at the offered lighter.

"Sure." The other grinned. "Was hoping you might."

Back at the table, the two men sat down opposite one another, leaned forward over their drinks; and spoke quietly.

"Laudi?" Curran asked (by this time he had already identified three others in the room whom he knew – two men and a woman, all on the "right" side).

The other nodded: a tall, rather thin Arab with greying hair, immaculately dressed in a grey business suit, his expensive leather despatch-case on the floor beside his chair. There was about him an air of total readiness: he had not troubled to mask *that*, Curran noticed. His name was Imad Farhal.

"Yes." He drank some coffee. "What brought you here?"

"The same. Only a watching brief, this time." Curran looked around him. "Plenty of muscle, I see."

"Here, sure. Wish someone'd persuade the bloody woman to accept protection when she's coming and going, though."

"Everyone I speak to beefs about that. I'd have thought you'd have forced her to accept it, by now."

Farhal smiled thinly.

"'Force' Laudi? That's a day you'll never live to see. And you're a lot younger than me . . . This time it's been even more complicated: her husband's with her."

"I know," Curran said. Then, "Are they close?"

"It wasn't an arranged marriage, if that's what you mean, like so many here. He has always been 'with' her in everything . . . He's a very brave man."

"Will they achieve anything, eventually?"

Sombrely, Farhal considered the question. (Considered also, Curran thought, whether to express any opinion on such a matter to a London-based agent.) Finally he said, "Off the record, Curran, there's some reason to believe that the meetings she had yesterday have more than an average chance of leading to some positive development."

Curran grinned across at him.

"By God, that's phrased pretty carefully," he said, "they'll be co-opting you for the Diplomatic soon . . . Can I come back to you later on it?"

"Give me four or five days."

In silence the two men finished their drinks. As he put down

168

his glass, Curran asked, "When you checked the Groups, before Laudi came, did you come up with anything? Is there anything planned? Any suggestion at all?"

"Nothing." It came fast, a total rejection. "Nothing, as far as I know."

"Did you check *all* the Groups?" But he knew they must have done.

The Arab looked up quickly, curiously – "You know something?" he asked.

"I *know* absolutely nothing," Curran said immediately. But this was a man he had a lot of time for, a man he trusted. "Khaled Namur." He put the name quietly between them, watching the other's face. "You know him?"

"I met him, once, and know *of* him, of course . . . FFCP mob, about halfway up the ladder of power and would like to get the rest of the way fast . . . Why?"

"Do you know if he's got any particular reason to go for Laudi? Did his Group ever suffer at Laudi's hands, or anything like that?"

"They didn't," said Farhal with total certainty. "They're not among those who did." He smiled his thin smile. "Believe me, the people you're thinking of will all be damn glad when Laudi's plane gets off that strip of concrete out there and they can move about freely again!" He looked down at his watch. "Three-twenty," he announced briskly. "I'll be moving along. She should get here around three-fifty." He got to his feet. "Thanks for the coffee."

But when Farhal had left, Curran remained unconvinced: his sixth sense still gave him no peace, insidiously and inexorably linking the name of Khaled Namur with his sudden feeling of mounting threat . . . Khaled could be working *by himself?* – But for what reason – personal vendetta? Personal revenge? – But revenge for what? It would have to be for something big, clearly. But Laudi was a woman who had been in the public eye for many years; who during and after the civil war had made many enemies, self-interested men who saw their plans placed in jeopardy by the journalist's fearless outspokenness and had therefore (and often openly) sought to destroy her. There could not be many *secrets* in the life of a woman like Laudi; and *no one* could keep that sort of secret for long, not in this country at this time . . .

Curran got up and prowled restlessly around the lounges and shops and show-cases of the departure area: the official guardians of Laudi's safety were well-placed and as alert as ever. Anticipating the announcement of the boarding-gate for the 4.30 flight to Paris, many travellers were gathering up children and hand-luggage, checking handbags and travel-documents; there was a perceptible lift in the atmosphere, the excitement of imminent departure quickening the tempo of people's minds and actions . . .

The boarding-gate was announced at 3.35, and passengers trooped off obediently to be body-searched and have their hand-luggage ruthlessly turned inside-out.

Laudi had not arrived yet: that was obvious to Curran from the continued presence of the security men, from their carefully preserved yet always fluid positioning to ensure – as far as was humanly possible – that the target would be protected from all angles . . . As Curran watched, he could feel their alertness intensify, could feel the air tingling with the nervous energy of these men and women waiting ready to kill, if necessary – or be killed, if necessary – on the instant. The tension communicated itself to him and as he looked covertly at his watch his palms were sweating.

4.00. And still Laudi had not arrived. Then suddenly a voice came over the tannoy system, first in Arabic, then in French –

"Mr Sargent, please. Mr Sargent is wanted at the Information Desk immediately. Mr Sargent to the Information Desk, please."

And at once, unobtrusively but swiftly, the Security men began to leave the departure lounge. Curran moved fast too, crossing to the exit that he observed Farhal making for, stopping there, getting a cigarette going.

"What's happened?" he asked quietly as Farhal drew abreast of him.

Farhal's face was grim; but he paused long enough to say tersely,

"Laudi didn't make it. Strict hush on that." And then he was on his way again, out through the doorway quickly but without drawing attention to himself.

A new and different quietness settled over the long reaches of carpeting and carefully grouped chairs, gift-shops and bars: there were not many passengers yet for the 5.25 flight to

170

Karachi, and the last of those taking the plane to Paris were already out on the tarmac in the articulated airline bus heading for the Boeing 727.

Curran made his way out of the airport buildings, got into the parked VW; and sat thinking. But not for long: he knew quite soon what he wanted to do, and would do; and – *had to do*. Surely, in the name of everything worth believing in, *had to do*. He needed to know whether or not Tagarid was involved in whatever was happening/had happened round Laudi: it was his only lead. So he would go to her and ask her. And if she *were* involved, then somehow or other he would get from her *some*thing that might lead him to Laudi. It was unlikely she would know everything; but she might know *enough*. Please God, *she might know enough*.

171

13

"GET THE driver to drop you somewhere public, well-known and easy to get to," Khaled had said. "Close to your flat – but not too close. After that, walk . . ."

So Tagarid had done that, stopping the taxi on Bliss Street, outside the Librairie du Liban, and walking up from there. During the drive back to Beirut from the garage at Nabaya the tension and exhilaration of action had seeped away out of her body and brain. They had made the journey fast, the driver handling the car – another Mercedes, with the red number-plates of a city taxi – like a skilled maniac firmly convinced of his own indestructability; and had made no conversation. Now, the sunlight had left the streets and she felt enervated and strangely remote from her fellow-men and women, these people going home from shopping or from work, the store-keepers beginning to shut up shop and the street-traders sorting through their wares, covering their barrows with sacking and tarpaulins.

Thinking longingly of coffee and a bath, she slipped the key into the lock of the front door of her flat and let herself in: Fatmeh would be in, so she would have a bath while the coffee was being prepared –

But as she walked into the sitting-room, Matthew Curran was sitting in one of her armchairs, facing her. For a frozen second they stared at each other like hostile strangers. Then he got quickly to his feet, came to her, and put his hands on her shoulders.

She tensed but made no other move.

"Sit down and listen to me," he said, turning her towards the table, guiding her firmly to one of the straight-backed chairs beside it. "No!" – hard, his voice slicing across the protestations she began to make, and they died in her mouth – "Just listen!" He pulled out another chair and sat down facing her, and went on speaking, fast. "Did you take part in the kidnap-

172

ping – or killing – of a woman not long ago, this afternoon?"
She could not adjust. Stared at him, silent. But the thoughts
were whirling about in her head, in indescribable confusion –
"Tagarid?" He made his voice gentler. "For Christ's sake,
don't be afraid."

At once she pulled herself together.

"I'm not afraid," she said (though she had been). "Why do
you ask me that question?"

"Hell!" The one word escaped out of his tightly controlled
fury; but he knew he must keep her with him or he would learn
nothing. "I'm a Special Branch man, from London," he said
flatly. "An agent here for my Government" – to get the facts to
her *quickly*, that was important. "My job with SaxAir is only
cover. Do you understand? . . . This afternoon a woman – a
woman important to Lebanon – was expected at the airport, to
leave on the 4.30 MEA flight to Paris. She didn't make it. *Were
you any part of whatever happened to her between three and four this
afternoon?*"

She stared at him. She accepted his given truths about
himself, so suddenly revealed; but she was with Khaled
Namur, not with Matt Curran. And held her loyalties before
her like a shield, asking as of an enemy: "Why should I answer
that?" Coldly, and her face stiff and totally against him.

"I will tell you why," he answered roughly. "Because the
woman you moved against this afternoon was Rawa Laudi."

"*Laudi?*" – She repeated the name on a rising note of disbelief
and shock, then cried out, "*No!*", her face bloodless and
horrified, the one word both a rejection and a frenzied denial of
a guilt she already dreaded was hers. "*No!*" she cried out again.
"You're wrong, you have to be!"

"*Who*, then?"

"I don't know! Khaled said –"

"Namur?"

"Yes. He told me –"

Again he silenced her: "That's not important, *now*." And
then he said, quietly but with a terrible cold certainty, "It *was*
Laudi. Believe that."

She did. Stared at him, appalled.

"They're going to kill her," she whispered. "Question her" –
she shuddered – "then kill her."

And he knew she was his now, not Khaled Namur's.

173

"So – forget everything now except that *we must get to wherever it is they have taken her.*"

She thought: he's assumed I'll go with him; thank God for that. That small mercy. And with an effort of will banished the desolation and guilt that had her by the throat (the anger would come later, Curran thought, as he watched her).

"They snatched her on the airport road outside a shop called the Jardin Araman and I drove them away along the highway to Syria." She was fully in control of herself again, remembering objectively and striving to restrict herself to relevant facts only. "They switched cars outside a village – Talia!" She plucked the name out of her driver's visual memory – "Just beyond a small village called Talia –"

"Get your map, the large-scale one." He was on his feet. "We'll get going right away. Tell me the rest as we go along. We'll need torches, blankets maybe, a bottle of brandy, some water. Can do?"

"You get the brandy and water from the kitchen, I'll get the other things." She ran out through the doorway into the bedroom.

He was surprised to see Fatmeh in the kitchen; he had forgotten the girl existed. She was sitting at the table doing nothing, quiet; and looked up as he came in. A coffee percolator on the stove was muttering away gently.

"Fill a thermos with coffee, quickly," he said. While she did so, he put bottles of brandy and Naas water in a shopping bag; then added the flask when she passed it to him. Her face was yellow-pale, her eyes wide and blank: he realized she had heard everything that he and Tagarid had said in the living-room, that she felt the world of violence reaching out for her again.

"Go home as soon as we've left, Fatmeh," he said to her gently. "It's all right, nothing bad will happen to you or to us. Just go home." She did not answer; but he saw the slight shaking of her hands. And swore to himself as he hurried back into the living-room –

But halted in the doorway, stood watching with a sense of almost emotionless expectancy. Tagarid was kneeling by her desk and had just lifted her gun out of its drawer.

She felt his presence behind her and, closing the drawer, got to her feet, the gun held professionally in her right hand. But not pointed in his direction.

174

"No," she said, staring at him and her eyes cold and intent, "not against you. Perhaps not against anyone. But if I do use it, I will use it *for* Laudi. Even if she is already dead."

As he moved forward into the room, breathing again, Curran was glad that the anger had already begun in her.

"You're armed?" she asked.

He nodded, his hand sliding up instinctively to the automatic holstered under his left arm, his thought touching the razor-sharp clasp-knife in his pocket which had served him well on one or two occasions in the past.

"You're ready?" He took the blankets from her, left her to carry the torches. And they went out of the flat, together.

. . . When the night closed in they were already well beyond the confines of the city, climbing up into the mountains.

"Seven-fifteen," he said, peering at his watch in the light from the instrument panel. "They've had her three and a half hours."

She made no answer. Only asked tightly, "Are we all right for petrol?"

He jerked his head towards the rear of the VW.

"There's a ten-litre spare. We always keep it topped up . . . Tell me about the car-switch now, and anything that happened after that which might be useful to us."

She told him, giving him as much detail as she could.

"When the blue Datsun drove off, and I followed it for a bit, alone in the Mercedes, it turned left off the main road," she said. "I'll be able to find the turn, but they might be anywhere along there . . . *Anywhere!*" For her, the word drawing pictures of unending emptiness and unending pain . . . *No, there will be an end to the pain* –

"So there are two of them with Laudi," Curran said. "Describe the other man, the one who drove the switch car."

She began describing him, seeing him in her mind's eye, but stopped almost immediately, exclaiming: "*Lamarés!* That's the name – this young man mentioned a place called Lamarés. As he stood beside the car, he said, 'We've got enough gas to get to Lamarés and back to Beirut.' It must be the name of a village, they must have planned to take Laudi there . . . *We may be in time*, Matt? Maybe? Now we know the name of the actual place?"

175

"Thank God you remembered it, anyway. Go on about the young man. It's good to know who you're up against."

When a minute or two later she stopped speaking (having haltingly described the "feel" of the man as well as what he looked like) it seemed to her that the silence within the car had acquired a new dimension, it was not merely an absence of sound, there was something terrifying in it.

"Do you know him?" she asked.

"I think so. His name's Tallal Kazzara. He's got a brother, Ali Kazzara; Ali's Khaled's right-hand man."

"There's more, though, isn't there?" she said.

After a moment he told her. It seemed to him she should know the full extent of what she had been part of.

"He's a psychopath," Curran said. Then, "That's what Khaled uses him for. I suppose you could say that's how he pays him."

The map folded in her lap to expose the area they were driving through, checking it by torchlight, she got them to Talia and, beyond it, while Curran drove, identified the long narrow lay-by where Laudi had been transferred to the Datsun. Stopping a few seconds there, they studied the map together, briefly: a turn-off to the left was marked, and, a few kilometres along it, a place called Lamarés. Beyond Lamarés the road worked its way on through the mountains, linking two or three other hamlets as well as the one they were looking for with the main road.

In the event she recognized the turn-off easily enough when they came to it, and directed him on to it. The roadway unmetalled now: surfaced with local stone pounded deep into the ground by the wheels of countless trucks and tractors, it gleamed pale and clear in the sweep of the headlights, creamy-yellow streaked with dark red where it was overlaid with topsoil; it was a rough ride from time to time, but it held few dangers.

After a while, looking out of her side-window, she saw the summits of far mountains where a minute before had been only the night; and even as she watched, their darkness deepened against the soft radiance pearling the sky behind: it would be moonrise very soon.

"The moon's coming up," she said, obscurely relieved by

176

this promise of better light – then immediately questioned her feelings, "is that a good thing for us, or bad?"

"Hard to say," he said. "Depends what's happened."

Suddenly she straightened in her seat. It was as if everything peripheral, the horror and the guilt and the fear, shrivelled and fell away from her, leaving her mind and body clean and poised and *ready* (as a new and purpose-built weapon is when the wraps are ripped off). She felt a new hard confidence in herself; and was glad.

"Matt. D'you suppose we might actually *meet* them?"

"Coming back, d'you mean?" But he went straight on without waiting for her reply. "I've been thinking about it. On the whole, it doesn't seem very likely. What they came here to do doesn't take very long."

Her hands clenched where they lay in her lap.

"But – Khaled said they had questions to ask her," she suggested softly. "That would take time?" And the pain, she thought but did not say, the pain designed to stretch out the time before dying, to punish and humiliate, that would take time too: but *she may think the agony has been worth enduring if we get to her before they finish it.*

"They've nothing to ask her," he said sombrely. "They snatched her, to kill her. For no other reason."

"But, what have we come for then? If there isn't any hope?"

"*Christ*, what else can we do?" he snapped. "Sit back in your flat and drink coffee while I get on the phone to a few people?" Then he bit down savagely on his anger; and after a moment said quietly, "There's a chance we'll get to her before they finish her off. They must've had her at this place Lamarés since around 5.30 . . . It depends, really, on how long Khaled allowed Tallal," he added, with a terrible absence of expression in his voice.

"We haven't – planned what to do," she said.

"How can we do that?" His face profiled against the outside night, tense, strained. (And, she thought, suddenly identifying what was in him: *loathing*. He has a gut-loathing for men like Khaled. For Tallal, yes; but for Khaled, who's not "warped", it is something far deeper.) "Whatever we do will have to be on the spur of the moment," he said. "When – if – we meet them, you take your lead from me but do whatever it seems to you will help to keep us in command of the situation. Don't hesitate to use your gun . . . That's all we *can* do," he concluded. "If it comes to meeting them, let's try and come out of it alive."

They drove on in silence. The track turned in towards the mountains, began climbing, at first gradually and then more steeply; and the light of the risen moon – just under three-quarters full – showed them the valley they were in narrowing, the hillsides towering above them on either side of the track, covered with low-growing scrub and trees, slabby grey rocks poking through the undergrowth and gleaming coldly in the moonlight.

"Those are wild cherry trees up there," she said suddenly. "These hills must be lovely in the spring, all sorts of tiny flowers, and the cherry-blossom . . . It's very like this round Al-Ain."

He made no answer. Went on driving with care and concentration.

To Tagarid, the world outside, the world of these mountain villages, suddenly very real: *this* is my country, she thought, my Lebanon. Beirut is nothing to me, a mere accident in my life and in the life of my people. *This* is *mine*. It is here that I live and may quite possibly, and in the immediate future, die. That is as it should be –

"This must be Lamarés!" he said suddenly.

His voice cut across her thoughts. They had reached the top of a rise and she stared out through the windscreen down the road ahead. Saw low houses straggling along the roadside, already close, cultivation to right and left, and on the hillsides trees planted in clumps and lines, as windbreaks.

It was Lamarés: the name roughly daubed, white against a darker-coloured signboard. And as Curran let the car roll on down the slope a huge, snarling animal-shape suddenly rose up out of the ditch at the side of the road and launched itself at them, began running parallel with the car, barking furiously, hackles up, ferocious wolf-muzzle close beside the car window, lips curled back from vicious-looking fangs –

"Jesus!" Curran wound up his window fast and put his foot down. As the car gathered speed the great beast paced them for a short distance then stopped abruptly, stood baying after them. "His territory, I suppose."

"There'll be more in the village," she said.

It was a small place, only a dozen houses, all with outbuildings, and yards enclosed within high stone walls; the houses were tight-shuttered against the night, no light showed anywhere.

"We go on through," Curran said. "Then pull up." He had his gun out, in his hand on the steering wheel, and sat crouched forward a little over the wheel, staring out ahead and from side to side.

More of the heavily built farm-dogs pursued them through the village; thick-coated against the winter, snarling and feral-eyed, they chased the VW until it was well beyond the last habitation; withdrew then; in the mirror Curran saw their shadows turning back, saw a fight break out among them as the roused ferocity sought outlet . . .

"Stop, now!" she said suddenly.

He did, leaving the engine running; and switched off the lights.

"There's a building a little way off the road, on my side," she said, pointing. "Maybe derelict."

He stared out in the direction in which she was pointing; and saw the silhouette of dark jagged walls: a square barn-like building standing by itself with low trees to one side, the walls pitted with yet darker holes where once there might have been windows and a door.

"They wouldn't have taken her into a house *in* Lamarés," she said. "That's highly unlikely. Remote villages like this, the people never get involved in *anything* to do with *any* of the Groups – it would divide their village, and that would destroy it . . . But they'd take her into a building, wouldn't they, if they could? Not just out on a hillside?"

"Probably. It's somewhere to start looking, anyway. Bring the torches, leave the rest."

It was cool outside the car. And silent. Walking through rough grass and undergrowth they approached the ruined building with the moonlight in their faces; and after pausing outside – to listen and take stock – went in through the broken doorway. There were two rooms only, both roofless. The first was empty, its rough stone floor littered with rubbish and part overgrown. Curran picked his way across it, using his torch, and through the narrow opening into the back room. She followed.

In this second room, too, the floor was of stone; but here part

179

of one wall had fallen inwards and there was rubble everywhere, fallen stone, mortar. Except in one corner, which had been cleared and where the stones were blackened by the lighting of many fires –

But Curran had smelt a smell he recognized. He moved cautiously across that rubble-strewn floor, hunched forward, his torch held out in front of him, peering at the ground; and after a moment, squatted down and brushed his fingers over one of the dark stains he could see on the floor near the fireplace. She watched him straighten up and then he held out his hand towards her: his fingertips were covered with blood.

"They had her here!" he said.

She said nothing, feeling sick. Made her way out ahead of him, stumbling once, into the night once more. Stood with one hand over her mouth.

He wiped his hand roughly clean on grass, held her arm for a few moments, hard. She was trembling, eyes narrowed, looking in the direction of their car. Eventually she broke away from him, deliberately.

"We've got to try to find her, haven't we," she said huskily. "She could still be alive." It was a half-question, made because she needed something to hope for.

"It's possible, just," he agreed. "And we have to try, as you say; if she's still here." Quietly, he reasoned with himself, out loud. "They had no reason to think anyone would follow them, or not for a long while. And they would want people to find her body. So they might not have dumped her far away."

Working separately and to a rough pattern, agreeing to meet back at the ruined building at fifteen-minute intervals, they began to search outwards from that place. When they were out in the open the moon gave sufficient light; only when they went in among the trees did they need to use their torches.

Her first area of search was on that side of the ruin which was furthest from the village; a roughly square stretch of broken ground, it was bounded by the road and reached up to a double line of well-grown trees planted on the slant across the hillside – to mark a boundary, perhaps, or as a windbreak – and ending in one fairly large copse. She worked her way over in that direction quite fast because the moon laid its clear light across the open land and the rocks and boulders and gullies were not big enough or deep enough to hide a body, though once or twice a shadowed darkness lured her closer, fearful – to reveal only its own emptiness. But when she was in among the trees it was different. These were scrub-oak and willow and stood quite widely spaced, some ten metres or more in height, others low-growing, and many of their branches drooped down nearly to ground-level, thus creating beneath themselves "caves" of secrecy and darkness. A woman's body could easily be concealed there, the darkness used to cover it like a shroud. She searched such caves grimly, using her torch, pushing branches aside so that its light stabbed into the hidden places; but each time found nothing. And the frustration building up inside her like a coiled, silent scream. Moonlight making a brilliance in the occasional open spaces among the trees, reaching in to create strange, twisted shadows everywhere; then, after a while, moonlight reaching into her imagination also so that as released branches swished back into their places it seemed to her that this place was laughing at her, soft sibilant laughter, mocking. She wanted to weep, she wanted to run, but she did neither: she went on looking.

And found the body of a woman. They had tied her to a tree-trunk close to the edge of the clump of trees, the ropes running tightly around and around her waist and upper body; her head was fallen forward on her breast and in the torchlight her long black hair streamed down to mask her face. Her blouse was ripped and torn open, covered with the dark stains of blood; and more blood had dripped down her skirt and legs to form a dark pool at her feet.

Tagarid ran. Dared not call out, but stones moved under her feet and Curran heard her coming before she reached him. Ran to meet her, grabbed her and held her by the shoulders, forcing stillness upon her as she told him, gasping for breath.

"Is she alive?" was all he asked, already moving off down the slope in the direction she had come from.

And she, following close: "I don't know."

And then no more words. At a stumbling run they headed for the stand of trees; and when he reached them he waited for her to catch up with him, gestured for her to lead the way. She made one mistake but corrected it swiftly, and they came to the tree where the woman hung bound.

Standing body to body against her, working clumsily but fast, Curran cut through the ropes using the knife from his

181

pocket, going more carefully as he got to the last few strands, bracing himself to take the weight as the body, freed, slumped forward against him. He wrapped his arms round the woman and supported her, stepping back as Tagarid tried to help him, and together they eased her gently to the ground. Kneeling quickly beside her he lowered his head to her chest to listen for a heart-beat, at the same time brushed the black hair away from the smashed and bloody face –

"Alive." The one word seemed to stay in the air as though frozen there. For a second Curran himself seemed frozen too, looking down into that shattered face; then his eyes slid away over her chest, her waist, and his hand went down to the right-hand side of her body as in a curious gesture – instinctive, protective, entirely useless – he sought to pull the remnants of her blouse up to cover her exposed breast

– checked the movement suddenly, then thrust the cotton stuff away again from her body, down and away from her right breast and side.

"This isn't Laudi," he said harshly. "She may have looked like Laudi, but it isn't her."

Holding the torch for him, but her face averted, Tagarid whispered: "What do you mean?"

"This is a woman *impersonating* Laudi –"

"*How do you know?*" The words jerked out of her.

"Laudi has scar tissue under her right breast and down her right side," he said. "Burns. Playing with matches when she was a kid. Plastic surgery in London but the scars are still there. This woman – has no scars." And now he pulled the stained blue cotton up over the woman's body.

"But – Khaled would have known?"

He shook his head. "Unlikely. Only Security know. The family kept it secret – the mother blamed herself." He scrambled to his feet, stood looking down at the woman. "But she would have told him she wasn't Laudi," he said grimly. "She would have been under instructions to tell, once they had put time and distance between them and Beirut. But even after she'd told him, Khaled still let Tallal loose on her." He turned away abruptly. "Let's get moving," he said. "You stay here. I'll get the blankets – we'll have to get her to the car, somehow." And he went off down the slope, fast.

She knelt down and straightened the splayed body of the

woman who wasn't Laudi; and saw that both her hands were raw and blackened pulp, hands out of bloody nightmare. Identified the appalling smell then: *acid*. First the knife, and then acid . . .

14

THEY WRAPPED the woman in blankets and carried her down the hillside, Curran taking the bulk of the dead weight, Tagarid cradling her wrapped legs in her arms. The man and the girl moving in a tense watchful harmony, each striving to maintain a oneness of movement and so prevent sudden shocks or wrenches to this tortured body of an unknown woman.

At the car they eased her into the back; then, after she had retched and been sick at the side of the road, Tagarid got in and tucked herself into one corner, lifting and gathering the woman's head and shoulders to her so that her own body pillowed hers, would shield her as much as possible from the bruising, jarring bumps of the road. Before starting up the car, Curran poured a little brandy into the top of the Thermos flask, added water and handed it to her.

"Try and get a little into her mouth," he said. "And have some yourself."

"I thought you shouldn't?" she said, taking it from him, nevertheless. "Not, someone unconscious."

"By God, she needs *something!*" Curran said. "Just let it moisten her lips, trickle a little down her throat."

While she did that, he tipped the brandy bottle to his mouth and took two quick swallows. Felt revived a little, after that.

"Have some yourself," he told her again. "It helps."

But she shook her head, firming herself back into her corner on the back seat, bracing herself there as best she could. And then he quickly stowed away the flask and the brandy, got into the car and started the engine.

He turned the VW, and they began the journey back. The last of Lamarés' ferocious guard-dogs pursued them to the perimeter of his territory; and then in the driving-mirror Curran saw the splendid and savage beast standing statue-still

184

in the moonlight, saw his image dwindle then finally merge into the dark blur of the village on either side of the pale streak of road. But Lamarés was a very small place and he did not see it for long; soon, could see back there only a broad valley and the sweet shapes of the mountains and over all a beauty of moonlight.

"The hands," she said after a time, all horror in her voice. "Why did they do that?"

"Because she wrote against them, I suppose," he said. "Because she was a journalist. Or they thought she was. Or because it didn't matter to them either way. They were angry, they had something special prepared, and used it. They must have cut her hands about first and then poured acid into the wounds." He was telling her all of it because at that precise moment he could find in his heart no pity for her and wanted her to suffer and know the full extent of her guilt. "Then they must have dragged her out of the building and tied her to the tree; shot her a couple of times in the stomach, after that, and left her to die . . . Khaled," he said bitterly. "Your 'leader' and man of action – Khaled."

They were on the main road before she spoke again.

"I did not know," she said, "I did not know they were going to do, *that*."

He knew then that he had got what he wanted: she was suffering. And for a moment a terrible and savage satisfaction possessed him.

"No one has the right to give another person the means to an end without first making sure that they know what that end *is*!" he said harshly. "It's a monstrous thing to do." Then, after a pause, he spoke almost gently; for he had acknowledged the ugliness of his own satisfaction and, disgusted, had driven it out of himself. "Leave it now," he said. "There are still important things to be done and there's only us to do them."

She eased her cramped body into a different position before she spoke again.

"We can't take her into the city like this," she said. "They'd have us at the first checkpoint, and it might take hours before we got free. What shall we do?"

"I'm going to try to set something up," he said. "There was a good-sized restaurant-bar just the other side of Talia, if I remember. We passed it on the way up."

185

"Yes, The Canary" she said. "It's fairly well-known."

"It'll have a phone I can use, won't it?"

"Of course."

"So we'll drive into the car-park there. You stay in the car. I'll go inside, buy a drink, and phone a man I know."

She did not question him further. It already seemed to her that they had been driving through this night for ever; and yet at the same time her mind kept projecting into her consciousness a sort of film-sequence of the events she had been part of that very afternoon: again and then again the yellow water-truck backed out into the road and the pictures-inside-her-head flicked on and on in their appointed progression. The sequence always stopped with the Datsun turning off the main road; she saw the blue car on the narrow track leading away into the hills enclosing Lamarés; and the pictures stopped there. But she *knew* now what had come next . . . Then, after a little while, the sequence would start again. She had no control over it.

Curran parked the VW well away from the brightly lit entrance of The Canary; and went inside. It was spacious and well-appointed, but almost empty. Monday-evening empty. So the barman served him brandy at once, and directed him to the public phones.

Only one of these was enclosed: shutting himself in, Curran dialled the special number that would put him in contact with Farhal – if the Security man were available at all, at this hour of night. A harsh, aggressive "Yes?" answered his call; and he quoted to it the special identification number that was his and his alone. Waited, then; and after a minute or two Farhal came on the line.

"I've got the woman who took the place of the one we were all waiting for this afternoon," Curran told him. "She's yours if you'll come and get her."

"Alive?"

"Just."

"What's in it for you?"

"No questions asked about the getting – *ever*. That's all."

"Agreed."

There was a brief pause. And Curran sensed the hand over the mouthpiece, visualized Farhal firing orders at other men down there in the city, those men springing to act and the action coalescing swiftly into a meaningful shape . . .

Farhal came on the line again. "We'll come out in an unmarked ambulance," he said. "Flashers and sirens for the journey back. We'll have a doctor and a nurse with us. Now tell me where you are."

Forty minutes later a grey Renault van turned into the parking area outside The Canary and Curran, seeing it from the bar, thought: by God they've made it fast. He left his second brandy half-finished on the bar, raised a hand to the barman, and went out. Walking quickly over to the parked van, noting the indistinct shapes of three men in it as he approached, he went straight to the driver's window.

"We'll drive out now, you follow," Farhal said, who had done the driving himself. "About half a kilometre back there's a place to pull in – watch our indicators, and pull in behind us. We'll transfer her there. Is she still alive?"

"Yes. Where's the real Laudi?"

"Safe in France. With her husband. I'll give you the details later. Let's go."

Tagarid waited outside The Canary while the white VW followed the big van away into the night. She stood in the shadows under an ancient, heavy-leaved loquat tree; leaning back against the trunk, thought about nothing and gave thanks that the pictures in her head had ceased. She heard the siren start up in the distance, not far down the road, and then swiftly die away into the dark silence. I hope she lives, she thought; please God she'll live.

Curran came back for her then; and in the front seat of the VW now she let her exhausted body relax, closed her eyes against the moonlit world outside (she had had enough of moonlight). And for her the drive back to the city passed in a blurred half-dream wherein questions echoed unanswered and answers floated unclaimed in a silent void . . .

He stopped the car outside her flat. She opened her eyes; sat forward then, suddenly and completely awake and a strange peace in her, an *empty* peace. Recognizing it as that, she murmured to herself, "Pax Romana – they make a desert and call it peace." Then, without looking at him, said, "If you come up, I'll fix you some coffee and sandwiches." And waited for his answer, knowing that for them this was a

187

watershed: his acceptance or refusal would have little to do with coffee and sandwiches.

He switched off, leaned his forearms on the wheel and, for a moment, put his forehead down on top of them. Then he looked up and sat staring out along the well-lit road ahead. After a moment he said, "I'd like that. Thank you."

In the flat they took time, to clean themselves up. Tagarid changed, coming up from the bathroom in housecoat and sandals, her face wiped clean of make-up. Then together they went into the kitchen.

In the living-room, they sat down opposite each other, mugs of coffee and a plate of sandwiches beside them. She had turned off the ceiling light: two silk-shaded standard lamps made a soft radiance that was kind to tired eyes and to faces thinned and sharp with strain.

"We both know a man called Khaled Namur," she said into the quiet, "only he seems to be two different people. Please tell me what kind of man the one you know is because I don't know him and I think he is the real one."

So he told her. His words were stark and sought to soften nothing; and she believed them.

And sat quiet for a while when he stopped talking, deliberately and mercilessly forcing herself to accept the knowledge that she had been totally and pitilessly used.

"You've told me what kind of man he is," she said eventually. "But still, knowing and coming to terms with all that, I do not see why he abducted and killed – tried to kill – Rawa Laudi. For what reason? What was the *motive* behind it?"

"That I can't answer yet . . ." He let a silence drift between them for a while, drank coffee and ate a cheese sandwich. When he spoke again, his voice was level, warning. "He's a totally ruthless man, Tagarid," he said.

She looked across at him and her face was almost expressionless, faintly mocking perhaps.

"You've made that quite clear," she said.

"And you know what follows from that."

"Yes. You mean that if he finds out that I – changed sides, he may kill me. Or have me killed. Because of what I know."

"That's exactly what I mean."

"How can he ever find out?"

Curran made a small, open-handed gesture: who knows that?

188

And then said, levelly, watching her closely, "He may simply *ask you*."

She laughed: no warmth in her laughter at all.

"It will be very easy to lie to him, if he does," she said. And then added with brooding savagery, lashing out at herself with the words, "It would be even easier to tell him the truth, yes, I'd like him to know . . . But even *my* naïvety isn't that immense, not quite."

"And if he asks you to act with him again?"

"*Never!* Not with him again, or as part of anything with which he is connected, not ever . . . Tell me if you find out *why* he did it, will you?"

"I won't have that much time."

It reached her, dragged her out of the closed world of herself.

"Why not?"

"Well, obviously Khaled's penetrated my cover. The news won't take long to get about. I'm more or less ineffective as of now."

"You'll be leaving Lebanon?"

He nodded; paused, then said, "Come with me, Tagarid."

She got up and switched off one of the lights, then drew back both curtains. Stood looking out of the window.

"I shan't marry again, you know," she said. And then when he had come to stand beside her, touched his arm with gentleness and went on, "I thought perhaps you would go on hating me for ever. It's a very big thing to me, that you don't."

"For a short time, at Lamarés, I despised you for what you'd been part of, yes . . . But not *you*."

Outside, the moon rode high and the mountains of the Lebanon were limned dark against the sky, their lower slopes starred with the lights of roads and villages.

"Will you do something for me?" she asked.

"If I can."

"Tomorrow, I'd like to go up to Al-Ain. I want to see Ibrahim. Could I have two days' leave? Come back into the office on Thursday?"

So everybody uses everybody else, it is only a matter of degree, how much they use them, he thought wryly. And said, "Why not. I'll fix it with Mustafa."

189

15

S HE LOOKED at Mount Lebanon from the window of her flat
and the long line of the summits was etched clean against
the deep blue of the sky: six o'clock in the morning, and in the
Lebanon yesterday was hot humid summer but today is autumn
and the air is cool and clear.

Driving out of the city was comparatively easy: it was
Tuesday morning and the commuter traffic was streaming
nose-to-tail into the business heart of West Beirut, not out of it
. . . Once in the mountains – Talia, Nabaya behind her – she
drove quite slowly, watching the shapes and colours of the
sunlit slopes change continuously as the road worked its way
towards the Beka'a. In the villages the slow tides of life ebbed
and flowed as people traded and mended, bought and sold; and
in the cultivated fields men women and children were tending
the red soil or gathering in its produce.

Down into the huge valley, through Shtura, past Zahlé.

Knowing that her coming would be marked and the news
passed on, she drove through the village and on to the place
where the big tree held its shade ready; and, having parked the
car off the road, walked down to an outcrop of slabby grey
boulders and sat down in the sunshine. The rock was sun-
warm; and there was a peace in her because she knew exactly
what she was going to do. She tilted the scarlet denim sun-hat
forward over her eyes and waited without impatience.

He came as he had come the first time she had brought Matt
Curran here: striding easily, sure-footed over the rough hillside. And when they had exchanged greetings, seated himself
on a rock a little way from her, facing her.

She told him at once, briefly and objectively, what she had
come here to tell him: how she had taken her revenge for the
murder of Hisham, how in London she had made a death for

Hisham's death. The facts were quickly told, and he listened without interruption, though he turned his face away from her almost as soon as she began, and looked out across the valley during the rest of the telling.

She stopped speaking; and in a little silence watched a lizard slip out onto a grey rock in front of her and begin to bask in the sunshine, his camouflage so perfect that as soon as he was still he was almost undetectable.

"Why do you tell me this, Madame?" Ibrahim asked then.

She looked across at him.

"Because you are Hisham's friend and I want you to know."

He turned and smiled at her, a slow smile with love in it.

"Truth for truth, Madame," he said quietly. "You are Hisham's wife and I want you to know."

Her skin prickled, her heart and body tensed and her eyes clung to his.

"What?" The word only a breath.

He kept his voice quiet and easy.

"Hisham was a highly placed member of the ACP," he said. "The pro-Iraqi anti-Syrian Baathist Group. For a short time after the civil war he stayed out of the politics that kept the Lebanon divided; he kept out entirely. But then he decided that the time had come, there was no alternative: a man had to make a decision and identify himself with one faction or another. It seemed to him that any man who cared what happened to this country had to do that and so work for something positive to emerge. He joined the ACP; but though he quickly came to a powerful position within its hierarchy, he kept himself always in the background because he wanted to go on with his medicine . . . The policies he helped to form and then promote were anti-Syrian: Syrian connivance was behind his murder, but the killing was Lebanese politics too, and one of the killers was Lebanese."

She looked away from him as he stopped speaking; and after a silence said, "In fact, *now*, I'm glad he was like that. In the end, as a last resort, you have to combat violence with violence. It's the only way to defend what you value, isn't it . . . And you, Ibrahim?" she questioned softly, tautly, suddenly aware that there was a new "feel" to him. "Are you still a man of peace?"

He got up and came towards her and she stood up to meet

191

him, hearing the sun-brittle grass of the dead summer rustle and break under his boots as he drew close. As he looked down into her face his eyes were narrowed against the brilliance of the sunlight, against the midday heat coming off the slanting, stony hills.

"The land and the village, these are my life," he said. "Beirut is nothing to me. But if men come from the city and deliberately kill a man of the village, we will have blood for it. And if the law does not give it to us, we take it for ourselves."

"Have you, taken it?" she asked intently.

"We are a slow people," he said. "We do things in our own time; but, *we do them* . . . We have a list of the people who were involved in the murder. There are four names on it. Two were local men and one of them is already dead."

"I should have known, shouldn't I?" she murmured. "I should have known *you*."

All he had ever wanted from her was in her face then. Looking at her gravely, he took it into himself.

After a moment they began to walk up towards the road, side by side.

"Will you act with us if we need you?" he asked as he opened the door of the car for her.

"Yes." At the wheel, she looked out at him as he closed the door and stood quiet, watching her. "I should have come here in the first place, shouldn't I?" she said. "His place . . . Thank you, Ibrahim. I'm going to the villa now. Could you come there tomorrow morning? With your advice, we'll get the land ready for winter-planting again."

She drove away then; and at the villa opened the shutters and the windows wide in preparation for living there again.

Curran spent Tuesday morning at the office, the last hour of it with Mustafa Bashir. The Director, urbane as ever, listened politely as Curran informed him that he would be leaving in about ten days' time. Bashir had known from the beginning that his Assistant's job had been engineered by the British as a cover for his other activities, but he did not know the particular nature of those activities: Beirut was a hive of agents and intrigue and, although Bashir was ready to assist those organizations whose broad aims he respected, he never asked questions whose answers might leave him dangerously well-informed.

192

Now, he merely expressed regret at the Company's loss, and invited Curran out to dinner for the coming Saturday.

"But you'll be coming round tonight, won't you, the Reception for Abdel Kader Krim?" he went on. "I suppose that since you're leaving us so soon now there's not a lot of point in your meeting him, but come anyway, you'll help things along socially, his wife's Scottish, as you know . . . Will London be sending anyone out in your place? I'll keep the job open if you like. As you know it doesn't really exist in its own right, though a nice office goes with it." He smiled his businessman's smile. "You've saved me a lot of work, in fact. I wish you were staying. The men who've used the 'job' before never did a stroke!"

Curran grinned and paid the required return compliments – meaning them, though, for he genuinely liked Mustafa Bashir as a man, and respected his undeniable business abilities.

"Tagarid Kurban can do most of my work, providing you keep a watching brief," he said then.

Bashir looked up at him sharply.

"She's staying on in the Lebanon, then?"

Curran suppressed a smile, and questioned back: "Had she thought of leaving?"

But Mustafa Bashir did not respond, as Curran had expected him to, with amused dismissal of the subject. Grave-faced, he said slowly, "She must be very careful. Things have been happening up at Al-Ain, the village where her husband was murdered . . . A man has been killed; it appeared to be an accident, but there have been rumours that it was a revenge killing, with village people involved. Mrs Kurban must be circumspect. It has emerged, you see, that her husband was politically committed."

"And, Mrs Kurban too?"

"The politics, no, I don't think there's ever been any suggestion of that. The other matter, I have no idea, no idea at all; but in the Lebanon nowadays . . ." He let his unfinished sentence drift away; and then passed the ball blandly back to Curran, saying quietly, "You can never tell where the lightning will strike next, I believe you say in your English idiom."

"I think it's really more along the lines of a statement to the effect that lightning never strikes twice in the same place."

"Ah." Mustafa Bashir nodded. "Put that way, it really has no relevance at all to what we were speaking about, has it?"

Continuing their friendly talk, they returned – by an un-
spoken but perfectly understood mutual consent – to business
affairs. And Curran left very soon, then. As he went out of the
Director's office, however, the warning implicit in Mustafa's
remarks concerning the Al-Ain affair came back into his mind,
and he thought with a certain grimness: perhaps he was right,
put the way I put it the saying I used probably has no relevance
to what we were overtly talking about; but by God it probably
has a whole lot of relevance to what we were both very careful
not to mention, namely the possibility that there is going to be
further killing worked into the pattern of events now develop-
ing at Al-Ain, and, if that is truly to be the case, then Mrs
Tagarid Kurban may find it extremely difficult not to become
actively involved . . . Surely, after the terrible eye-opening she
had received during the course of the abduction and rescue of
"Rawa Laudi", Tagarid had learned her lesson and would do
her damnedest to stay clear, he told himself. But would she, in
fact, do that? And what *sort* of lesson had she actually learned?
She was up at Al-Ain now, with Ibrahim Selim doubtless, who
was perhaps a "man of peace". Perhaps? Perhaps, indeed – in
all things which did not directly concern his village, which was
also "hers" . . .

So when Curran went to see Farhal that afternoon he had
questions to ask about three matters, not two. And all his
questions were answered, because Farhal knew himself deeply
in his debt.

16

THE WEATHER stayed cool and the city was grateful for that because it meant people did not need air-conditioning and, therefore, with luck, there might not be any power-cuts. Throughout Wednesday morning the people moved about their city with a tentative happiness, rejoicing in the freshness of the air, bargaining at the fresh-produce stalls with renewed vigour, agreeing with neighbours that the nights recently had been a bit quieter, perhaps the "situation" was improving . . .

At 3.30 that afternoon, Khaled Namur was working in his back room at La Paloma. He sat at the desk with an open file in front of him and a pen in his hand; a small pile of letters lay by the desk-calendar awaiting his attention, and noted on his desk-pad were four telephone numbers he ought to call that afternoon. But he was finding it impossible to concentrate on the paperwork. Throughout the remainder of the previous Monday night when he had driven back from Lamarés and dropped Tallal off in Raouché, down by the sea, throughout the whole of Tuesday (how long a day can be with its vast blocks of hours, its morning, afternoon and evening, each to be lived through until the next News programme), he had waited with tightly controlled impatience. But now it was more than half-way through Wednesday and *still* there had been nothing about Laudi on the media. All Tuesday, and even through this morning, he had accepted this total silence, telling himself with grim satisfaction that naturally at first the authorities would try to keep secret the killing of such a woman, partly because they feared the reaction of an outraged populace, partly (no doubt) to give themselves time, hoping to catch those responsible for the crime so that when at last they *had to* release the news they could at least put the evil-doers on show and thus divert the public

195

rage away from themselves and their own shortcomings . . .
But now, he could not stop his mind returning to the continuing
silence, probing it –

He put down his pen and sat back. And with intense concentration – *this* was not hard to fasten his mind on! – thought his
way again through the torture and killing of Laudi, the securing
of her body where it would be certain to be found but equally
certain not to be found too quickly, and the entirely uneventful
return journey of himself and Tallal to Beirut. Laudi *must* have
been found by now – even the nearness of the body to the village
was enough guarantee for that! – but until the assassination had
been made public, Khaled Namur was entirely powerless to
initiate the moves by which he hoped to gain from it what he
desired –

The woman had said she wasn't Laudi, had said something
about a scar – plastic surgery scars below her right breast and
down her right side – scars which Laudi had and she hadn't,
which proved she wasn't Laudi. But that was an old trick: "a
scar", if you please; he had never heard of Laudi having any
scars, which he would have done, surely, if that had been the
truth . . . An attractive woman, Rawa Laudi, he thought. It
had been a pity in some ways to let Tallal mess her about –

His phone rang, and he answered it: the caller was the
information-broker, Asif Jammal, who said that he had further
facts available about Matthew Curran, if Mr Namur was interested?

When a price had been agreed on, Khaled hung up and sent
immediately for Zayroun.

"I'm going off duty at four," the driver said, standing
sullenly in front of the desk, staring at Khaled with resentment.
"Chawki's coming on then. Can't it wait until he gets here?"

"Take the car, then," Khaled said impatiently. "I trust you
more than I do Chawki." Which was not true but served its
purpose: Zayroun grunted and went out, slamming the door
behind him.

Zayroun got into the black Mercedes and swung her out into the
stream of traffic with his usual aggressive arrogance. Drivers in
post-civil war Lebanon were uninhibited by the traffic-laws
because there were no police on the streets to enforce them, but
most people admitted and practised a degree of unselfishness;

but to Zayroun, the most enjoyable part of driving was to confront other drivers and force them into submission.

So, now, he sped through the city, driving on his brakes and horn – the streets busy at this time of day, people out shopping, visiting friends – his progress punctuated by the squeal of tyres, by the furious hootings and shouted obscenities of those he made trouble for.

Turning, as he often did on this route, into the one-way Rue 34 he set off down it counter-traffic – which afforded him both a short-cut and a self-gratifying exercise in machismo – with his horn blaring to warn anyone coming the opposite way to pull in or back up to let him through. But about halfway along it he came face to face with another car, a sleek and immaculate white convertible, which did neither. The two cars faced each other, the vehicles parked nose-to-tail along both sides of the street making it impossible for either to pull in to let the other pass: obviously, one of them would have to back.

For a full minute they hooted at each other, to the amusement of various passers-by and two or three boys who had been kicking a ball about along the narrow, broken pavement. Zayroun observed the driver of the car opposing him to be an elegantly dressed man wearing sunglasses, saw the thick-banded gold of the watch on his wrist: and his fury mounted. Bloody bossman, he thought, reckons his cash'll get him anything he wants, well *I'm not bloody backing for him!*

And, hot with rage, he got out and advanced on the convertible, stood shouting in through the open side-window at the driver. Passers-by were gathering round now, people were looking down from the balconies of the tall blocks of flats flanking the street, and a crowd of kids watched, grinning hopefully.

The well-dressed man got out and faced Zayroun, leaving the door of his beautiful car wide open to its luxurious, pale-green interior.

"My name is Said Amhaz," he said coldly. "You will back out of this street and get out of my way."

Zayroun recognized the name: this man was second-in-command of a rival Group, the ARRC. Sullenly, he stood his ground, and swore at him; he was by nature a foul-mouthed man, and had great facility.

Deliberately, Amhaz unbuttoned his elegant pale jacket,

197

drew an automatic pistol from the holster at his waist and shot Zayroun in the shoulder, sending him crashing backwards to the ground.

People ran: they knew this kind of trouble, they fled from it and no one shut their doors against strangers running from gunfire-in-the-streets.

"I shall take the number of your car," Amhaz said, re-holstering his gun and adjusting his jacket over it without haste. "I can assure you that you will never drive any sort of vehicle in this city again." And he turned contemptuously away from the fallen man.

But he never reached his car. Zayroun had his gun out and he shot Amhaz three times; the last shot went straight into his brain and he clawed at the air and fell. As he lay on the patched asphalt his death-blood ran into the gutter, discolouring the water pooled there where, earlier, someone's water-tank had overflowed.

As fire along a powder-trail to a barrel of gunpowder, news of the shooting travelled to the main command-post of the ARRC: at 4.10 a wild-eyed militiaman with a Sten-gun in his hand charged into the utilitarian whitewashed hall.

"They've killed Said Amhaz!" he shouted. There was an immediate, stunned silence, the half dozen armed, uniformed men turning to him in amazement. "They shot him in the back! On Rue Thirty-Four. I heard shots and saw people running –"

His comrades surged into movement and grouped tightly round him, fierce-faced, questioning; and he told them all he knew. When he named names, they looked at each other grimly.

"A cretinous FFCP driver, and in the street for everyone to see!"

"He shot Said *in the back!*"

"It's an open challenge to us!"

"Only one way to answer that!"

"– strike back, immediately –"

"That driver – if we're quick we might get him, he might still be there, we can dispose of him straight away –"

"Right!" The leader there interrupted incisively (a tough man, thin-mouthed, known both for his courage and his ruth-lessness). "The driver."

198

He took three men; and they got to the scene of the killing fast. But Zayroun had already been driven away to a doctor by the time they arrived. No one was walking in that one-way street, and in the flats overlooking it every door was shut, every curtain drawn. For a moment the four men prowled, frustrated blood-lust flaring in their restless eyes. Then, at a word from the leader, they gathered round him, a tense, fierce group.

"The killer was a driver for Khaled Namur," he said. They nodded grimly, fingering their guns, their eyes feral now; and listened avidly to a very simple plan. Simple, direct, deadly: the men and the plan had much in common.

Making their way swiftly – and each separately – to the block of flats on Mikdassi street where Khaled Namur lived, they regrouped there and walked into the square, marble-floored hallway together, drawing their guns as they went. The concierge's wife was sweeping the floor outside the open door of her small flat beside the lift; at the sound of their boots she looked up – and froze, yellow-faced with fright and her mouth half-open.

"Get inside, shut the door and keep quiet. Move!" Close to her, the leader gestured with his gun. She dropped the broom and fled into her flat and, at another gesture, one of the gunmen followed her to make sure she didn't use the phone.

Khaled lived in the flat occupying the entire third floor. Surging out on to the landing there, the three men took out the single bodyguard seated beside Khaled's door before the man had a chance to raise any sort of alarm, clubbing him senseless with the butts of their guns. Then they went into their planned action. The leader shot the lock off the door, his two men used their heavy boots on the smashed and splintered wood – the door gave at once and they were through the entrance-hall of the apartment and into the reception-room beyond before its occupants had done more than get to their feet.

Khaled and a girl, neither armed. They had been sitting on a big settee upholstered in dove-grey velvet; and now stood in front of it with a dreadful, awkward stiffness, staring at the levelled guns. It was a large room, richly furnished and its colours quiet; the late afternoon sunshine filtered in obliquely through the white muslin drapes masking the windows, enclosing the people in a soft and pleasant radiance.

"Who's the woman?" the leader of the gunmen asked.

For a split second Khaled hesitated, wondering whether to lie or tell the truth, but knowing that it would make no difference; he knew this sort of man because those of his own Group were basically the same. If they had come here to kill, they would kill: in a situation like this, it was that simple.

"My cousin," he said.

The leader walked up to him, held the gun close to his body and shot him three times; and, as Khaled collapsed to the floor, turned to one of his men, gestured to the girl.

She was tall and dark, narrow-faced and fell-eyed, elegantly dressed in lilac silk; as the gunman came close to her she spat in his face. And died a second later with two bullets in her head.

They found her papers in her purse: name Dina Alameddine Dhaibo, religion Druze. This puzzled (and worried) them for a moment: a Druze girl with Khaled, certainly, therefore, no "cousin". Had Khaled allied himself on the quiet with factions within the Druze community? If so, the matter should be borne in mind. On the other hand it might merely be a personal thing. But with a Druze? Unlikely. It mattered very little either way to them, but the occurrence should certainly be reported . . .

They left the apartment then, went down in the lift and walked out into the street. There was no one to see them go; at the first gunshot the people of Mikdassi street had gone to ground. (You shut the fear in with you; but at least you kept death out.)

Four killings by 5 o'clock that day: all over West Beirut the shop-keepers have slammed down their steel shutters, the street-traders have hidden away their produce, the people have locked their doors and moved as far away as possible from their windows for they have seen what flying glass can do to the human face.

As the sun moves down the sky towards the horizon, a quietness broods over these streets. Quietness should be a beautiful thing but this quiet neither possesses nor gives beauty: this is a city with fear pulsing just below the skin, for its people have given it over to the gunmen and the quietness is a true and terrible emptiness, it is the silence of non-existence, of a deep withdrawal from life; it is a denial of life.

Daylight begins to fade from the sky. Now, men move

through the streets, singly or in groups of two or three, and a few cars speed along the roadways. All this movement is limited and purposeful: the militiamen of a dozen different Groups are gathering at their command-posts scattered over the area, weapons are being issued and plans prepared. Already there have been a few exchanges of fire between the FFCP and the ARRC but these are only, as it were, *practice*, a declaration of intent; really, each man – each Group – is waiting for the dark. It comes. Dropping down over the city with tropical sudden-ness, and there is no moon yet. Then, it begins. The fighting has no overall pattern, it is gang-warfare. Local commanders lead attacks on the positions of other local commanders – with whom they may or may not have some immediate difference of opinion – then return to base (perhaps) to find their own post has been overrun during their absence, its buildings wrecked by hand-grenades and its defenders either dispersed or taken hostage – to be beaten-up, probably, but kept alive (for the moment) because they may be useful later to trade-in for captured friends. This warfare is many separate battles, some of them fought on the run through the poorly lit streets, some of them static, rocket and mortar attacks on strongly held, sand-bagged positions with well-guarded approaches; and all the ugly din of war is present because the Groups are financed from many sources and are well-supplied with weapons and ammunition of all kinds; burp-guns, bazookas, heavy stuff, it is all there . . . Sometimes, silence holds for half an hour or more, but it contains no peace – it only masks the build-up to some further violence.

The moon rises; and on the rooftops the snipers take up their positions, watching the shadowy places where a man may hide. Some of them do not fight *for* any Group: they are there because they want to kill. *Anyone.*

By midnight, West Beirut is a maelstrom of violence. The Groups are wild in the streets, the gun-fever has swept the men along on its own rip-tide: hysterical and volatile, they no longer have even the pretence of belonging to fighting-units, they are well beyond the control of their own appointed commanders, they have degenerated into voracious packs of killers out for blood, gathering round any leader-of-the-moment who will give them that . . .

In the small hours the Security Forces admit the situation is completely beyond their control; the APF is appealed to – and respond (in their own time) by sending in the "Saiqa" battalions.

Therefore, silence comes to the city; and stays.

For these men are élite troops; savagely trained units of destruction, they deal with all militiamen ruthlessly and impartially, for they are Palestinians in Syrian pay. They hate everyone, and everyone hates them.

They go in with overwhelming firepower and obliterate anyone and anything that stands in their way.

Therefore, dawn breaks on a silent city.

A burst of gunfire breaks that silence once: an FFCP militiaman, trudging back filthy-tired and wounded from an earlier long pursuit into enemy territory that fell apart when he and his comrades were ambushed and decimated by a Saiqa commando, stops suddenly as he sees the body of a uniformed militiaman huddled into itself against a housewall at the side of the road. He cannot see the face; but the uniform is the same colour as his own. Squatting down, he moves the body because he has to know. The face that rolls bloodily over to stare lifelessly into his own is that of a longtime friend. He hunkers down beside the body; and weeps. His weeping is entirely silent: and after a while, he stops. Getting to his feet, he lifts his own weapon and points it at the sky, then fires a burst of valedictory shots to his friend's memory. Momently, the silence is ripped apart; it returns swiftly. And through it the militiaman trudges on through the paling, dawn-cool streets of the city he lives in.

17

COMING AWAKE suddenly and completely, Curran stared for a second at the totally unfamiliar room, deep-piled pale carpeting and scarlet upholstery – The angle of viewing also puzzlingly odd, he must be lying on the floor? . . . Then everything slipped back into place: this was Mustafa Bashir's flat; early the previous evening, during a quiet period, he had walked over here from his own place for the Director's Reception for the Egyptian Abdel Kader Krim; but then as the evening progressed the fighting had intensified all over West Beirut. Mustafa's party had been sparsely attended and most of those who had come left early, but two or three of the host's bachelor friends, like Curran, had stayed on for a more relaxed couple of drinks together, expecting the trouble to die down: but when they finally decided it was time to break it up and go home, to walk the streets would have been suicidal . . . So here he was in a pair of Mustafa's silk pyjama-trousers, and across the room from him another recumbent form humped, like himself, under a large duvet.

The five men listened to the radio News over coffee: news out of the shock-numbed city unable to believe what it had done to itself. No real facts out of West Beirut because no one had yet begun to assess casualties and damage inflicted; the men of peace were dazed with guilt and sleeplessness, the militiamen were licking their wounds: and both were counting their dead . . . By nine o'clock the city had declared a day of mourning.

And as Curran walked in the warm, hazy sunshine, away from Raouché towards the area of West Beirut where he lived, it seemed to him that he walked through an abandoned city. The roadway and pavements were littered with glass and debris, with shrapnel and spent bullets; walls were newly fallen or

203

pitted with bullet holes, cars overturned, and the interior of
The Speakeasy gaped open, charred black where a bomb or
rocket had blasted it apart and set it on fire, flame marks
streaking up to the top of the six-storey building above and the
air fouled with the stink of burnt-out timber. He saw no other
person walking in the streets; every shop was shuttered, the
gates and doors of all houses and offices were padlocked; the
balconies of the apartment blocks were empty, and as he passed
a huge pile of rotting garbage two brown rats were still foraging
about contentedly in the smoking filth, undisturbed that morning by man-the-enemy (who is also man-the-provider).

He had told Mustafa Bashir he would drop in at the office to
check that all was well there, for already it was known that a
great deal of material damage had been done. He took the long
way round, a route that enabled him to pass Tagarid's block of
flats: there was apparently no damage done to it, and he went on
his way with one fear at least gone out of him. And when he
reached the splendid block housing the SaxAir offices he found
it had escaped with minor damage; and rang the bell and
hammered on the shut and padlocked gates until the watchman
appeared and let him in.

He pulled back the curtains of his own office up on the ninth
floor, turned the air-conditioning up to high; then, deciding to
ring Farhal to get at least a preliminary yes or no to the favour he
was going to ask from him, sat down at his desk and did so.

Rather to his surprise he got a line at once; and the call was
answered by Farhal himself.

"I won't take up much of your time –" Curran began.

"God, that's the one thing I have and to spare this morning,"
the clipped voice interrupted. "In West Beirut, you and I are
probably the only two people actually at work. And before you
go on, let me tell you something. Khaled Namur's dead."

"How?"

Succinctly, Farhal told him. Told him also what had led to
the killing.

"You're telling me that last night – that bloody madness –
was sparked off by an argument about who should give way on a
one-way street?" Curran demanded in total incredulity.

"That's right, it was . . . You have not been in Beirut very
long, have you, my friend?" Farhal added grimly.

"Christ! But that's unbelievable!"

204

"The truth has to be believable, surely? But I grant you the aftermath of civil war sometimes produces truths that are hard to comprehend . . . What did you ring me about?"

"For a favour. You don't have to make any promises yet. I'm only asking about feasibility for the moment . . . Can you get a Palestinian refugee the papers to leave the Lebanon and go and live in the States?"

"Providing there is sponsorship the other end, these things can be done. Is it a man or a woman, and are there political or criminal connections to be taken into consideration, or not?"

"Woman; no politics, no crime."

There was a short pause, then Farhal said, "Provided you can get the clearance through Washington, yes, it doesn't sound impossible. I'd want a lot more detail first, naturally. And no promises. *Possible*, though, yes. And I owe you, Curran. Come back to me later on it, will you?"

Curran rang off then, and immediately dialled Tagarid's number, thinking she must surely be up by this time.

The phone was answered at once.

"I'm so glad you're safe," she said. "I got back here about three in the afternoon, yesterday, and I rang up but you weren't in . . . Matt, what about the woman, the woman we brought in? Is she still, alive? And, *who is she?*"

"She's alive, yes. In Intensive Care . . . I've got a lot to tell you," he added soberly. "Can we meet? Everywhere's closed, cafés, offices, everything."

"Come round here and have some coffee," she suggested.

As he walked down Hamra he wondered if what he was going to tell her about Khaled Namur would make any difference, if it might make her answer differently, should he ask her again to go with him to London.

She let him in and the coffee was already prepared, Turkish, the scent of it aromatic on the air. Her caftan was of cream-coloured silk; it flowed about her as she moved yet clung to the curves of her body. She looked very beautiful to him. They sat down in armchairs, and Fatmeh set the small cups down on low tables beside them.

"Tell me about it, then," she said, lighting a cigarette. "The woman in Laudi's place, who was she?"

"Leave that for a moment," he said. "There's something I

205

should tell you first." He saw a watchfulness come in her eyes, a stillness in her face. "Khaled Namur's dead," he said, because it was not possible to talk about other things first when you brought the news of a man's death to someone whose life had been very closely linked, for a time anyway, with his.

She put down her cigarette in an ashtray, carefully; and got up and stood looking out of the window, her back to him.

"How?" she asked quietly, after a while. (And he remembered that between Farhal and himself the first exchange about Namur's death had been exactly the same. Perhaps that is because anyone who knew Namur had always expected him to die a violent death, he thought.)

He told her the way the terrorist had died. When he fell silent, she turned and looked at him.

"*He* was given a quick death," she said bitterly. And after a moment, went on, "So I'm safe now, aren't I? He was the only one who might have guessed, guessed true even in the face of my lies." She moved away from the window and sat down again. "That is a terrible reaction, isn't it?" she said, staring at him intently. "A man is dead and my first thought is that his death gives me a kind of safety. But in some strange way he had – for me – already *ceased to exist* . . . What was his *reason* for wanting to kill Laudi?" she asked.

"The lust for power, influence," he said. "He knew that to bring off such a coup successfully would be sure to bring him to the notice of the real high-ups in the FFCP, at least one of whom, probably, had a grudge against Laudi. He would have ensured, of course, that they came to know it was *his* work, the plan and the execution of it both entirely *his* . . . A man capable of doing what Khaled *thought* he'd done would be marked for advancement from then on."

"Nothing else?"

"No."

"How can you be sure?"

He looked at her silently for a long moment; and then said, "I'm not going to give you names. I can't."

She looked away. "I didn't really need to ask that," she said carefully. "When I think back, now, about Khaled, it makes a sense. I made myself see in him what I *wanted* to see."

As they sat then in a quiet almost-companionable, the conviction began to grow in Curran that something important to her

206

had occurred up at Al-Ain: it seemed to him that she was different; he sensed in her a sort of personal wholeness, a sureness that was new.

"How much do you in fact know?" she asked then. "About what really happened, *before* the event? The afternoon of the abduction of the woman who took Laudi's place?"

"I know all that actually took place, I think," he answered slowly, "though there's probably a lot of peripheral stuff I know very little about."

"Tell me, then. There's been nothing about it on the media."

He got to his feet; and as he told the story, moved over to her desk, where he sat down again.

"It was cleverly done. Simple really, but clever . . . That Monday morning the real Laudi and her husband attended her mother's funeral. There were, naturally, many of her relatives there, and most of the women were heavily veiled. And when they drove away from the ceremony afterwards, they had already made the switch: the woman who got into Laudi's car, with Laudi's husband, was actually a cousin of hers, a woman of roughly the same age and like her in general appearance, enough like with make-up to deceive any but the most discerning eye. This woman – her name's Al-Mawi, Jeannette Al-Mawi – she's done the same thing before on occasion, and is in any case a member of the security forces . . . Well, she proceeded from then on as 'Laudi'. But the *real* Laudi got into one of the other cars and was driven straight out to the airport. She got there perfectly safely around midday and went straight to a private room which had been reserved for her, where she stayed until it was time for her to get on her plane. When it was time and the Security men gave her the go-ahead, she simply boarded the plane – with or without her husband, I'm not sure, he may have taken a later plane – and left."

"So the husband's safe also?"

"Oh yes, no problem. He and Laudi are now in Paris again, together."

"And what was the other woman – Jeannette Al-Mawi – what was she supposed to do when she got to the airport?"

"After the funeral she went off with the other relatives to a family lunch at the place Laudi had been staying . . . Later, at the airport, if she had got there, she would have been held up at Emigration on the pretext that her travel-papers were not quite

207

in order, and taken into a separate office supposedly so that they might be checked further. In reality, of course, she would simply have remained there until the Paris plane, with the real Laudi – and her husband, probably – safely aboard, had taken off; then she'd have gone home."

"But it didn't work out like that, for her, did it? . . . She must be a very brave woman indeed."

Curran got to his feet again and stood gazing out of the window.

"I've been told she *venerates* Laudi for what she has been trying to do, is still trying to do, for this country," he said.

"But, she put her life on the line! You say she's done the same sort of thing before – well *every time*, Matt, *every time* she was putting her life on the line!"

Below him, Curran saw the city built around its crescent harbour.

"Apparently there's another reason, also," he said after a moment. "It goes back to the civil war. I don't know the full story, but during some of the bloodiest street-fighting in '76 Laudi risked *her* life in an attempt to rescue Jeannette Al-Mawi's two teenage sons from a burning building. She didn't succeed. The boys – they were part of the fighting and were wounded, you see – were both eventually killed." Below him, close to the sea-front, the fire-gutted shell of the multi-storey Holiday Inn faced black-windowed out over the harbour. Very blue the water. "It was down there," he said, "March '76, when the Palestinians and Leftists finally took the hotel . . . Ever since then Jeannette Al-Mawi's been thanking Laudi for what she tried to do."

"For me, it takes bravery into a new dimension," Tagarid said quietly.

"She and Laudi have lived a closeness that could do that. It was because of this closeness and mutual respect that Laudi would actually permit Jeannette Al-Mawi to take her place on occasion. They were both aware of the risks, and accepted them."

"She's still alive, you said. What are her chances?"

"She'll live, they say." He did not elaborate.

Tagarid did not press him further; only said, after a pause, "Matt, up at Al-Ain I learned that Hisham *was* involved in Lebanese politics. He was –"

"I know it all, don't worry," Curran said.

She stared at him. Then asked tightly, "And, *how long have you known it?*"

It was, he could see, an accusation; but he smiled, brushing it aside.

"Since Tuesday afternoon."

She smiled at him then. And asked after a moment, "From the same man as all the other information?"

He nodded. "He owed me," he said, "and he owed me because of what you and I did on Monday night. That's why it's *yours* as well as mine . . . Who told you about Hisham?" Though he knew who it had to be.

"Ibrahim."

Only the one name; but he felt her suddenly on guard against him, a tension in her, a withdrawal. So he knew he had to warn her. He went and stood behind her chair, leant down to her but did not touch her; and spoke quietly.

"The man who owes me told me something else," he said. "About Ibrahim. You should warn him. *The Syrians know*, d'you see. They know that the people of Al-Ain have compiled a 'Vengeance' list. They know that the local man who has already died was *killed*. They have no proof, but the Syrians *know* . . . So they are waiting for the next move. When it comes, they will be ready to strike back. And *they will be hard and sure and totally merciless.*"

She turned her head, shifted in her chair, and looked up at him then. Had realized *why* he had told her, had realized that he was aware that she might have committed herself now to Ibrahim Selim and the village.

"Thank you for telling me," she said. "I'll pass the message on." She smiled at him; and then went on slowly, her eyes holding his. "So, we must wait. We *of the land* are not men and women to risk our own lives and those of our friends uselessly; we believe, and always have done, in survival, not in the 'heroic' throwing away of lives in dramatic gestures. That is something for Beirut, but not for us . . . But, one day, you may count on it, *we shall have those men whose names we have noted down.* One day, we will make the Syrians wish they had never set eyes on a village called Al-Ain."

He noted the "we"; and struggled against it.

"It's not *your* concern!" he said, as persuasively as he knew

209

how. "Leave it for Ibrahim Selim, for Hisham's family, *his* people . . . Come with me, my love, to London."

"You still haven't understood, have you?" she said. "I'm not leaving Lebanon. Maybe when we belong to ourselves again – maybe, after that. If we win that much in my lifetime. But not now."

"So what *are* you going to do? Now?"

"What Hisham did."

"Join the same Group? Tagarid, *please* –"

"No! *You*, please." But then she questioned: "Did you listen to the News in Arabic on the radio or on TV, yesterday or today?"

He nodded. "I always do."

"What were they reporting?"

"Nothing in particular. A car-bomb –"

"Yes!" she cut in passionately, "a car-bomb – so I do have the right to tell you, *please*, to try to understand. The Syrian Army has started shelling Zahlé: the town in which I spent many years of my life, when I was a child. They've been shelling the town for two days now, using rockets and heavy artillery. The people of Zahlé are living in their cellars – or, of course, dying in their streets – water and food and medical supplies are already running short, *yet the media of Lebanon have reported not one word of this to the outside world!*" She got to her feet and faced him. "Zahlé is under full-scale bombardment by a foreign army which is supposed to be keeping the peace – and in Beirut, twenty-five miles away, most people *do not even know* . . . Change the names to Brighton and London, Matt," she said quietly. "Wouldn't *you* try to do something about it?"

"Yes," he said.

"So." She leaned towards him. "Instead of asking me to join *you*, what *I'm* asking you to do is: *join us*."

After a moment he shook his head sadly and turned away.

"I can't do that," he said.

Hearing her say, behind him, "I didn't think you could."

EPISODE: Two days later

4 p.m. Tagarid came out of the entrance to her apartment block
and turned right, towards the Sidani Street crossroads: Fatmeh
had forgotten to buy apples, and perhaps there would be
mangoes from Egypt; also she needed fresh yoghourt . . .
Checking over her shopping mentally, she drew level with the
small jeweller's shop bomb-blasted some two months earlier,
open again now
   – stopped. Shock-frozen. That other world-of-the-past
crowding in, menacing *possessing* her: soft lights and coffee,
khaki uniforms and the smell of whisky and
   – *that face.*
Breathing fast and shallow, mind-bound to the past, she
stepped softly up to the poster-photograph displayed in the
jeweller's window and stared into those pictured eyes and for a
second it was as if he were raping her again, but then her brain
registered the blue and black border to the photograph, the two
other posters beside it
   – he is dead! she exulted. These are the "martyrs" of that last
violence and he is dead.
   After a moment she smiled into the eyes of the dead man; and
then turned and walked away and went shopping.

AUTHOR'S NOTE
THE LEBANESE CRISIS
1948–1981

Phase 1. 1945–1975. After the Second World War the French gave up their mandate on this corner of the former Turkish Empire and a precarious constitution for the new State of Lebanon was agreed on which allowed a say in government to just about every element from among the embryonic country's many disparate social and religious factions: Maronite, Greek Orthodox and Greek Catholic Christians; Sunni and Shi'a Muslims; Druze. A balance was struck which held – at times very shakily – into the seventies, and the country prospered, becoming a banking and commercial centre, also a richman's playground, for the whole Middle East. But, after 1948 – again after Black September 1970 – the Palestinians kept coming, at first invited in by successive Lebanese governments for humanitarian reasons, then more and more grudgingly accepted. Other Arab states gave the Palestinians no freedom at all, no rights of citizenship or land, so they gravitated to the one country in the region in which they might hope to re-make their lives and from which they might continue their struggle against those they saw as the usurpers of their homeland. With outside help they armed themselves, becoming a state within a state, and the Lebanese could not agree on what to do to stop them, did not have the power or the ruthlessness to kick them out, so that, inevitably, the carefully contrived unity among the various ideologies and interests in their country fell apart. Leaders like Gemayel, Chamoun (both Christian), and Kamal Junblatt all had "their solutions" but would not ally together; with total cynicism other Arab countries played one faction off against the other to keep the problem localized and out of their hair; to the south the Israelis, with their bitter self-confidence and fire-power, played no one's game but their own. At Ain Rummaneh, a suburb of Beirut, in February 1975, a hideous incident occur-

212

red, and the powder-keg exploded, the Lebanese went for each other and for the Palestinians in their midst. The small Lebanese security forces could not, or were not allowed to, cope, and the civil war began. Junblatt, a Druze and possibly the one man who might have held things together, was assassinated, probably by Syrian agents.

Phase 2. March 1975 – December 1976: Civil War. In two years the cost was 40,000 known dead, downtown Beirut razed to the ground, the country terrorized and ruined. During that time occurred the ghastly siege of Tell Zaatar, the massacres at Quarantina, the destruction of Damour. Gradually a pattern emerged, as cease-fire after cease-fire proved short-lived, as half-hearted efforts by Arab "peace-keeping" forces came to nothing, as government followed ineffective government, as the refugee problem became catastrophic and the butchery continued: in the north-west the KATAEB and the AHRAR (Gemayel's and Chamoun's people, Israeli-backed); Beirut split down the middle – the Green Line – between Christian and the many small and diverse Muslim groups; the Palestinians (Syrian-backed) all over the south; the Druze up in their mountains keeping their heads down; the rich valley of the Beka'a bordering Syria a kind of no-man's-land. In December 1976 the Syrian Army came in in strength, ostensibly to protect their Lebanese Muslim "brothers" from massacre at the hands of the Christian forces, and a sort of peace was imposed upon the country by force of arms. All parties settled down to lick their wounds and re-equip. In preparation for the next round, or rounds, to follow.

Phase 3. 1977 – date. The next rounds have not in fact taken place, yet. In 1979 the Syrians, by now cordially hated and mistrusted by all Lebanese, went for the Christian KATAEB in northern Beirut but failed to dislodge them. Later the same year, also in northern Beirut, the KATAEB turned on Chamoun's people, their erstwhile allies, and ruthlessly crushed them, thereby establishing a strong and united Christian enclave from Tripoli to the Green Line. In late 1980/early 1981 the Syrians, content now perhaps to contain the powerful and well-armed Christian forces, flattened and destroyed the isolated Christian city of Zahlé on the edge of the Beka'a, thereby very nearly provoking a war with Israel; and the Palestinians continued to build up their strength in the south, continued their sporadic attacks into Israeli territory, thereby inviting massive reprisal and alienating the bulk of the population in that part of the country, the formerly sometimes downtrodden Shi'a, whose party, the AMAL, began gradually gathering its strength and who now seem to be moving towards an accommodation both with the KATAEB and the state of Israel.

So what happens next? Who knows –

Not *the Lebanese*, at last united on one thing: that all foreigners should get out of their country and leave them in peace. Whether Muslim, Christian or Druze they are sick to death of the "Arab line", pan-Arabism, and the Palestinian Cause which they once genuinely espoused, and want only to be allowed to run their own affairs – complex as these may be – without outside interference.

Not *the Israelis*, who are determined that Lebanon should not continue to provide a base for incursions into their territory but revert to being a peaceful and unthreatening neighbour along its northern frontier, as it was in the 1950s and early 1960s.

Not *the Syrians* (manipulated and egged on by Moscow), who are cynically content to keep the Lebanese crisis "on the boil": the land of Lebanon providing them with a partial buffer-zone between their own country and their Israeli enemy, from which their clients, the Palestinians, may carry on the war both on their own account and on behalf of their Syrian masters. In the long run they also want the Beka'a Valley for themselves.

Not *the Palestinians*, who are still searching for a homeland, somewhere, and see their best hope of getting this to be in territory which formerly was southern Lebanon. They fight on to achieve this, hating both their enemies and those who help them (for their own ends), taking dreadful advantage of a country and people too weak, as yet, to monitor and control their activities.

214

Not *the United Nations*, whose tiny peace-keeping force in south Lebanon has neither the mandate nor the firepower to achieve very much.

In the face of all this, what chance in fact do the Lebanese have? Some, perhaps. They are a gifted and resilient people with a long, long history of re-establishing themselves after periods of foreign domination. May God help them.

February, 1982